through infinity

Libby Austin

Copyright

Cover Design by: Indie Solutions by Murphy Rae

Editing by: Book Peddler's Editing

Formatting and Design by: Book Peddler's Editing and

Allusion Book Formatting and Publishing

through infinity

Libby Austin

table of contents

Dear Reader,

Thank you for taking the time to pick up this book. There are a few things I would like you to know before you begin reading:

First, if you are looking for a book where the heroine meets the hero, who happens to be the college football star, on the first day of college, this is not that book;

Second, if you are looking for hot, raunchy sex (WOHOO! Good for you.), this is not that book;

Third, if you have a problem with gay people or drag queens, this is not the book for you.

Fourth, if cussing or vulgar language offends you, this is not the book for you. There's no need to message me about how many times this happens. I've already counted for you; it's much easier in a Word document. Fuck appears thirty-five times. Shit appears fourteen times. Damn appears thirty-one times. Bitch appears twelve times.

Fifth, I'm not a medical professional. I've done my best to make the situations realistic, but they may not go by a medical textbook. If you want to read such, I hear Gray's Anatomy—the textbook, not the TV show—is good for that.

Finally, if you want to read about a mature woman rediscovering love, then I hope you take a chance on *through infinity* and enjoy it.

through infinity & beyond…

dedication

To the loves of my life,

I love you more…

I love you through infinity & beyond…

& I'll love you forever & a day…

For my grandparents,

I wish each of you had

lived long enough for me

to appreciate you.

prologue

*L*ife is a funny thing. It has many different meanings. Merriam-Webster's Dictionary lists twenty-one different definitions for the word 'life' in the noun form alone. People describe it in various ways. What constitutes life has been debated and argued over in living rooms, on the streets, and in courtrooms for decades. People have died to save life, and others have killed for the very same reason. I think most people would agree that life holds value, even when they can't agree as to what that value represents.

Is there anything more valuable than the thing you lost once it has been returned? Is it appreciated more upon its reappearance? When the shininess of its recovery wears off, will its greater significance remain or dull over time?

I've pondered these questions and quite a few more over the course of the past months. I've had a lot of time to think and a lot of empty space to fill up. I'd like to think the challenges I've faced made me stronger, if not a few pounds lighter. There should be something to show for the hard work and dedication we had contributed.

What I know is that life is a fleeting, precious gift that should never be taken for granted. Didn't someone important once say, 'That's why today is called the present'? No? Maybe I read it in a greeting card, but the sentiment remains the same no matter who coined the phrase. Don't get so caught up in what's going on around you that you forget to appreciate everything, including the stuff that seems like nothing. You never know when the most mundane occurrence will become the most significant. It's a lesson I've taken to heart, because, to paraphrase Reba, 'The heart won't lie.'

I woke up one day and everything I knew had changed, not just changed, it had disappeared into a clouded ether of tangled thoughts and missing pieces. My life had become a puzzle. Unfortunately, all of the pieces weren't there so that I could put the puzzle back together.

My life began the day I died… Wait, let me rephrase, my life as I knew it began five days after I died.

chapter
one

Why won't somebody turn off that damn beeping? It's driving me up the fucking wall! Those were the first thoughts I remembered having upon waking. They flashed through my mind before I could summon the strength to open my eyes. That incessant noise annoying the crap out of me was probably what drove me toward consciousness in the first place.

Grunting and groaning with the effort it took, I finally raised my eyelids, only to quickly shut them. Certainly I'd had worse hangovers in college, but I couldn't say I remembered one at that moment. Dear God, I thought as the brief flash of light set off an explosion in my head. The desire to cry flitted through my mind, but it was trumped by the thought of how much effort it would take to cry causing even more pain than the light did.

"Babe… Babe, can you hear me?" Great, now some jackass is yelling. Doesn't he realize I have a hangover? Is it necessary to speak at the top of his lungs? "Babe, can you squeeze my hand? Please, just squeeze my hand," the voice kept pleading. What I truly wanted to squeeze was his windpipe, but if it shut him up, I'd squeeze his hand until gangrene set in.

I squeezed as hard as I could squeeze. That one little squeeze felt like it took a Herculean effort. I heard the voice say, "Oh my God! Oh my God!" Then another loud buzz right in my ear, which caused me to flinch and jerk my head, which, in turn, caused me to wince and moan. Another voice, female this time, yelled, "Can I help you?" I wanted to scream, 'What's with all the damn yelling?' But that would kind of defeat the purpose, wouldn't it? Plus, I didn't have the strength to get the words out.

By this point, I was getting really tired. Between the breathing, the wincing, the groaning, and the squeezing, I was exhausted. The beating in my head pounded to the rhythm of some unknown death metal music, so, as the fogginess of unconsciousness called to me, I decided to accept the offer for peace and quiet a little while longer. Just as I was about to slip under into a nice, numb cocoon, I heard the male voice say, "My wife squeezed my hand."

WIFE! WHAT THE FUCK! I'm not married, I thought, as I

tried to jerk back to consciousness, but the pull was too strong for my weakened body, so under I slipped once again.

chapter
two

The next time I awoke, the band playing in my head had shifted from death metal to a parade march. There was a very vague recollection of waking prior to that moment that would crystallize soon enough.

Cautiously, I opened my eyes. Looking around, I ascertained I was in a hospital room, which seemed like an odd place to be at the time. I couldn't quite figure out why I was in a hospital room when I was only suffering from the world's worst hangover. Being admitted to the hospital for drinking too much seemed unlikely. Other scenarios floated around my brain, but I couldn't quite get a grasp on any one of them.

Eyes flickering around the room, I took in the ambience—the hideously bland wallpaper, a tacky seascape, and the ugly, vinyl chair—or lack thereof, as the case may be. There was a pulling sensation on the left side of my face, like glue stuck to my skin. I also realized there was something in my nose, which seemed to be connected to the pulling on my cheek. Once I realized it was there, I wanted it gone. I tried to swipe at it several times, but my right hand didn't want to cooperate. My arm would raise and move, just not in the direction I wanted it to go.

Since my nose swiping was such a success, I decided to try and sit up. Maneuvering my left arm was much easier than my right. I'd pushed up about three inches off the bed when my head started to swim, and I fell back to the bed, which caused the throbbing pain inside my head to flare.

It was time to regroup and figure out what the hell was going on. Lying there, I took slow deep breaths and concentrated on being as still as possible.

After the beating in my head relented a little, I called out, "Can somebody come help me?" Unfortunately, what I heard was, "Gn swumwolly umm ewp mwhee?" I tried to speak again…and again my words came out jumbled. Why couldn't I speak? I was able to think fairly clearly, but the words didn't come out of my mouth the same way. However, I wasn't about to give up, so I kept calling out.

After a couple of minutes or so, I noticed a guy carrying a cup part the curtain and walk toward the recliner. He glanced my way briefly, but continued on his path for a split second—about the time it took for his brain to process the scene he'd taken in—then, almost comically, he whipped his head around and stumbled over his feet, barely maintaining his grasp on the cup as he abruptly turned in my direction.

If it hadn't been for the uncertainty of the situation, I would have thought he was good looking—a little older than I would normally go for, but attractive all the same with blue eyes, tanned skin, closely cropped blonde hair, broad shoulders, and a thick chest. It looked like his waist was trim, but it was hard to tell with the loose T-shirt he wore. His eyes were widened in surprise as he walked over and perched on the edge of my bed. His hand trembled as he set the cup down on the rolling table and gently grabbed mine.

He swallowed a couple of times before he finally spoke. "How are you feeling?" Fairly innocuous question, but, honestly, I wasn't sure. I had to contemplate my answer before answering. In thinking about it, I realized my abdomen was a little sore along with the ever-present headache. Worst of all, my throat and mouth were very dry.

"Wahmher," I croaked as I tried to ask for water. I could tell he didn't understand what I'd said, so I cupped my left hand and raised it to my mouth, hoping my motions conveyed I wanted something to drink.

Realization dawned on him and he said, "Oh, water—um—let me check with the nurse. I guess they need to know you're awake again." He reached to the outside of the bed rail and pushed a button to contact the nurse, I assumed, as a beep rang out.

It wasn't long before a speaker crackled. At my wince, he reached for the controller and lowered the volume just as the voice on the other end asked, "Can I help you?"

"Um…yeah…she's awake and trying to talk. She wants some water."

"Okay, give the nurse a moment. She'll be right in."

"Thanks."

Based on the furrowing of his brow and toughness around his mouth, there looked to be a debate going on within his head, but then he asked, "Do you know where you are?"

"Yeh. Howpawiwhal."

"Hospital?" he repeated what I said. I still didn't understand why I was unable to talk, so I nodded slightly to indicate he'd guessed correctly. "Yes, you're in the hospital. Do you remember what happened?"

I cautiously moved my head from left to right. It was then that I posed the question I wanted the answer to most. "Oo are oo (Who are you)?" He was taken aback, but the nurse walked in before he had time to answer.

"Hi there," she greeted me in a cheery voice. "We've notified the doctor on call that you're awake. He should be here in just a minute. How are you feeling?"

Well, wasn't that the question of the hour. "Door," was my response, but I was trying to say sore, so I tried again. "Ore," I said a little more forcefully as I concentrated on forming my words.

"Sore?" she repeated, and I nodded yes. "We'll give you something for that in just a few minutes, but we want to let the doctor examine you first." She and the unnamed guy glanced at each other. An uncomfortable silence settled over the room as my gaze jerked back and forth between the two of them and they seemed to look everywhere but at me. The nurse busied herself checking the machines and tubes and wires connected to me before documenting her notes on a strange looking TV screen connected to a keyboard.

Not a second too soon, a man in a white coat strode into the room. He pushed back the curtain like he was unveiling a statue or something. All I could see was a narrow view of a wall with a wide window and an open door showing a few people walking back and forth to places unknown. I was relieved. His arrival seemed to be what everyone was anxiously awaiting.

"How's our patient this evening? Feeling rested after your extended nap?" Oh great, this doctor thought he was a comedian.

"Ore. Waw wahappwin wo whee?" I wanted to know what happened to me.

"I'm Dr. Ludlow, one of the doctors assigned to your case. Let me do an exam first, then we'll discuss what happened. Okay?" He gave me a cheerful, reassuring smile. I felt anything but reassured. Things got more unsettled as the minutes dragged on. He completed the physical exam and began asking questions. "Let's start with some simple questions. What's your name?"

Truthfully, I had to think about it longer than I should have, but then I announced, "Awwal Duhwin (Apple Dumplin')." He nodded his head and asked me to repeat it. And I did. "AW WAL DUH WIN!" I couldn't talk very loudly, but I said it with certitude.

"Apple Dumplin'," a male voice behind the doctor clarified. The guy knew what I was trying to say. It didn't seem like it should be my name, but it was the only one that came to my mind when the doctor asked. But how did this guy know that? And who the hell was he?

The doctor glanced over his shoulder and nodded his head before turning his attention back to me. I was beginning to feel like a bug under a microscope. Something told me I didn't like bugs, so the idea of being one was a little off putting. "What are your parents' names?"

"Arawl and Ehwhen Odens (Carl and Ellen Owens)."

"Good. What street do you live on?"

"Hahwan (Holland)."

"Very good. Are you married?" All three of them were studying me intently, making me feel like everything hinged on this question.

"No," was my automatic response. Although I couldn't see all of him, I watched the guy's shoulders sag as he sort of deflated. He stared up at the ceiling for a few seconds and then drug his hands down his face as he drew in a deep breath. When the guy looked back at me, he gave me a tenuous smile. There was no doubt my answer hurt him, but I had no idea why.

The doctor proceeded with his next question. "How old are you?"

This answer required a little more thought. I was pretty sure I was twenty-three, but I remembered being in the habit of saying that before I turned twenty-one so it matched my fake ID. Once again, it appeared to be the only reply that popped up. "Whenny-fwhe (Twenty-three)?" My answer came out as more of a question than a definitive answer. Once again, something told me I had failed this doctor's quiz.

"Okay, we're going to order a CT scan in order to get a better idea of what we are looking at." He turned to the nurse and began to give her instructions, "I want a CT scan and—"

"WOMWOWHEE WHELL WHE WHAWS GOWIN ON!" Since I was becoming agitated, my blood pressure was going up, which caused my head to pound even more.

The doctor patted my leg and spoke in a calm tone. "Settle down for me. We're going to get a couple more tests done before I can give you a full answer, but I'll explain as much as I can right now. You fell a few days ago and bumped your head. It appears you may be experiencing a bit of memory loss. Nothing to get worked up about. You're in good hands, and we're going to do our best…" I stopped listening to him as my thoughts and heart raced, which caused the throbbing in my head to escalate to pounding.

I bumped my head? Memory loss? Things were a little fuzzy, but I knew who I was and all that, right? Didn't I? My eyes darted to the guy to see if he would give me some answers. I'm not sure why, since I still didn't know who he was, but it felt like the natural thing to do, like he was there to reassure me.

My head started to feel woozy again, and I became very tired. Before I could stop myself, I slipped back into the blackness once again.

chapter three

$\mathcal{A}$ couple of days later, I was still trying to wrap my head around the diagnosis and all the other information the doctors had laid out for me. Out of everything, the most terrifying thing was how frightened I felt. Each time I thought back to the day when my life changed, my heart raced, my breathing became erratic, and I would sweat. The psychologist assigned to my case said these spells were panic attacks. Luckily, the doctor had already started to show me ways to cope at the onset of a panic attack.

With conscious effort, I slowed my breathing; in through the nose and out through the mouth. Focusing on the mechanics of breathing allowed my mind to break its runaway train of thought and center itself once again. After a few minutes of regulated breathing, I began to contemplate my new reality. I thought back over the past few days to that moment I'd learned how I came to be in the hospital.

The day after I'd woken up for the second time, a meeting was scheduled to go over my diagnosis and develop a treatment plan. I'd woken up the evening before, slightly ahead of schedule. Waking up ahead of time was out of character for me; I'd always loved to sleep. However, I'd been sleeping for days and desperately wanted answers to what was going on with me. Sensing that I was anxious upon waking for the third time, it was decided that I'd needed to be informed of what had happened and what would most likely be my immediate diagnosis and overall prognosis rather than waiting for the scheduled meeting.

My little ICU room had become quite packed as more people in scrubs and white coats had filed into my room. But the people I'd recognized immediately were my mom and dad. I'd started to cry as soon as I caught sight of them. Theirs were the first familiar faces I'd seen since regaining consciousness. I'd wondered where they had been and why they weren't with me when I'd woken up in the hospital, but I forgot those questions as soon as I laid eyes on them.

They'd immediately made their way to my bedside; Mom on one side and Dad on the other. They gently raised me up off of the thin mattress, being cautious of all the wires and tubes attached to me, and cradled me in their arms, all the while murmuring reassurances. I'd tried to ask where they had been, but my speech was still slurred on top of the boohooing. Both had kept assuring me it was going to be okay.

Finally, Mom had drawn back just a bit, wiped my face, and told me to calm down so I could listen to the doctors. She'd always been the steady and strong one. People thought it was men who kept everything together and running smoothly. They'd never met someone like my mother or my granny. These women were forces to be reckoned with, and even though I was a grown woman—at least I was pretty sure I was—when Mom pulled out her Momma voice, it was time to shape up and listen.

When my tears had dried, I'd taken a moment to look at my parents. I'd known they were my mom and dad. There'd been no doubt about it, but they'd looked different than I remembered. Mom sported a full head of blonde hair. Last I could recall, she'd merely had highlights to hide the gray. Her motto was, 'just because you were growing old gracefully, didn't mean you couldn't give it the good fight'. And Dad had the most beautiful snow white hair. He'd looked more like my grandpa than my dad. Both had a few more wrinkles and lines than I'd remembered, but they were most definitely my parents.

The answers appeared to be right in front of me, but I'd been unable to add everything together. All of the information had been jumbled in my mind, like I had all of the components but was missing the formula.

Then my mom said, "All right now, Candy, we're going to listen to what the doctors have to say and then make a plan. So, you keep calm and know that we're right here with you. Okay, baby girl?"

My brows twisted in confusion. She'd called me Candy. While it had sounded familiar, it hadn't fit like Apple Dumplin' did, so I'd told her, "Awwal Duhwin wy wahm (Apple Dumplin' is my name)." This had actually caused my parents to laugh. Dad had especially thought it was funny.

Dad had chuckled and said, "No, Candy, your name is Candice, but I call you Apple Dumplin'. It's my pet name for you. Jason told us that was what you said your name was, and I can't say I really believed him, but hearing you say it actually makes my heart a little lighter." He'd hugged and squeezed me in his excitement. I hadn't been sure who Jason was, but I'd been sure I would find out when one of the doctors got around to talking. "Everything is going to be just fine, Dumplin'. Don't you worry. Now let's let the doctors tell us what's going on in your noggin."

Knowing they were there to help me through whatever was going on, I'd felt a bit more secure. As Dr. Ludlow had begun to introduce everyone, I focused on the conversation at hand. The last thing I'd wanted to happen was another spell. I'd been afraid they would sedate me again and I might never find out what was going on.

"Candice, we met earlier, I'm Dr. Ludlow." I'd nodded my head as he spoke. "I'm the neurologist assigned to your case. This is Dr. Farquhar, the on-call doctor from your OB/GYN's office. Next is Dr. Vermillion. She's the psychologist assigned to you. Then we have Donna Sellhorn. She'll be your case manager. It's her job to coordinate all of your different therapies and such while you are in the hospital and rehab then help you transition and facilitate your care once you return home. And, of course, we have Jason." Oh, so 'the guy's' name is Jason. I liked the name; it fit him.

Dr. Ludlow kept talking while I'd studied the guy, and then Dr. Farquhar explained step by step what had transpired prior to my awakening. Awakening sounded rather dramatic, but it was how I'd felt at the time. "Five days ago, you were brought in to the emergency room for severe vaginal bleeding and a head wound. We ascertained that your uterus had ruptured. This apparently occurred while you were standing on a step stool. We aren't sure if due to the sudden blood loss, you lost consciousness and fell or if you stumbled and fell. Either way, you fell, striking your head on the counter top.

"You were taken into surgery, and had a partial hysterectomy; however, the surrounding tissues, including your ovaries, were unharmed, so they were not removed. We aren't sure why the uterus ruptured, but given your history of gymnastics and the previous abdominal surgical procedures, it is not unheard of for this to happen."

I hadn't recalled having any abdominal surgeries, so I'd been even more confused. The surprising emotion had been sadness. A hysterectomy at twenty-three? I would never be able to carry a child. I mean, twenty-three-year-old me hadn't been sure if I'd wanted kids. I'd known I hadn't been ready right then and there, but to have the possibility taken away, before I'd ever had the chance, was heartbreaking.

At that point, Dr. Ludlow had taken over the explanations once more. "There were a couple complications. You went into cardiac arrest during your transport to the hospital. As a result of the cardiac arrest and lack of oxygen to the brain, you suffered some brain damage, which is what is affecting your speech and the movements of your right arm. Treatments for brain injuries have come a long way in the past couple of decades, so we expect that with speech, occupational, and physical therapy, you'll fully recover the movement of your right arm and your ability to speak clearly. These symptoms should begin to improve over the course of the next few days and then more so once you're in therapy."

My head spun. My brain'd had a hard time making sense of everything he'd told me. It'd been overwhelming and frightening. Those emotions must have shown on my face, because he'd interrupted his explanation to offer some words of comfort.

"I know this is all overwhelming, Candice, but hang in there with me. I want to lay all of the facts out for you first, and then we'll address any questions you have. Okay?" He'd paused for my response. Nodding my head as my parents hugged me and patted my hand, I'd given him permission to continue. "A brain injury could account for some memory loss and confusion; however, given the extent that your memory seems to be affected, we believe you are suffering from amnesia—more specifically, retrograde amnesia."

Amnesia? What the heck is he talking about? I know what's going on around me. I know who my parents are. I remember my friends and going to school and my job. I remember my apartment and my cat Boo Radley. As my mind had kept going over all of the things I'd known, the inconsistencies had also flashed by; why my parents looked older, and who the Jason guy was, and how I hadn't seen myself in a mirror. Why hadn't I seen myself in a mirror?

While I had been thinking about all of this, Dr. Vermillion had started talking. I hadn't been paying much attention to her until I'd heard, "your husband". My head snapped up to stare at her as I'd started saying, "OO? Oo? Uswan? Oo?" There had been a moment of uneasy silence before the guy—Jason—stepped up.

He'd definitely been unsure, but when he'd reached for my hand, my mom had let it go willingly. The guy—Jason—had grasped my hand in a handshake. As he nervously shook my hand, Jason had said, "Hi, I'm Jason Woodruff, and I've had the honor of loving you and being your husband for just over fifteen years."

Shock. Absolute and utter shock was the only way to describe that declaration. I'd been frozen in place. The room had kind of spun around me, and if it hadn't been for my parents holding me up, I would have collapsed back on the bed.

The guy… I didn't know why I had kept referring to him as 'the guy'. I'd known his name, but he'd been 'the guy' for as long as I could remember. Granted, that had been less than a day, but at that point it had been enough to be engrained.

Anyway, Jason had turned a little and looked back over his shoulder. He'd spoken quietly, so I couldn't make out what he was saying, but Dr. Vermillion had nodded her head. As Jason had turned back to face me, he'd swallowed and gathered his composure before he'd started to speak again. "We've been together just over seventeen years, and," he'd paused to swallow again, looking like he could be sick. Jason had drawn in a couple more steadying breaths and continued, "And we have four kids."

WHAT THE FUCK! HOLD THE PHONE! STOP THE PRESSES! Whatever somebody says when they need to stop the crazy train had to be said. Hadn't it been just five minutes ago I had been preparing to mourn my inability to ever carry a child, and now I have four? FOUR? Four? FOUR? FOUR! I'd contemplated passing out just to keep from thinking about it. I mean, I couldn't even keep an aloe plant alive, and I was responsible for not one but four human beings?

Everyone had taken my reaction in stride. My parents had murmured more encouraging words, and Jason had continued with his description of his—I mean, our—children. My reaction to the news had to break his heart. Who wants to see the person they call the love of their life in tears at the news of your marriage and children? I can only imagine myself in his place, and I can't blame him for any of the emotions he'd felt. Honestly, I wouldn't have blamed him if he'd turned around and walked out of the hospital room without a backwards glance. He hadn't, though, Jason had kept on talking about his—our—four children.

"Damaris is thirteen, and she studies dance. She's definitely a born leader. Rissa—umm, that's what we call her—will take in anyone and any creature, much to your dismay, under her wing." He'd chuckled a bit at the 'much to my dismay' part.

"Sybany is eleven. I'm pretty sure that one day she will rule the world. She's never met an obstacle she couldn't conquer. Your love of gymnastics rubbed off on her; she'd live in the gym if she could. She's the quietest and most reserved of the kids.

"Xavier is our oldest boy. He just turned nine a couple of months ago. He's our resident rock and roller. He's been playing the drums for two years and the guitar for four years. He wants to try out for a performing arts school. Music is in his blood, he says. Although, I'm not sure how, since neither of us has any musical ability whatsoever.

"And last, but not least, is the baby of the family, Dawson. Dawson is… Well, Dawson marches to the beat of his own drum. He's five and is convinced the world is here just for him. He has an enthusiasm for life that if we could bottle it, we'd be billionaires. While Sybany is taking over the world, Dawson will be leading the resistance. He's a non-conformist."

The entire time Jason spoke to me, a small smile graced his lips. More importantly, it had lit up his eyes. You could tell how much he loved and adored his—our—kids. The pride had radiated off of him as he'd talked about them.

I'd still been so discombobulated and had no idea where to begin or what to ask or anything. Where did I begin to connect with four people I'd given birth to, but had no memory of? I'd co-created four souls, yet I'd remembered none of it. How could that be? What was I supposed to do?

I'd done what I would like to think any person in my position would do; I'd wrapped my arms around my momma and cried like a baby while she held me.

chapter four

$\mathcal{C}$rying didn't solve anything, but it sure could make you feel better, unless you had a residual headache from a head injury—then crying is not so *muy bueno*. The aftermath of my breakdown hadn't been attractive. The doctors had been kind enough to step out of the room to allow us privacy as a family to deal with this information. They'd confirmed the appointment for the next morning in the conference room, where we would come up with a detailed treatment plan. But how do you make up for someone's lost life?

My parents and Jason had let me cry everything out. I wasn't even sure what all I'd been crying about because at the time I hadn't known half of what was going on. Since I had no frame of reference for being a mother or a wife, I didn't actually know what I was missing at the time. My emotions had had a hold of me, and they'd decided to go for a ride on the craziest roller coaster ever.

Mom, Dad, and Jason had been patient and encouraging. I'd heard everything they told me: *"It's going to be okay." "We'll figure everything out." "You aren't alone."* But I hadn't really been thinking about anything right then. It had been like my brain turned off everything except my ability to breathe, cry, and produce copious amounts of snot. The sight had not been a pretty one—not pretty in the least.

Through it all, they'd remained strong. There'd only been space for one basket case in the room. As my tears started to lessen, my mom lifted my chin and began wiping my tear-stained face. "Dry your tears, now. You've had a good cry. I understand that you're overwhelmed and having trouble making heads or tails of everything, but your family is here. We love you, and we'll be beside you. You'll never have to do this alone. So, chin up and let's start dealing with the situation at hand."

Hiccupping, I'd focused on calming down. I'd thought about all of the things I'd wanted to know: what year is it; am I a good mom; did I learn to cook without requiring a visit from the fire department; how did I end up with four kids—well, obviously, I knew how, I just hadn't known *how*; did I visit Europe or Australia; what about my brother and sister; do I have more nieces and nephews; how old am I—yeah, how old am I was the question I'd decided to ask.

"Ow ole m Iya?" I'd asked, holding my breath for the answer.

I'd done some basic math. The last age I'd remembered was twenty-three. Jason had said we'd been married fourteen years, so that put me at least thirty-seven.

"You're forty," Mom had answered.

"Fowhee?" I'd repeated in disbelief. The tears had started to build again, and I'd steadily tried to beat them back.

Later on, as I would begin to tell the story to others, I'd realize some people were quite pissed off at my reaction to learning I was forty. How dare I be upset at being forty? Didn't I realize how lucky I was to be forty? Didn't I realize how fortunate I was to wake up at all? I should think about the people who didn't, and then maybe I would just be grateful to be alive. As I looked back to document my journey, I could agree with them; however, in that moment, it was so overpowering. In what seemed to be the blink of an eye, I'd lost seventeen plus years of my life.

As I'd sat there in my ICU hospital bed, the last memory I had of thinking about getting older was contemplating how old I would feel at thirty. Forty was downright ancient to my early twenty-something self, who had been just beginning to come into her own and discover what adult life was about. Virtually half my life was gone; wiped away without a trace. Except there were traces. There'd been plenty of evidence that my life had progressed beyond the age of twenty-three—the husband and four kids, for instance. I'd needed a crash course on my life. How was I supposed to move forward? Who was I supposed to cling to? So far it had been my parents, but I couldn't ignore 'the guy' for much longer. Addressing him and the life we'd apparently built needed to happen sooner or later. As my mom would say, it was time to put my big girl panties on and deal with it.

At the thought of panties, I'd realized the ones I wore were really thick, like a pad all over. Then it had dawned on me: I was wearing a diaper. I was a forty-year-old woman in a diaper. Umm, no thank you. Then I remembered that I had a tube in my nose. Relieved to have something else to focus on, I'd asked, "Yan yi gewa (When can I get clean)?"

"I'll step out and ask the nurse," Jason offered, quickly getting up and leaving the room.

While he'd been gone, I'd asked my mom about my brother and sister. "Dwee and Wawwy (Andy and Meri)?"

"Andy is still with the fire department, and Meri runs her own day spa. Andy and Laura divorced, and he remarried about eight years ago. His new wife's name is Johnna. They work really well together. He has a daughter with Laura named Cheyenne, who's fifteen. Meri and Don are still together. Don kept the gym, but he focuses more on Crossfit now. That's a newfangled kind of workout that people are crazy for. They have two boys and a girl. Bryson, Jenelle—do you remember Bryson and Jenelle?" She paused to wait for my answer.

"Ywa, waywees (Yes, babies)."

"Well, they aren't babies anymore." She'd laughed in affection. "Bryson is twenty and in his sophomore year in college. Jenelle is seventeen and about to graduate from high school. She can't decide what college she wants to attend just yet. Then they have Riley. He's the same age as Damaris. They're very close." There'd been a brief pause, like she'd been trying to think of what to talk about next. The fear that someone died had crept in. My grandparents would be in their eighties or nineties. I'd had trouble remembering their ages.

"Wawwy en Wiwwl Wahnwy (Pappy and Little Granny)?" When I was growing up, Little Granny was just Granny. As Bryson began to talk, he'd called her Little Granny, I guess because she's smaller than my mom, and it stuck. You would think he would have called my mom Big Granny as a result, but no, he called her Kitty.

Kitty was Bryson's first word. He loved to say that word. Everything became kitty. Every time he said kitty, we acted like he had solved world peace or something. The beauty of being the first great-grandchild. Eventually, it was whittled down until just my mom was Kitty. All of the grandchildren in my immediate family, which, at the time I remembered, were Bryson and Jenelle, called my mom Kitty instead of Grandma or Granny.

"Oh goodness! Those two are still getting into trouble. They fight like cats and dogs. Pappy likes to pretend he's more hard of hearing than he is, and Little Granny gets irritated with him. She likes when she can put him to work; otherwise, he gets into mischief. He and Dawson are two peas in a pod. They're together a lot." Mom had then proceeded to name off the family tree; who was still kicking, who was six feet under, who got married or divorced—or, in some cases, both, who had kids, who bought a house, which of my five aunts was still arguing about who'd created the family favorite—tump soup.

For the record, it was Pappy who came up with the recipe. My aunts argued over who'd given it the name. Why anybody would want to argue over coming up with the illustrious name of tump soup, I never understood, even before I lost my memory. But that's family for you, or at least my family. Personally, I don't blame Pappy for pretending to be deafer than a doornail. If I had to listen to those seven—yep, six daughters and one wife—women, I'd act like I couldn't hear, too. They also had five sons. Some are adopted and some are biological. Nobody is sure who is who, because they didn't make a big deal out of it. They're all just brothers and sisters.

In some cases, it's obvious, and occasionally a person would feel the need to point that out, like no one else had ever come to the same conclusion. Family legend has it that Granny got so mad with one person, who wouldn't drop the subject, that she shouted she'd had an affair with the milk man. At the time, Pappy ran the family dairy farm. It was quite the inside joke over the years. While the woman tried to figure out the puzzle, Granny had walked off.

The nurse walked in followed by Jason, which snapped me out of my brief trip down memory lane. Memory lane…ain't that funny? I guess at some point I would've come to a sign that read *Dead End*.

"Candice, the doctor gave the okay to remove your feeding tube. That's the tube in your nose. How are you feeling about using the restroom? Do you feel the sensation to urinate?"

Well, now that ya mentioned it, "Wes."

"All righty then. Let's get this NG tube out first. We're gonna leave your IV in to make sure you are staying well hydrated. Then we'll take a short stroll to the bathroom." The nurse kept talking as she pushed a few buttons on the machine that held a bag of white liquid and clamped the tube. She laid out a few things on a tray, pushed it up close to the bed, and then came close to the head of the bed. "Okay, I'm gonna raise you up, then I'm gonna loosen the tape." After I was in the correct position, she said, "Dad, since you're on the other side, I want you to hold this little basin right here. I'm going to remove the tube now." She'd moved the kidney shaped dish under my chin. Right about the time I'd wondered about why I needed a puke basin for a nose tube, I found out so enough. HOLY MOTHER FUCKING GAG REFLEX! "Breathe through your nose. It will pass quickly." I would've glared at her if my eyes hadn't been tearing up.

After she'd disposed of all the tubing and paraphernalia, she calmly asked, "You ready to mosey to the restroom?" I nodded. "Okay, we're gonna take this a little slower. As the doctor said, you don't appear to have any paralysis, but let's take this nice and easy, since it's your first attempt to walk. There's no prize for who gets there first. Which, by the way, will be me, since I'll be in front of you," the nurse said with a little laugh. Obviously, trying to lighten the mood with humor. She'd already pulled the covers off my legs and helped me carefully swing my legs over the edge of the bed. "Good girl. When I tell you to, I want you to slowly lean your upper body toward me and place your hands on my shoulders. Once I'm supporting your weight, you're going to slowly slide forward until your feet touch the floor. Then you will slowly straighten up as much as you feel comfortable. Don't strain yourself, okay? After you're standing, Jackie is going to walk behind you. You'll feel her hands at your waist." I looked over to see a nursing assistant standing off to the side. She must be Jackie.

Trying to remember all of the instructions, I'd extended my left arm to the nurse's shoulder. My right hand missed the mark and landed on her forearm. She'd just smiled and moved it higher. "Don't worry, we'll work on your dance form later." Nurse, whose name I hadn't remembered from earlier, was kind of funny. I'd wondered if I'd learned to dance in the past decade and a half.

It seemed like it took forever to make it from the bed to the tiny bathroom, but everything worked the way she'd said it would. An eternity later, our awkward trio stepped into the restroom. I'd felt like doing the Rocky pose in triumph, but thought better of it, since I hadn't wanted to land on my ass.

We'd maybe been about half a foot into the bathroom when I turned my head to the right and saw my reflection for the first time. There I was, or so I had been told. The reflection staring back at me wasn't the one I'd recalled. The hair was longer and a redder color than the brunette I was born with and remembered. Even though I had been out of the sun for a few days, I could tell my skin tone was paler than it had been. Guess my days of basking in the sun without a care were long gone. My face was a little thinner, and there were definitely more lines than I'd had in my early twenties. I'd looked down because the most surprising thing was my boobs were notably bigger. *Well, there's a new development.*

I'd tried to take everything in stride. There wasn't much I could do about my looks at that moment. Maybe I would be able to shower soon. Mom could brush my hair at least. I'd always liked to have my hair brushed. Turning back to Nurse, I indicated I was ready to move forward.

"Candy, Jackie is going to reach in and undo the tabs on the adult underwear." *Adult underwear? Woman, it's a freakin' diaper. Just because you call it something else doesn't mean it changes what it is.* Once that was done, the rest had been pretty effortless.

I sighed deeply and sank back into the bed. Getting to the bathroom and back to the bed had taken a lot of energy. After getting situated, I'd closed my eyes and rested.

"We'll be bringing in dinner soon. It will be a soft, bland meal. If you tolerate that, we'll be able to start adding other foods." I'd cracked my eyes open to acknowledge her statement, and she smiled and left the room.

Dad stood beside my bed. He'd leaned over and kissed my forehead. "Dumplin'," he kind of grinned at the name, "now that you're back with us, I'm going to head back to the house for a bit and check on everything. I'm sure you're worn out and need some rest. I'll be back in time for visiting hours tomorrow morning. I've got a lot of good news to pass along." He gave me another kiss on the head and walked over to my mom. They gave each other a long hug, a brief kiss, and a look that said more than words could express. I'd always known I was very fortunate to grow up with so many great role models for love and marriage.

Jason, Mom, and I looked back and forth between each other. Since I hadn't wanted to hear any more about the family tree at the moment, I got my mom's attention. "Om."

She smiled and said, "Yes, baby?"

I concentrated and replied, "Ush air," while making a brushing motion with my left hand.

"Sure, baby." She hopped up and opened a drawer in the bedside table. Mom extended the brush to me, but with a shake of my head, I'd rejected the offer.

"No, eww ush, eez," I'd requested.

"Wow, it's been a long time." But she'd stepped closer and gently began to stroke the brush through my hair. Each stroke had lulled me a little more, and soon I'd fallen asleep.

The sound of the dinner tray being delivered interrupted my slumber. Those few moments between sleep and waking were filled with a wonderful numbness and possibility. It was the moment before reality rushed back to life. That's exactly what happened when I'd opened my eyes and connected to a set of blue eyes I was becoming familiar with.

"Did you sleep well?" he asked. I nodded my head in reply. "Would you like some help with your dinner?" I nodded my head again.

There was a cup of broth, which was steaming when I lifted the lid, and a plate of congealed scrambled eggs. But when you haven't eaten in days, it's pretty appetizing. Until I saw the green Jell-O. I groaned out loud. I hate Jell-O, especially any color that isn't red. In my world, the only Jell-O that's edible comes in a plastic shot cup and is made with liquor.

Jason laughed. "Not feeling the Jell-O?" I'd shaken my head. "Good to see some things don't change, huh?" He'd given me a reassuring smile. For the first time, I noticed his dimples. I'd finally taken a good, long look at him. It's not nice to stare, but I'd desperately wanted something to register. Jason was a handsome man and built the way I favored. He had broad shoulders and a classic square jaw. Given what I could see, Jason was definitely a hotty.

He'd cut the scrambled eggs into small, bite-size pieces, then he'd helped me position the fork in my left hand. I was naturally right-handed, so this was going to take some effort. One would think that switching hands to eat wouldn't be that hard, and it isn't, per se, but it does take some getting used to. Whenever my hand would wobble, Jason was there to offer support. Holding my cup of broth or wiping my mouth when liquid dribbled out, whatever I needed, he'd done it without hesitation.

I'd managed a few bites of eggs and took a few sips of broth. That was all my stomach could handle. I made sure I steered clear of the green Jell-O. Watching as Jason cleared away the dinner tray, I'd wondered what we would talk about. Maybe he would turn on the TV, since I couldn't talk very well.

He'd surprised me by pulling out a laptop and plugging it in before he set it on the rolling table. At my confusion, he'd said, "We thought it would be easier for you to type. You can still talk as much as you want, but this way if you are getting tired or stressed out, you have a backup."

"Yaz weep (That's sweet)." I'd hoped I was smiling and not grimacing. The right side of my mouth was a little numb, like after you've been given a shot of Novocain, so it was hard to tell if I was moving it.

His grin was huge. OH MAN! Those dimples. Now, there I'd been, without a memory of almost half my life and I was drooling— quite possibly literally—over a guy's dimples. I'd needed my head examined. Good thing there was a shrink already lined up for the job.

"I wish I could take the credit, but it was mostly your mom's idea. She said there was something similar in a book you made her read about a guy who didn't speak." He'd finished setting everything up. This laptop was a little sleeker and thinner than the kind I remembered, but the basics appeared the same. He'd even added a mouse I could easily use with my left hand. It was almost identical to the mouse I'd remembered using.

"Eya owws (My mouse)." His thoughtfulness about the little details meant a lot.

"That was a no brainer. You've used the same kind of mouse for eons. Even have a couple stocked away in case the one you're using breaks. We just needed a left-handed version. Your Amazon Prime subscription came in handy." He'd laughed at the obvious joke I didn't get. I wasn't sure what Amazon was other than a river in South America.

There was a long pause. What do you ask 'the guy'? The one you fell in love with, married, and had children with. Easy was best, so I'd typed, **Where's my mom?**

"She went to grab a quick bite to eat and to pick up a few things she thought you might need."

Okay, so what now? I'd known what twenty-three-year-old me would've wanted to do, since I was alone with an attractive guy, but that wasn't the prudent thing to do at that moment, nor did I feel very attractive to institute flirting.

Instead I'd typed, **How did we meet?**

He'd grinned and said, "My sister introduced us."

What's your last name again?

"Woodruff."

I'd wracked my brain for a name. It was on the tip of my tongue. Tracy? Casey? Lacey? Macy? MACY! Macy Woodruff. I typed, **You're Macy Woodruff's big brother!**

By this point his grin was huge as he'd replied, "That's me, but I try not to claim her too often." Even his eyes held humor, and there were those damn dimples. Jason's dimples should come with a warning label; Caution: When dimples are present, may cause women to act stupid.

Just then a few pieces of the puzzle had started to slip into place. Macy was my little sister in our sorority. When I'd seen that she was not only from my hometown but had attended my high school, I'd known I wanted to be her big sister. At the time, I hadn't put two and two together with the last name. Woodruff wasn't super common, but it wasn't rare either. And, well, math was never my strong suit. Macy and I'd clicked right away. She was the little sister I never had in real life.

One day, she and I had been talking about people we knew and our relatives. It's a Southern thing. We either had to figure out how we were related by being sixty-seventh cousins eighty times removed or who we knew in common. Macy talked about her brother Jason, who happened to be a Marine. As she'd talked about him, it had occurred to me who her brother might be.

I'd transferred into my high school midway through my sophomore year after my dad had retired from the Air Force and we moved back to my parents' hometown. It was a hard time. I'd been painfully shy and awkward with a mouth full of braces, no fashion sense, and bad skin. The highlight of my day, every day, was Geometry, which was saying something considering my aforementioned math talent. Directly in front of me sat the object of my first real crush, none other than Jason Woodruff.

When I'd divulged this information to Macy, she'd pulled out her photo album and opened it to a photo of her brother. Without a doubt, there was my crush. She'd laughed her ass off after pretending to get sick at the thought of her brother being lusted after. Lust after him I had—well, as much as any naïve fifteen-year-old can. I'd been mortified when she'd announced she couldn't wait to tell him, and I had begged, on the honor of the sisterhood, that she never mention my crush to him.

That was when the next revelation hit me: Jason Woodruff, my crush, had seen me in a diaper and God only knew what else. This was every high school nightmare come to life! Oh my God! My face had to be beet red. Life was so unfair; I'd survived a ruptured uterus, a blow to the head, brain trauma, and cardiac arrest only to die of embarrassment. As my mind spun, I'd hurriedly typed, **Have you been here the entire time?** And then I silently prayed, *Please say no, please say no.*

"Pretty much. I didn't want to leave in case you woke up." His face had grown a little concerned. "Babe, why is your face so red? Normally, you turn red when you're embarrassed or the like, but it kind of scares me after everything that's happened." I'd covered my face with my hand. Could the floor open up and swallow me, please? "Babe, look at me." Jason gently, but firmly, grasped my hand to pull it away from my face.

He'd switched hands and then raised his hand to my chin to turn my face. Making eye contact with him had been too embarrassing, so he'd said again, "Babe, look at me." He'd waited until I made eye contact before he spoke. "Candice, when I said my vows, I meant them. You're the love of my life. I'll be beside you no matter what. Some days will be better than others, but there is nothing that could ever make me love you less or move from your side, unless you tell me to go, and even then, I will still support you. You may not know the depth of my love for you right now, but my love will never waver. I'm here to stay. Got it?" I'd barely nodded my head, but he'd accepted it with another ravishing smile. "Besides, we have four kids, and I saw three of them born, not to mention had an active role in creating all of them. There isn't anything you have that I'm not intimately acquainted with," he'd said with a laugh.

*Oh yeah, the four kids…*crossed my mind. *Wait, did he just refer to our sex life?*

Grim Reaper calling, party of one. Cause of death: mortification.

Getting over myself and my embarrassment had taken a few minutes. Though I'd wanted to know more about how we became a couple, I was more curious about the kids. They'd seemed like a safer topic anyway, as long as we didn't discuss their conception.

Do you have pictures of the kids? I typed.

"How about I show you your Facebook page? You have tons of pictures on there." Jason had started clicking buttons on the laptop.

I'd remembered the Internet. I had just upgraded to a cable modem. It took forever for a web page to load on dial-up, so I'd been pretty stoked with the cable modem's speed. A couple of my classes for my master's program were going to be offered online, and I was looking forward to them. But I'd had no clue what Facebook was or why I 'had' a 'page'.

It didn't take long before a web page popped up. Jason typed my name in a search box. Next thing I'd seen was a picture of me and him… and four kids. We'd all been making silly faces. It looked like everyone was having a lot of fun in the picture. As I'd been studying the picture, he pointed out who each of the children were from left to right; Dawson was beside me, then came Damaris, Sybany, and Xavier standing next to Jason.

Why do they have such odd names? Okay, that may not have been the nicest way to ask about their names, but, seriously, they're weird.

Thankfully, Jason had laughed before answering. "They are unusual, I'll grant you that. Damaris is named after my grandmother, whose name is Melva, which means gentle. We wanted to honor my grandmother but didn't want our daughter to have to go to school with the name Melva. Out of the list, we picked Damaris—Damaris Kathleen. Kathleen after your granny.

"Sybany's name was simply a name you liked. It was the name of the sister of an elementary school friend of yours."

What's her middle name?

"Leandra. After your Godparents, Lee and Sandra."

Okay

"Xavier is named after me and my dad. Jason Xavier III. We call him Xavier because my dad goes by J. W. and I'm Jason, and you said hell no to J.J., because there were already two J.J.s in your family and more were sure to come.

"Dawson is named after your dad's dad, who was named with his mother's maiden name. It was either Dawson or Wilson. Wilson is my mother's maiden name. Wilson didn't really fit, plus we didn't want people to think he was named after the volleyball from the movie *Cast Away*, so we chose Dawson and used my grandfather's first name, John, for his middle name.

"You said staking claim on a name in your family was all about who got there first, so you wanted each of their names to have a reason that no one could argue with, and I think you accomplished that."

At least I didn't name him after the TV show.

"We get that a bit, but, luckily, that show has been off the air for a long time," Jason said with humor lacing his voice.

For the next hour, we clicked through picture after picture and explained each one. There were thousands of pictures. He'd mainly focused on the kids, but showed me a few of my brother and sister and their families. I'd been amazed that all of this was there at the click of the mouse.

We'd kept going until my mom came back, wheeling a suitcase behind her. She'd brought photo albums, scrapbooks, and baby books. They hadn't had time to make a CD of everything, she'd explained.

As prolific as I'd been about putting pictures on Facebook, there were still quite a few physical pictures. The three of us spent the rest of the night flipping through the albums and books. I'd gotten to know bits and pieces of my lost life. There were times I'd lingered over certain photos, trying to remember what I had been feeling when it was taken, but there was nothing but a blank. Even as the sun began to light the morning sky, I'd still searched, only to be alluded.

People often say they wouldn't trade their experiences, good or bad, because they make them who they are. Half of my experiences were gone and might never return. If half the equation was missing, what happened to the total? If the experiences weren't there to learn from and make me who I was, then who was I? It was all so…unsettling.

chapter five

$\mathcal{S}$haking myself from my maudlin thoughts of the past few days, I decided to think about how lucky I was in this situation. I had been transferred to an in-hospital rehab to begin my therapies five days after I woke up from the coma. The team of doctors handling my case thought it would be best to transfer me to inpatient rehab for the beginning of my recovery and then transition me to outpatient. As Dr. Ludlow had predicted, my speech and use of my right arm had rapidly improved even prior to me being moved, so I couldn't wait to see what would happen with therapy.

We'd all met in a big lounge the day I was transferred to the rehab. It was a very comfortable and relaxed environment. Since I had already been filled in on my condition, everything was focused on my recovery. The physical and occupational therapy team were introduced, along with a speech therapist. Thankfully, they'd all had their names embroidered on their shirts. At times, recalling new things was somewhat as problematic as remembering my old memories. The attitude in the room was positive and uplifting. If anybody thought I couldn't make a full recovery, they'd never said so.

The therapy schedule was going to be heavy. I would see each therapist every day. As long as I was progressing, I would be allowed to go home in a week or so. Then I would return for outpatient therapy.

The next day, I'd made it through my first day of therapy. By the end, I'd been physically exhausted. The great thing about focusing on my therapy was not having to think about the situation. Well, I'd tried not to think about it, but part of my situation was with me every step of the way.

Jason never left my side. He'd escorted me to every therapy and sat off to the side, taking everything in. He asked questions and gave me encouragement when I needed it. That came to an end with my final therapy session of the day when Jason was asked not to accompany me into this particular therapy session.

Dr. Vermillion opened her door and smiled my way. "Hi, Candice. Ready for the head shrinking to begin?" I'd grinned at her description. The image that popped into my mind was of a miniature head on my shoulders. Maybe my head would shrink enough to fit my shrunken memory.

I'd nodded my head and said, "Es." My speech was already clearer. The speech therapist said that wasn't unusual in these types of cases and would continue to improve. The advances in brain injury treatment made great strides in helping patients recover at a much quicker rate than before.

"Well, let's get you in here and get started. I'm going to have Jason wait out here while we talk first. Then we'll have him join us in just a bit. That sound okay with the two of you?"

I looked over at Jason, and he gave me another one of his reassuring smiles. He picked up my hand and kissed it, then said, "I'll be here waiting."

Placing my hands on the walker I now used since my balance was a little off-kilter at times, I stood up, balancing myself until I felt steady, and then carefully made my way across the small waiting area. It took a minute for me to cross the distance. It was hard not to have performance anxiety when it felt like everyone was watching every step I took, and walking with a walker wasn't natural in the least.

I'd already figured out how lucky I was, not just for surviving but the family support I had backing me up as well. I would have expected it from my parents. Jason, however, was the surprise. There was no doubt he cared very deeply for me. His every action showed how much he cared. He helped me eat, he helped me go to the bathroom, he helped me do anything and everything that needed to be done. He never wavered. Jason was a good man, and I was very fortunate that he loved me. I only wished I could remember loving him and not just crushing on him.

After I was seated in the chair, I'd pulled out the laptop. Even though my speech was improving, there were times I had a hard time getting the words out. The more tired I became, the harder speaking clearly became. The day's efforts had already worn me out.

Dr. V opened the session by asking how my first day had gone. "Good. I's a wot o' work," I answered, wanting to sound positive about the day.

"Yes, it is. But we all have faith you can do it. How are you feeling about everything that's happening?" She waited patiently and didn't press as I tried to get my thoughts in order.

"Scared…oderwhehmed…worried…woved…bwessed." I told her I felt scared, overwhelmed, worried, loved, and blessed. When I was done, I looked up at her, waiting for the next question.

"Those last two aren't so bad. How about we talk about the first three things you described. I know it seems obvious, but explain to me why you feel that way?" Her voice was kind. I could tell she was trying not to add to my stress, but her job was to uncover how I was feeling and help me deal with those emotions. She couldn't do that if I didn't tell her the truth. "You know I won't share anything with anyone that you don't want me to."

Since there was a lot to say, I'd started typing.

Jason mentioned bringing the kids to see me. They've been worried about me. He and my parents think it would be good for the kids to visit with me, so I can start to get to know them and reconnect.

I paused to think about what I wanted to type next. Sometimes being honest with yourself was the hardest thing of all. Then, on top of that, sharing those thoughts and being afraid of the judgment wasn't easy.

I don't remember them. There's no connection. I've tried to search my mind to see if there was some residual feeling or memory of them, but there was nothing. What if I never feel anything for them? What if I can never be their mom again? How are they going to understand why their mom doesn't love them anymore?

By the time I typed the last question, I'd started sobbing. Dr. V handed me a box of Kleenex. She waited a couple of minutes for me to calm down before she spoke. "Candice, everything you're feeling is normal. Your memory is of a woman who wasn't married and didn't have children. This is all a big change for you. Your memory may come back, it may not, or it could partially return. We can't predict the future. We're going to establish a support team for the children and Jason, and we'll all do our best to help them understand. There will be bumps along the way, but I have no doubt that they can be addressed with love and honesty.

"Try to think of it like a stepparent for now. When someone

meets a person who has a child, they have to learn about that child. They grow to care about the child. Love isn't always instantaneous, even when we give birth to a child. It's not something you can force."

I try to remember that, but then I feel guilty. I feel guilty about putting everyone through this. Why didn't I know something was wrong? Shouldn't I have felt pain? I just don't know what to do with everything.

"I know, and we are going to help you with that. You've got more people cheering you on than you know. I've never seen a room fill up with cards and flowers so quickly. You'll need a U-Haul to get everything home when it's time to leave," she'd finished with a little laugh.

It was true assertion. As soon as I was moved out of the ICU, flowers had started to arrive. Every time my parents came to see me, they brought more cards and letters and drawings.

The cutest card was from Dawson. He'd drawn a stick figure Mommy with a helmet. His card read, *Sorry you bumped your head. You should wear a helmet.* And he'd included a picture with *this is me* written on the back.

Dr. V and I talked a few more minutes, and then she'd invited Jason to join us. He came in and sat down right beside me on the couch. We'd discussed the best way to reintroduce the children. It was decided that my parents would bring the kids to the rehab. The kids and Jason would meet with Dr. V and the team first. She would coordinate getting as many of my team there as possible. That way the kids could ask any questions and the team could address them prior to me joining them for our reunion.

So there I was sitting in my room, waiting for the time to go down to the rehab's lounge. I felt like I was going into the biggest job interview of my life. This was worse than the fear of standing up to give a speech and looking down only to discover you were naked.

I had so many fears. What if they didn't like me? What if they asked me something I didn't know how to answer? What if I got overly emotional? One of the side effects of my head injury was my emotions were out of whack. They went to extremes. I watched a commercial last night and started crying because it was so sweet. It took me an hour to stop crying. I hoped I didn't do those kinds of things with the kids.

"Babe—Candice—they're here. Are you ready to go?" Jason's question snapped me back to the present, and my palms began to sweat as I nodded and said yes. The three days since my first therapy session with Dr. V hadn't been long enough to prepare myself for this meeting, but I doubted any amount of time would've been enough.

chapter six

Sitting there in the adjoining room to the lounge alone since Jason left were the longest five minutes ever gave me too much time to over-think what was about to happen. He'd gone to go meet the kids in the lobby and bring them up to the lounge. My support team was already assembled and were chatting among themselves. They'd dressed casually. Everyone was making an effort to make the kids as comfortable as possible. I sat behind a one-way mirror that faced into the lounge. I would be able to see and hear everything the kids talked about. And I admit, my mind was starting to run away with itself.

Luckily, before it got too far down the track, the door behind me opened and my dad walked in. He leaned down and gave me a huge hug. My body relaxed so much, I'm surprised it didn't slide to the floor.

"How're ya doin'?" Dad asked as he sat down.

"Good. Nerbous." During my down time, I'd been studying the scrapbooks and Facebook, hoping for recognition. My desire to learn as much as I could about the family I'd created couldn't be quenched. I was anxious to see what would happen when the kids arrived.

"Aww, it'll be fine, Candy. They're your kids, but don't worry, they got enough of Jason to keep calm and not go ape shit." He smirked as he finished, and I'm pretty sure I'd just been insulted.

"Ey, I habn't done 'razy in..." I hesitated because I was unable to remember. "...'ince I 'an bemember." I laughed, and my dad joined in. He'd successfully distracted me from my pending panic attack.

As we were laughing, the door to the lounge opened and in walked my four children. Sybany and Dawson entered the room like they were getting ready to conquer. Damaris and Xavier were a little more hesitant but still brave in the face of the unknown. They were followed by Jason and my mom. Mom immediately sat down.

You know the person that every eye in the room is drawn to? That would be Dawson. He had a presence, even without his—shall we say unique—sense of style. The kid wore purple shorts, a pink and yellow striped button down with the sleeves rolled up, lavender suspenders, deck shoes sans socks, a fedora, and a cape. When he walked in, he reached up and tipped his hat while saying, "Good morning." Then he proceeded to walk around the room, shaking hands and introducing himself. Dawson had more self-assurance in his little body than most grown men. Later, as I thought back, I would realize he didn't look at the people when he introduced himself to them.

Sybany said, "Hi, I'm Sybany," and sat down with her arms crossed and a blank expression, which seemed out of place on her young face. She was dressed casually in cutoffs, a band T-shirt, and flip-flops. Her dark brown hair, similar in color to what mine used to be, was in a messy ponytail. Picking at the fringe of her cutoffs, she didn't meet anyone's eyes. Based on her closed-off body language, her attitude was…disinterested.

Speaking quietly, Damaris introduced herself then sat next to her sister. Her hair was blonde, like Jason's. Even at thirteen, she was elegant. She moved with a subtle grace.

Dawson's flashiness had drawn my eyes, but then I took in my other son as he stood next to his dad. There was no denying their resemblance. I had no doubt that when Xavier smiled, dimples identical to Jason's would pop up. He waited until Jason walked over to sit down before he took a seat.

I reached over and grabbed my dad's hand. The anticipation was killing me. The wait wasn't long. After everyone was seated, Dr. V immediately started the introductions. Everyone else went around the room, introducing themselves.

Then Dr. V addressed the kids. "I know your dad and grandparents have talked to you about your mom's condition. Do y'all have any questions?"

As I watched through the one-way glass, there was a prolonged silence, like no one wanted to be the first person to speak.

When it seemed like none of the kids wanted to be the first, Damaris asked a question. "If Mom can't remember," she hesitated for a few seconds, like she was trying to find the right words, "how does she know who she is?"

"Honestly, we aren't really sure, Damaris. There is so much we don't know about the brain. Amnesia works in different ways. The way it is with your mom, it seems that most events before a certain period of time remained. Even in the period of time she remembers, she has difficulty remembering some events. Things like speech and motor coordination, how a person uses their hands and legs, are stored in another area of the brain," Dr. Ludlow answered her question.

"Will she know who we are?" This question was raised by Xavier.

Dr. V responded, "She knows who you are now. Your dad and grandmother have shown her pictures and told her lots of stories about y'all. Do you understand the difference in her remembering you before the accident and her knowing who you are now?" She waited for him to respond, but Dawson spoke up first.

"So'd she can know'd new stuff?" Dawson piped up.

"Yes, but even some new things are difficult for her right now."

Then he said, "Talon at school said she was a veg-ge-table. What does that mean?" Tears started to pool in my eyes.

Before anyone else had the chance, Jason responded, "Son, that's not a nice way to talk about anybody. Talon probably heard someone talking out of turn. I don't want you repeating that kind of thing. It's an unkind way to describe someone who can't respond for whatever reason. Your mom is capable of quite a lot, and with our love and understanding, she'll continue to heal, whether she gets her memory back or not. Understand?" Dawson nodded his head and looked deep in thought.

"Can Mom walk and talk?" Sybany quietly asked.

One of the speech therapists answered. "Yes to both. Although her speech is slurred and she has to think about what she says a little longer, it's getting better every day."

"The same with her mobility—walking. Your mom is using a walker, but soon we expect her to move to using a cane. Then she'll progress to walking unassisted. We have no doubt she will return to normal physical activity. She's dedicated to her therapy. You guys are a great motivator," the physical therapist told them.

"Sooo she doesn't wemember da time I dared Fwog ta hit da window wid a bat 'cause da awarm wady said it wouldn't bweak?" The look on Dawson's face was hopeful while Xavier looked like he wanted the floor to swallow him. Given the expression on each boy's face, I was pretty sure the story had been different after the actual event.

"Buuuussssssteedddddd," Sybany teased her brothers. Jason looked like he could strangle the boys. Everybody else in the room tried to stifle their laughter. Since we were in a separate room, my dad didn't bother trying not to laugh.

My mom admonished Dawson as gently as possible by saying, "Dawson, just because Mommy doesn't remember the things we've done in the past, doesn't mean we should take advantage, and we definitely don't need any more busted windows."

Dad looked at me and said, "Grandchildren are the best payback for the things your children put you through." I was sure it was, if you were the grandparent.

"What can we do to help Mom when she comes home?" Damaris asked, getting everyone back on track.

"Do little things for her. If you see her having difficulty, ask her if she needs help. Encourage her and be patient. She'll be coming back for therapies, and she'll have to practice things at home. Having a partner will be good for her." Dr. V paused a moment then said, "Be proud of your mom. She's working really hard. She may not be like other moms, but she's doing her best."

All of the kid's nodded their heads.

"Is there anything else you would like to know?" Jason asked, and they all shook their heads.

The hour was at hand; it was time to meet my children. I stood up and asked my dad to help keep me steady as I walked. I wanted to enter the room without using the walker. I wanted the kids to see that I was getting better. I didn't want them to be any more worried than they already were. Dad and I slowly made our way to the door of the lounge. Our journey was slow, but I made it without stumbling. My equilibrium was getting better, like everything else.

As Dad and I walked carefully through the door, Dawson yelled, "Mommy," jumping up and rushing over to me. Dad kept me upright when the impact of the five-year-old connected with my lower body, arms wrapped tightly around my waist.

There were more tears welling in my eyes. Dawson's hug was so touching, but at the same time, I was upset because I couldn't remember anything about him other than what I had been told. His hat had fallen from his head during our collision, so I rubbed my hand over his hair. My contact soothed him in a way I was unfamiliar with but seemed natural just the same.

My dad spoke up and told Dawson that I needed to sit down. I looked up and saw the other children standing there with varying expressions of uncertainty on their faces. I knew this moment wasn't about me, so I said, "No, not until I get a chance to hug everyone." That was all it took. Within seconds I was in the middle of the most heartfelt group hug. Dad stepped back but stood close behind in case I lost my balance.

I have no idea how long we stood there hugging each other, but that was the moment I felt like I could be a mother…I could be *their* mother. They deserved my best effort.

"This is the best hug ever!" I proclaimed to them. "How about we sit down and y'all catch me up on everything that's been going on?" We all made our way over to the couches that had been vacated when my team left the room to give us privacy. The kids helped steady me as we crossed the short distance. I glanced up at Jason, and there was a huge smile on his face. "What have y'all been up to?"

Dawson piped up first. "I'm playing soccer. It's so much fun, but you can't use your hands, only your feet." He bounced from foot to foot with his excitement.

"Oh wow," I responded, "that sounds like so much fun and lots of work." He nodded his head enthusiastically, jumping up to demonstrate how to dribble an invisible ball with his feet. When he finished, he crawled up in my lap, and I wrapped my arm around him.

"I'm playing too. Dad's coaching our teams, even though he never played soccer before," Xavier said with pride. "It's fun, but not as fun as my drum lessons, but you said we should be well rounded." He rolled his eyes, but then seemed to realize he was doing it and smiled, before saying, "But I really like playing."

I smiled and said, "I can't wait to see you play soccer and your drums!" I hoped I sounded as if these were the things I was most looking forward to because they were.

"The gym hosted the regional meet, but you missed it. I placed first in the all-around, the uneven bars, and the balance beam. I stumbled on my vault, and I needed to work on my beam work to make it stronger." I could tell Sybany was the most upset by what happened, but I wasn't sure why.

"Momma, it was awesome. Bunny was flying. It was so cool," Dawson exclaimed. Sybany smiled at her brother.

"Thanks, twerp." Aww, it was nice to see sibling love in play.

"I can't wait to see it," I told her, smiling. She gave me a small, crooked smile back. I noticed Damaris squeeze Sybany's hand.

"Damaris, what have you been up to?" I asked, trying to draw her into the conversation.

"I'm practicing for my next recital. We're doing an excerpt from Sleeping Beauty."

"That sounds exciting. What part are you playing?"

"I'm dancing the part of Princess Aurora," she says softly. Her voice was as gentle as she appeared. Dainty was the best way to describe Damaris.

I couldn't believe how active the kids were, and I couldn't fathom how there were enough hours in the day.

We talked for an hour or so, until someone suggested going to get something to eat. The kids requested to go to the food court down on the first floor of the hospital, so we went there. Much like their personalities, everyone wanted something different. Luckily, there was something for everyone. All of the kids seemed more relaxed. Sybany was reserved, but they all joked with each other and told stories for a couple of more hours until it was time for the kids to return home. The afternoon spent with the children had been the real beginning of rebuilding my life as a mother.

chapter

seven

$\mathcal{M}$y week in the rehab flew by. I worked hard at my therapies, and during my down time, I studied my recent history. Events were starting to register from the constant repetition, but there were still no memories to accompany the knowledge. I learned birthdays, first foods, first words, first steps, who played peewee baseball, and that they all thought magic fairy dust sprinkled around their beds at night kept the monsters away. Well, Dawson was the only one who still believed it, but the older kids went along with it so the tradition wasn't spoiled for him. Even in college, I'd never studied as hard as I studied those scrapbooks and Facebook. It was as if someone had given me the Holy Grail and I was determined to learn its secrets.

The kids took turns coming to the hospital to have dinner with me. Then we'd spend a couple of hours together. Each child picked the activity they wanted to do while we spent time getting to know each other.

Xavier came the first night. His dinner of choice: tacos. Based on the amount of food he ate, I worried about how we would feed him when he was a teenager. Jason wasn't a tiny guy, and Xavier was shaping up to be as big as, if not bigger than, his dad.

Our entertainment was a compilation video. Xavier had taken videos of all of his favorite drummers and put them together. I was floored by the array of performers. There was every type of drummer, from rock bands to symphonies. He pointed out nuances to each performance. What looked like people banging on drums to me was an art form to him. He explained how each one added to the music and how to compose music, layering each piece to make it tell a story. When I asked about why he was so interested in the history behind the music, rather than just playing the instrument, his answer surprised me.

"Mr. Seth—he's my teacher—says you can't really appreciate an instrument unless you know its history. Every culture has a drum of some kind. Drums have been used for thousands of years for thousands of different reasons," he explained, a sense of awe filling his young voice. It sounded like his teacher had a great desire for his students to connect with the musical instrument they played. "Plus, girls think drummers are cool."

Snapping out of my musings at that, I said, "Gurls? Why are 'ou worried 'bout what gurls tink? Don't gurls still 'ave cooties at ewwer age?"

"Mooom," he groaned, "only babies think girls have cooties. I'm nine, and I know that girls like musicians. It's just the way it is." Forgive me for not realizing that nine was a ripe old age. I thought boys were still tugging on girls' braids at that age. "Just look at Mr. Seth. His wife's hot, and he's a nerd."

"Xavier, don' c-awl 'ewole names," I scolded. Based on the picture I'd seen of Xavier and his music teacher, the description was accurate, but I didn't want him to think talking about people was okay.

"But Mr. Seth says he's a nerd. Why can he say it and I can't?" he argued.

"'Cause someimes 'ewole 'ay stuff 'bout themelves they 'on't wan' udder 'ewole to repeat. Is 'alld…itis cccalled…" The word wouldn't come to me. It was right there, but I couldn't grasp it.

"Self-deprecation." Jason spoke up.

"But being a nerd can be cool now," Xavier continued to protest. "Look at *The Big Bang Theory,* those guys are über nerds and they get hot chicks all the time. Well, except Amy Farrah Fowler."

I asked the obvious question, "Wha' does Bid Ban' 'eory 'ave to do wid calling 'ewole nerds?" Speaking slowly, I was able to enunciate my words much better.

"Oh, Mom, it's a TV show about this group of science nerds who like board games and comic books."

And that was how we ended up watching the first season of *The Big Bang Theory* on Netflix. I learned that being a nerd, along with Dr. Who, comic books, and dressing up as fantasy characters, was now cool. My, how times had changed.

The next evening was Damaris's turn. She brought a full meal, including dessert, with her along with a large rolling suitcase. Curiosity about the suitcase almost got the better of me, but I refrained from asking.

"Kitty made meatloaf, mashed potatoes, and corn. And I brought a surprise for dessert," she explained as she laid everything out.

We sat down to eat and the conversation flowed easily. Damaris filled us in on all the drama in the dance company. "So Bobby isn't talking to Tyler because he thinks Tyler was flirting with Adam, but Adam's not gay, so Tyler doesn't understand why Bobby is upset." Wait, is Bobby a boy or a girl? Not that I have an issue with it, but when I was thirteen I had no clue about things like this, and I definitely lacked the ability to talk about it without being childish.

"Is Bobby a 'oy or a gurl?" I asked in my stilted speech.

"Bobby is a boy, Mom," she says, like I should've known this, which I probably should have. "He and Tyler have been boyfriends for about two months, so he's really hurt. He said even if Adam isn't gay that Tyler shouldn't have acted the way he did. But, honestly, I think he just likes the drama. He can be worse than a girl sometimes." I felt like I was watching an after-school special mixed with a soap opera. I looked at Jason, who just shrugged his shoulders.

Once we finished dinner, the surprise dessert was a pint of Ben & Jerry's Ice cream. I stock piled pints and threatened anyone who dared to touch them. Damaris thought I would forgive her this time. She was correct. Thank God they hadn't retired the flavor, or I would have been up Shit Creek without a paddle.

After dessert, Damaris rolled the suitcase over. She had me sit in a chair and placed a footbath in front of me. "Daddy, will you start filling this for me then pour it in the footbath?" He grabbed the water pitcher she was holding and went to the restroom. "Make the water really warm but not hot," she called instructions to him.

After she got everything situated, she put a wrap on my hair and then rubbed a facemask on me. Then she pulled her chair beside mine and sat down. "I'm gonna start on your fingernails while your feet soak," she explained. Jason finished filling the footbath, pressed the start button, and placed my feet in the warm water.

In her Mary Poppins suitcase, she'd brought everything she

needed to give me a spa treatment. By the time she left, I felt like a new woman.

The night of Sybany's visit, it was raining. The dismal weather fit the mood inside my room. She'd selected her dinner of choice, and we ate in virtual silence as she stared at her plate. I tried to engage her, but her answers were mostly one-word replies. I didn't want her to feel pressured to talk to me, so I didn't push her for answers.

Not long after dinner, she asked her dad to take her home, saying she had homework to complete and chores to finish. I was sad to see her leave so soon.

I spent the rest of the night trying to read a book on my Kindle while I waited for Jason to return but failed miserably. I couldn't concentrate. My thoughts kept veering to Sybany and her reaction to me.

When Jason returned from taking her home, I asked him about her reaction to me.

"Sybany seems the toughest, but I think she worries the most. She found you when you fell. She had no idea what had happened to you. All she knew was you were bleeding really bad and wouldn't wake up." He squeezed my hand. "I think she thinks if she had done something different, then you might not have lost your memory. We've all tried to explain the circumstances to her, but she's having a hard time. We'll be there for her, though, and we'll make sure she understands that none of this was anyone's fault."

We were silent for a few minutes before I broached the next subject. "Jason, 'ow are 'ou here all the time? Don' 'ou 'ave to work? 'Ou won' ge' fiirred, wiill 'ou?" I had no clue about our financial situation. I didn't know what our jobs were, but I knew we couldn't afford to lose income right then. My hospital bills were going to be outrageous.

"It's okay, babe." He gave my hand another squeeze and began to rub his thumb over the palm of my hand. "I'm here because this is where I should be. We're very fortunate to have a large family to step in and help take care of the kids. Your mom and dad are staying at the house with the kids. They also have Mike and Beverly to help them out."

At my questioning look, he continued and explained who Mike and Beverly were. "Mike manages all of the maintenance and remodeling on the properties we own, and Beverly helps out around our house. We own several rental properties and other businesses. We manage all of that together. My 'job'," he used air quotes when he said job, "is working on custom cars at the shop I run with my dad." He grimaced and silently chuckled before correcting himself. "Technically, Mom and Macy run it. Dad and I just do what they tell us to; it's better that way." Jason raised my hand to his lips and pressed a kiss to my knuckles. "When you're ready, we'll sit down and go over the details of the business, but for now, I don't want you to worry about that. Our primary goal is getting you well," he finished with a smile.

Me getting well. What if I never got 'well'? Not wanting to talk anymore, I told him I was tired, and we got ready to go to sleep. He'd slept on a little foldout couch that was way too short for him since I had been transferred to rehab. Poor guy. He said he'd slept in worse places, so he wasn't going to complain.

My next visitor was Dawson. And true to form, he made the night fun. We went down to the food court because Dawson liked to be around people. He would talk to anyone about anything. He never met a lady he couldn't compliment. The first time he did it, I was shocked.

"Ma'am," he said to the lady in front of us, getting her attention, "jou hab nice wegs."

She murmured a surprised, "Thanks," and smiled at him. He tipped his hat in acknowledgment.

He was fashionably dressed in western wear today, including a cowboy hat, Wranglers, boots, western shirt, and bolo tie. There was a swagger in his step that hearkened back to John Wayne. I was surprised he didn't have on chaps to complete his outfit.

The next lady he complimented happened to be at the frozen yogurt machine. "I wike da cowor of jour hair. It's pwetty. It matches jour eyes." The thing was, he was sincere. He really thought the things he said. Then he reached for her hand and kissed it before telling her to have a good evening.

I looked at Jason and said, "'Haire does 'e geet dis?"

"I have no idea, but I think it's from watching old movies with Pappy."

We were going to need to watch out for the little ladies' man.

After we went back up to my room, Dawson said he had a special surprise for me. Since Damaris had given me a beauty treatment, or as he said, a booty tweetment, he wanted to make me pretty, too. I was a bit scared when he pulled out his Ninja Turtle lunchbox. Fortunately, all that was in there was his prized collection of tattoos. By the time he pronounced me fully decorated, I was sporting thirty-seven different tattoos, and he had nine, including one with a heart that read, *Mom,* on his small bicep.

chapter
eight

A week later the time had arrived for me to make a decision. My discharge from the rehab was scheduled for the next day. I needed to decide where I was going to live, which place was going to be home. My parents offered for me to stay with them, but I felt my place should be with *my* family. I was just a little uncomfortable with how it was going to work out, so I broached the subject with Jason.

My speech cleared up more each day. I still spoke slowly with careful thought and concentration, stuttering and dropping sounds, but I was much more understandable and could hold a conversation without needing to revert to the laptop. For clarity, I'm retelling my story from this point on without the awkward speech to save frustration.

"Jason, I think I should come home to our house." He said okay, and I continued, "But I'm a little worried about how things will be."

"Like what?" he asked, not giving any hint to what he thought should happen when I arrived home. His face was calm as he looked at me. I couldn't read any of his inner thoughts. He was still relaxed on the couch, but his attention was completely on me.

Under his gaze, I hesitated as I tried to think of how to phrase my thoughts. "Where will we sleep?" There, I said it. It was out in the open. There was no doubt I was physically attracted to Jason, but I still didn't know him. The thought of sharing what had been our intimate space when I didn't remember our life together bothered me.

"Umm, I guess I hadn't really thought about it. I can move into one of the guest rooms for a while," he offered, even though it was obviously not what he wanted based on the small frown that now turned his lips down at the corners.

"Do you think it will bother the kids if they see you sleeping in another room?" I know it seems like I only worried about the kids, but they had almost no choice in what was going on. We had to be their voice as well as our own.

Jason nodded his head in agreement. "It will probably bother them a little bit, but we'll explain it to them. We've taught them that a marriage is sacred and what goes on between two married people is based on love and trust. We'll have to explain that you don't remember those feelings just yet." He looked up and winked at me. "But I'll be working on that 'yet' part."

"What!" I was a little discombobulated. I'd been focused on trying to make sense of everything else. I hadn't been worrying about falling in love.

"Well, I did get you to fall in love with me once, despite your attempts to play hard to get." He laughed, and I lost any thought I had as I watched him. Jason was always handsome, but when he smiled and laughed, his eyes sparkled with mischief. "I'm pretty confident it could happen again."

Fidgeting with the fuzz on my pants, I gathered my courage and asked, "How did we fall in love? The last memory I have of you was saying hello at school and you looking at me like you had no clue that I was the girl who sat behind you the year before."

He grimaced a bit at my mention of him not remembering me. "Well, we met—again—your senior year of college. Macy invited you to our parents' house for their Christmas party. I happened to be home on leave. Macy introduced us, and you said 'hi' and blushed. I was intrigued by the blush, not to mention you were beautiful." He grinned and had a far off look in his eyes, as if he'd stepped back in time to that party. "Then Macy rushed you off to introduce you to our parents, and I spent the rest of the night trying to get a chance to talk to you. Every time I got close, you drifted away. Before I knew it, you were gone, and I'd missed my chance.

"The next day, I asked to use my sister's laptop when I saw it open and looked up your email address." He smirked at his sneakiness. "I sent you an email asking for your number. Two days later you sent me an email back, basically brushing me off." Me brushing Jason Woodruff off was unfathomable. "I wasn't giving up, though. I sent you another email asking you to help me pick out something for Macy's Christmas present. You sent me back a list, and I had to come up with reasons why everything you mentioned wouldn't work. Then I threw myself on your mercy and explained how our gifts had to be just right and have meaning behind them. It was all bullshit. Normally, I gave Macy a gift card, but I'd heard my mom say that to my dad and it sounded good, so I used it. I convinced you to meet me at the mall the next day." Humor filled his voice, but as he began to tell the next part, he started to bounce his knee.

"We met at the mall, which was a complete madhouse. But I was desperate, so we went shopping." A roll of his eyes emphasized the point of his desperation. "I produced a list of people I needed to shop for—I think I listed every aunt, uncle, and cousin I could remember and a few I made up—and off we went. We spent the day shopping for gifts. You'd ask all kinds of questions about the person receiving the gift, and I'd pretend like I was really into shopping. Each time I asked about you, you gave me really short answers. Even when we stopped to grab dinner, you were distant. Whenever I flirted with you, you seemed to get annoyed." The frown came back, and I wore one to match. I just couldn't get over how I would have withstood Jason being interested in me.

"At the end of dinner, we were standing outside the restaurant and I offered to walk you to your car. You told me 'no thanks'. I tried to argue and asked for your number. I wanted to ask you out on a real date while we were home." He glance up and gave me a bit of a playfully irritated look. "You said, 'Jason, it was really nice to see you again after all these years and you're just as good looking as ever, but Macy is my friend, and I'd like to keep it that way. I'm not interested in you having a fling with the nerdy girl you overlooked in high school.' Before I could figure out what the hell you were talking about, you told me to tell Macy and my family hello and to have a Merry Christmas. Then you turned around and walked away.

"I remembered Macy mentioning you had gone to our high school, but I didn't remember you. When I got home, I looked through my yearbooks, but you weren't in there, so I looked though Macy's. There you were. You'd graduated the year after I did, but I still didn't remember you. When Macy got home that night, I asked her if we had known each other. She refused to say anything and told me to ask you. I tried to play dumb, but she called me out on getting your email address and refused to give me your phone number and threatened to do bodily harm if I got it from her cell phone." He laughed, but I'm sure he wasn't laughing at his sister's threat at the time. I have no doubt the Macy I remembered would have made him pay the price.

"I emailed you and apologized for not remembering you, and I explained that I wanted to get to know you. I asked what class we had together. I figured that would be a good place to find something in common." His shrug was a boyish way of saying that should have been an easy conversation starter. "The email you sent back said, 'I'm sorry, class, I made a math error.' The class clicked immediately: Mrs. Dunlun's Geometry class. I went through all the girls I'd known in that class, but I'd gone to school with most of them since Kindergarten." His eyebrows drew together, as if he was mentally going over all of the female faces from the class. "Then I finally remembered the really quiet girl who sat behind me. She never said much, and I never paid much attention to her. I wrote you back with my discovery, and you responded with 'Ding! Ding!' That was it. I waited until Christmas Day to write you back and tell you what everyone thought of the gifts, and I asked you out for New Years, and you turned me down—again." This was punctuated with a pointed look at me.

"I moped around for the next week, which is why Macy took pity on me and invited me out with her and her friends. I accepted, hoping we'd bump into each other, but she quickly shot that idea down. Anyway, she lied, because after we'd been there for an hour or so, you showed up with a guy." The knee was bouncing again, but this time his hand rubbed up and down his thigh. "I cornered you and asked why you didn't just tell me you had a boyfriend. You said you didn't, and I asked why you came with a guy then. You looked at me like I was being an idiot, which I was, and said because you were friends with him. Right then the countdown to midnight started. You turned to walk away, so I grabbed your arm to turn you back around and kissed you. When I drew back, you wrinkled your nose and said, 'Not at all what I'd imagined,' and walked off. I went home ashamed of myself."

I wished I could offer him some sort of comfort that what happened was okay. Jason didn't strike me as the type of guy who would do something that would make a woman uncomfortable, but my lack of memory held me back.

"The next day, I sent you an email apologizing for kissing you and acting the way I had. Two days later, I left to go back to North Carolina, thinking I'd never hear from you again. But you did email me." The hand stopped rubbing his thigh, but the knee still bounced, and his thumb caressed my hand in a now familiar pattern. "You accepted my apology and said there really wasn't anything to apologize for. Somehow over the next three and a half months we progressed from emailing each other every day to talking to each other every day. When

Spring Break rolled around, I convinced you and Macy to invite a few friends up to North Carolina to stay in a condo a friend owned out on The Outer Banks.

"I was excited and terrified that you were coming. I knew I was developing deep feelings for you, but I wasn't sure about you because we hadn't talked about it. I knew you planned to move back to Mobile when you graduated, and I would still be in North Carolina. Long distance relationships are a lot of work.

"Anyway, y'all came up for the week, and I spent as much time with you as I could. The night before y'all were leaving to go back to school, I asked you to walk on the beach with me." He drew in a deep breath, and his eyes once again had that far off look. "We walked without saying anything for a long time. It was getting dark and you said, 'The evening star is out, make a wish,' and you closed your eyes. I had no doubt what my wish was, so I reached for both your hands and kissed you. It was the best kiss I'd ever had." He paused, reliving the memory for so long that I thought I would have to ask what happened next. I felt like I was reading a book and it ended with a cliffhanger. "I'd never felt the way I did up until that moment. I told you, 'I know we have a lot to work out and a lot more ahead of us, but, Candice, I'm falling in love with you. I just wanted you to know.' And you said, 'Okay.' That was it, 'okay', and you turned back toward the condo. I told everyone good night and left, feeling hopeless."

I wondered what the hell I had been thinking. The guy admitted he loved me and all I said okay. Even now I could feel our chemistry. I could only imagine what it must have felt like to stand there on that beach and have the guy I'd dreamed about tell me he loved me.

"The next morning before dawn, you called me and asked me to come down early. When I got there, you were sitting out on the beach, watching the sunrise. I sat down beside you. I was unsure of what to say or do. The sun rose higher and higher, and then you said, 'I'm not sure when it happened, but I know I love you, too. I didn't want to leave without telling you.' I picked you up, sat you across my lap, and kissed you for all I was worth." He grinned shyly and glanced over at me. I smiled a little at his memories as I tried not to think about the fact that I didn't have any of my own. "It was the best morning of my life, until Macy yelled that y'all needed to leave."

chapter
nine

$\mathcal{I}$ wished I could remember that time and all of those feelings bursting to life. How many people find their first crush years later and fall in love? It had to mean something. Fate had given us so much, and then it had been taken away. Life could be cruel. I thought about our first kiss and our second and all the ones that came after it. There were so many unanswered questions. All the things I didn't know about myself, let alone everybody else.

Nerves were getting the better of me as I sat at the curb in the hospital-mandated wheelchair, waiting for Jason to pull around. I was going home to a house I'd helped design, to a family I'd helped create, neither of which I could remember. I knew the general location of our house. It was close to my mom's family's original dairy farm.

As I was mentally retracing the drive to my family's farm, two cars pulled up to the curb in front of me. The first was a huge SUV. It must have been the size of a school bus. No sooner did it stop before the doors started popping open. All of the kids piled out onto the sidewalk.

Dawson yelled, "We comed ta take jou home, Mommy. Are jou suepwised?" He was bouncing from one foot to the other. It was cute that he still pronounced you with a j instead of a y.

"Yes, buddy, I sure am surprised." I chuckled at his enthusiasm. I looked around at all the kids and their various expressions of wariness and excitement. The fact that they weren't still innocent to the world and didn't share their youngest brother's blind enthusiasm made me a little sad for them. The doors to the other truck opened, and my parents got out and walked over to us.

Jason bent down to kiss my cheek and said, "I called in reinforcements. Needing a U-Haul to get all your stuff home was only a mild overstatement." Even though we'd given all of the bouquets of flowers and plants away to other patients, there was a ton of stuff that had accumulated over the course of my hospital and rehab stay.

"Movers at your service. Okay, boys and girls, let's get this stuff loaded up," my dad instructed, and all of the kids jumped into action. My stuff was loaded up rather quickly, and before I knew it, I was seated in the front seat of the SUV headed home.

The great thing about little kids is they're great for breaking tension. Dawson kept us entertained with stories about our dogs. It seemed we had quite a few—dogs, that is—and they were a source of a lot of destruction. "…but Aunt Melissa put a few of them in foster homes, so there aren't so many." Aunt Melissa? Who was Aunt Melissa? "She left da biggest trouble makers wid us, but she's working on gettin' dem wid experimenced peoples, so dey won't get as mad at da dogs."

While he continued to explain Aunt Melissa's plans for the troublemakers, I asked Jason who Aunt Melissa was. "She's one of your best friends. Y'all met when we lived in California and have been friends for over a decade. When we opened The Dog On It and it took off and expanded, you asked her to move here to run it. Now she coordinates the dog rescue as well."

Dawson spoke up from the back seat, "But we can't have cats 'cause Daddy's aller–allergit ta dem."

"You're allergic to cats?" I asked Jason.

He nodded his head and grimaced. "Yeah, sorry 'bout that."

"What happened to Boo Radley?" Boo Radley was the cat who'd adopted me. He started out as a squatter on my patio. I felt bad, so I would feed him. One day he darted inside my apartment when I opened the sliding glass door and never left. Guess he knew a sucker when he saw one. It took me a while to get used to having a pet, but I caught on eventually. One sky-high water bill, because he learned to turn the kitchen faucet on when he was out of water, and replacing the molding around the pantry door where I kept his food, were great teachers.

"He lives at Kitty and Paw Paw's. He used to be really skittish, but now he likes to curl up in everybody's lap," Damaris explained.

"How many dogs do we have?" I asked.

"We had seventeen, but we're down to five. A lot of people volunteered to foster when they heard what happened." Damaris continued to fill me in on all of the animal related topics. We had quite the menagerie, minus cats and reptiles. I'd drawn the line at reptiles and bugs.

It took about thirty-five minutes to make the drive home. Jason pulled up to a gate and pushed a button. The gate opened and we drove down a long driveway lined with pecan trees. When the driveway turned to the left to dip behind a hill, I saw our home for the first time. It was a massive Victorian.

"I thought we built this seven years ago," I stated, obviously confused because it looked older. It looked like a house I'd loved when I was a child. Any time we'd drive by that house, I would tell whoever I was with I wanted to live in that house when I grew up.

"We did. You showed the architect a picture of a house and said you wanted the outside to look like that house. I was pretty sure Jeff would quit before he got the house designed the way you wanted it."

The last few moments of the drive were silent as I took in the house that was our home. This was the place we chose to raise our family. It housed the memories that I'd lost. Too bad walls couldn't talk.

As we pulled around to the side of the house there was a large garage. Each bay had a wide garage door. "We had a double doors put in because you had a tendency to knock mirrors off in a single width garage." I wanted to defend myself, but it sounded like something I would do. I never had really bad wrecks that I could remember, but my fender benders with inanimate objects were legendary. He parked in the first garage bay. The kids jumped out of the SUV as if they'd been sprung from jail.

"Come on, Momma!" Dawson began to pull me toward the house. I tried not to stumble and caught myself on my new cane.

"Dawson, slow down. Be careful. Mom needs to walk a little slower," Jason scolded Dawson.

Dawson frowned and apologized, "Sowwy, Mommy, I forgot." I smiled down at him and squeezed his hand.

"I'm glad you're so excited I'm home, but we'll just have to go a little slower. You can give me the grand tour," I offered, hoping it would distract him from thinking about the reality of the situation.

"I already made jou a map," he proclaimed with pride; his little chest poking out.

We crossed through a wide glassed-in hallway with plants and flowers lining the sides. Dawson ran ahead to open the door at the end.

He held it while I made my way toward it, focusing on the small section I could see. I'd been focusing so intently that I hadn't realized Jason was right behind me until I felt an arm across my back and one at my knees, sweeping me up in the classic bridal hold. Getting my barring, I looked up to find Jason grinning, dimples in full effect. "I figured you don't remember any of the times I carried you across the threshold of our new home," he stated, "so I can get away with doing it all over again."

Damaris said aww. Sybany laughed. And Xavier said, "Dad, that's gross. Can you wait to do the mushy, sissy stuff 'til later?"

"This mushy, sissy stuff is how you catch a lady like your mom, so you better start taking lessons," his dad retorted.

Xavier scoffed. "I don't need those kinds of lessons, Dad, 'cause I'm gonna be in a band."

"Doofus, you need to be more than in a band to get a girl to like you," Damaris chided her brother while cuffing him on the shoulder and rolling her eyes.

"Whatever. Shawna already had Jessica send me a message asking if I liked her. And I'm not even in a band yet," he staunchly defended his position.

Jason sat me down in a chair at the table and turned his full attention to Xavier. "Xavier, you will treat girls with respect. I don't care if you like them or not, do you understand?" Jason's tone was stern but didn't hold any anger.

"Yes, sir."

"Besides, none of you are allowed to date until you're sixteen, so you don't need to be worried about who likes you and who doesn't. There's plenty of time for that later in life. Now, who's hungry?" he asked and a round of "me" and "I am" went up around the room. Right then, the back door opened and my parents walked in.

Jason walked over to a cabinet and opened it, revealing it was a refrigerator. He started pulling out lunchmeat and sandwich fixings. Mom walked over to start helping Jason, and my dad headed back out the door to start unloading the truck. I heard Xavier tell Sybany, "Shawna's like two feet taller than me. No way I'd like a girl who is taller than me."

To which she replied, "Don't worry, you won't always be a shrimp."

"I'm not a shrimp. I'm almost taller than you, so if anybody's a shrimp, it's you," he argued.

She shrugged her shoulders. "We can't all be the Jolly Green Giant."

"I am," Dawson said. "I'm gonna be da Jowwy Gween Giant when I growed up."

"Xavier, go help your Paw Paw, and, Sybany, go let the dogs out. Dawson, come and get Mom's drink and take it to her," Jason instructed. A chorus of "Yes, sir" followed by the shuffling of feet as each kid went to do as instructed.

Jason and Damaris carried everything over to the table. It took a couple of trips to transfer it all. There was a large assortment. Xavier and Sybany returned, and we all sat down to eat lunch. Lunch was filled with more chatter about the family happenings until Jason brought up me taking a nap.

"You all have schoolwork to work on and chores to complete. I'm sure Mom could use a nap. I'm going to move some of my clothes to the guest room to sleep in there for a little while," Jason calmly filled everyone in on the plan. He tried to set a positive, casual tone. Unfortunately, it didn't work.

Damaris asked, "Why?" Alarm transformed her normally serene face.

As she stood abruptly from the table, her hands clenched in fists, a visibly distressed Sybany blurted out, "Are y'all getting divorced now?"

And Dawson said, "Bu' Mommies and Daddies awe suepposed ta sweep in da same woom." He appeared to get agitated at the thought of Jason and me not sharing a room. His hands began to flap and tears formed in his eyes.

Since Jason had been taking the brunt of the discussions with the kids, I wanted to let them hear from me. "It's okay, guys. Daddy is just giving me a little time to get used to coming home. We're getting to know each other again."

Not believing the explanation, Sybany cried, "But you'll end up getting divorced. That's what Alissa's parents did. They had separate rooms and then they got divorced." Her fists banged on the table and her voice wavered as she made her point.

Jason tried to comfort her, but I could see it was hard for him because he was unsure. It was the subtle tenseness around his mouth and eyes and the strain in his voice that gave his feelings away.

"Kitty and I sleep in separate rooms some times, too. You know, on the count of she snores like a hibernating bear," my dad interjected, trying to be funny. He drew a few chuckles from everyone but my mom.

"Carl Owens, you take that back. I do *not* snore!" she exclaimed.

He laughed. "Yes, you do 'cause you won't use your CPAP machine."

"You said I looked like an elephant when I wore it!" She was getting into a hissy. I feared my dad might get a frying pan upside the head. Luckily, no frying pans were handy, so his head remained safe.

"I wike ellafunts, Kitty. Can I weared it?" Dawson spoke up and asked, having calmed down from the separate rooms issue. The idea of being an elephant was a bigger draw.

"Sure, baby. It messes up Kitty's hair when I use it," Kitty told him.

"Great! Thousands of dollars for it to become kid toy," my dad halfheartedly griped.

"Better spent on a kid's toy than on your tombstone at the moment." I think Dad decided he'd taken enough heat for the moment because he held up his hands in surrender.

Jason remained calm and looked each of the kids in the eye as he spoke. "Nobody knows what the future holds. We aren't going to lie to y'all: I'm sure we're going to have some tough times, but we're a family and your mom and I made vows to each other that we believe in. Neither of us is giving up, but sometimes we have to adapt to make it through a tough time. Besides, there's no way Mom would be able to move all of her stuff out of the closet." Everybody gave a halfhearted laugh at his last statement. No doubt they all got the joke at my expense.

Once everyone was calm, Jason told the kids to go start on their schoolwork and chores. Then he offered to show me to our room.

"Candy, we're just going to hang out here and help the kids if they need anything, okay?" my mom said, and I nodded as Jason and I started to walk out of the kitchen.

We walked through the family room, where Dad had set all of the suitcases and stuff from the hospital. There was a wide staircase to a landing, but we bypassed it and went down a hall, then turned left down a short hall that ended with a double door. Jason opened one door, and I stepped into a beautiful suite.

The room looked like it had come out of the pages of *Southern Living*. The furniture was what I think is called French provincial. The floors were the same hardwood as the rest of the house with a few pale silver and cream rugs scattered across the floor. The draperies that hung over three French doors that took up one wall matched the ice blue damask bedding. The upholstered couch and chairs surrounding a large cream-colored fireplace had the same fabric. The room was exactly what I had dreamed of when I'd pictured my dream house.

"There's not much of you in this room, is there?" I stated to Jason.

"Nope, but I got my man cave and garage, so the rest of it I didn't care about. I did help pick out the mattress, though," he said with what I was coming to know as his trademark smirk.

I chose to ignore the bed comment and asked where the bathroom was so I could freshen up. In reality, I needed to pee like a rushing racehorse. Jason pointed to two sets of double doors on the left. "The second set is the bathroom. The first set is one of the doors to your closet," he told me.

I walked over and opened the second set and walked into a bathroom that was bigger than my first apartment. Centered on the right wall was a claw foot bathtub. It was framed by a huge cathedral window with a chandelier hanging above. There was also a large walk-in shower with multiple showerheads. Overall, the bathroom was over the top.

"Rick helped you design it," Jason volunteered. That explained loss of my friend. It was so unfair.

"I don't know, babe. I didn't know the answers then, and I still don't. I know, for you, this is like losing him all over again. But I know you. You've been my best friend for over sixteen years, and I'm not going anywhere. I promise." I knew that wasn't a promise Jason could make, but I understood and appreciated the sentiment.

After a few minutes, I dried my eyes and drew in a deep breath. "I guess we should get back to our guests, shouldn't we? Rick always did love a good dinner party," I said with a sad smile at the thought. As I stood up and looked at the bathroom I'd previously thought was beautiful but somewhat overdone, I knew I would never change a thing. I could almost hear Rick's voice as he said, 'Listen, Candyland, when you have the choice between good and all right and bigger and better, always go bigger and better. Bigger is *always* better.' I told Jason, "Just let me brush my teeth."

He waited for me while I cleaned up and then reached for my hand as we walked back to dinner.

The rest of the night was subdued, but I did my best to smile and have a good time. I knew the next day was going to be worse.

After therapy the next day, I asked Jason if we could meet Devon. Jason called Devon, who said he would meet us at their house. Jason turned toward Midtown, but he stopped at the Krispy Kreme. "We'll have a little bit of time before Devon makes it to his house. Let's get a snack," Jason suggested.

"When did they build this one?" I asked. This was a much newer Krispy Kreme than the ones I remembered.

"It was before we moved back from California. It's the only one now," he answered.

"There isn't one on Government anymore?" I asked, not believing the ones from yesteryear were gone.

"Nope."

"What about Highway Ninety?"

a lot. Rick had been my best friend since high school. He was also as gay as they came, so it explained a lot of the grandeur to the bathroom. "I'm going to start gathering some of my clothes to take to the guest room." Jason opened one of the doors on the left wall and stepped inside. I decided to find a toilet in this bathroom on estrogen overload. Thankfully, it was the first door I opened.

I'd finished my business and was washing my hands when Jason walked out of his closet. "This is your closet," he said, pointing to the door next to the one he exited, "if you want to change into something more comfortable."

"No. I think I'm just going to go lie down," I said and turned toward the bedroom.

"The remote to close the curtains is on your bedside table."

I said okay, even though I didn't know which side of the bed was mine, and left the bathroom. The thought of him moving out of the bedroom was depressing. It felt like we were taking two steps back, but at the same time, it didn't feel right to share a bed with him.

Damn it all to hell! What had I done to deserve this? Did I not appreciate everything I had been blessed with? Is that the reason, God? Are you trying to teach me a lesson? Was I too focused on material possessions and what we could achieve?

As I crawled into bed, there were no answers forthcoming. I pulled the comforter up to my chin and cried. I thought I was being quiet, but I must have made noise, because I felt Jason's body behind mine. He slid an arm underneath me and the other over me, drawing me back into his embrace. "It's going to be all right, babe. We've had hard times before. Shhh." He continued to murmur loving words while he held me. Eventually I drifted into a deep sleep.

For the first time, when I awoke, Jason wasn't there.

chapter
ten

I freshened up and then went in search of caffeine. Caffeine and I had a longstanding love affair, which predated the point at which I lost my memory. Right then, I was willing to make a bargain with the devil himself to get an ice cold Dr. Pepper without ice.

As I walked back into the bedroom, I noticed the pictures grouped together over the fireplace. In the center was a stone plaque that read, *There's no place like home.* Surrounding the plaque were photos in all different sizes. Every photo was in color, making them stand out against the soft color pallet of the room.

Each picture spoke to the love that had created this family.

A picture of younger versions of Jason and me as we lay in bed. Given the angle, it had been taken by one of us. Most likely Jason. He was smiling and laughing while I had my head on his shoulder. My smile not as big but just as satisfied.

One of me standing in front of a window. The sunlight shining through my nightgown, outlining my heavily pregnant body.

Jason kneeling in front of me, kissing my pregnant belly. His cover about to fall off of his head. A cover is a hat in the Marine Corps.

Jason asleep in bed with a curly haired toddler on one shoulder and an infant on the other, her butt propped on his arm. All sleeping with their mouths open.

The girls playing dress up. Huge dresses, tons of jewelry, and enough makeup to make a drag queen shudder.

Me in my wedding dress, sitting on a couch. Jason's head in my lap, my hand cradling his face, his hand pressed against mine, our other hands clasped together, resting on his chest, the two of us gazing at each other and sharing a laugh. I wondered what we had been laughing about at that moment.

Jason and Xavier on a tractor in the pecan orchard.

A picture of all of us crowded into a hospital bed with a baby Dawson, I figured, since there were two little girls and a little boy in the picture. Our first complete family photo.

A small baby dressed in a white T-shirt and a pink hat cradled in each of our hands. It was the only photo like it on the wall. There was a sweet sadness to it. I wondered which of the girls it was.

Jason, Xavier, and Dawson peeing off a balcony. I shook my head, thinking, *Boys!*

All of the kids in a pool, grinning with Kool-Aid mustaches.

There were so many, and I wanted to know the stories behind each of them. This was the only place I'd seen most of these pictures. They weren't in baby books or on Facebook.

Stepping away from the wall documenting our life over the past seventeen years, I continued on my quest for caffeine and headed to the kitchen.

I'd slept for about three and a half hours, and the noise level in the house was substantially louder than when I had laid down. As I stepped into the family room, I could hear adults in the kitchen and the squeals of kids outside accompanied by the sounds of splashing in the pool. I looked out the patio doors and there were more kids out there than just mine. A few people sat around chatting. I wanted to see who was in the kitchen first before I tackled who the people outside were.

When I stepped into the kitchen, there was a loud squeal and then I was wrapped in arms that smelled like honeysuckle. My sister said, "I'm so glad you're home and we can see you finally." I had asked that nobody but my mom, dad, Jason, and the kids visit while I was in the hospital and rehab. I'd wanted to focus on my relationships with them.

"Yes, I am," I responded, unsure of what else to say.

She pushed me back, but held on to my shoulders. "Damaris did a great job freshening you up, but, honey, we're gonna need to get you in for an overhaul. You just let me know when you can come in, and I'll make sure it happens," Meri instructed me.

"I have therapy every day, but I'm sure we can fit it in somewhere." I wanted to reconnect with my sister. At least I remembered her—mostly. She smiled widely at my answer.

"Oh without a doubt. I'll tell Mom, she'll make sure your skinny behind gets there." Then she let go so the next person could step up to greet me.

I met Melissa, her husband Juan, my brother's new wife Johnna, Tonya, and Bethany. Tonya and Bethany were part of our home school group, and we had become good friends. I met their husbands and kids. Mike and Beverly introduced themselves. Lee stepped up to hug me. Sandra, my Godmother, had passed away from breast cancer my junior year in college. Macy hugged me and introduced me to her husband Jeff. At our introduction I said, "Oh are you the architect that almost quit on me?" He laughed and said yes, but that he didn't since it gave him an excuse to be around Macy because he was waiting for her to dump her boyfriend so he could have a chance. Funny how things work out.

While I slept, it had been decided to have my core group of friends and family over for a cookout to welcome me home. Everyone was laughing and having a great time. They took turns telling me stories about our lives together. It was very nice, but something was missing. It took me a while before it dawned on me; it wasn't something that was missing, it was someone. I'd done my best not to question why he hadn't shown up at the hospital, convincing myself he was respecting my wishes or maybe he'd moved away for a job.

"Where's Rick?" I asked, and everyone stopped eating. I knew at that moment my hope that he had just moved away for a job was fruitless.

Jason was the one to speak. "Rick was killed in a car wreck three years ago. Devon wanted to wait a while to see you because he knew you would ask."

I felt sick. I pushed back from the table and ran for the only bathroom I knew of, the one in our bedroom, barely making it before I lost everything I had eaten that evening. Once I stopped dry heaving, I realized someone was holding my hair for me. A hand held a wet wash cloth out to me, and he said, "Wipe your face, babe." I did as he instructed then sat on the floor, crying out my sorrow. He picked me up, sat in the same spot I had been in, and held me in his lap, doing his best to console me.

Through my sobs, I cried out, "I don't understand why, why did God have to take the one person who knew me better than I knew myself? He was the best of everything. Why take him?" I wailed at the

"Nope. I'm afraid this is it," he confirmed.

"That's just sacrilege. We should be ashamed of ourselves for coming here."

"I get your righteous indignation and all, but we're talking doughnuts here, and not just any doughnuts but the world's best doughnuts, so can we just forget about the being mad because it's not tradition part and just get a doughnut?" Jason pleaded.

I nodded my reluctant consent. He'd given me so much, I could relent on doughnuts, so we went in and ordered three mixed dozen. "You said it was polite to take a gift when you went to someone's house for the first time," he explained. "And if we show up at home without any for the natives, we may not make it to dinner."

"How would they know we had doughnuts?" I asked, genuinely bemused. I thought if I could hide my antics from my parents, then the reverse should be true. In reality, I hadn't fooled my parents about any of my antics, and there isn't much that gets past kids.

Jason looked at me with pity, like the look you give someone right before you say bless your heart. "They smell it on you. It's like they have a sixth sense that can sniff out when you've had something they want or done something they wanted to do. But like most animals, if you keep them fed, they're pretty happy and under control," he observed. I had a lot to learn about children.

That's how we ended up carrying a box of doughnuts to Devon's front door. It's odd that people always bring food to the house of someone who dies, and here we were doing the same thing; it just happened to be three years later.

I was nervous to meet the man that my best friend had loved. What was I supposed to say? Should I hug him? Were we hugging-type friends? I mean, with Rick, there were always hugs. But I didn't know Devon from Adam's house cat.

In the time we stood on the doorstep of the charming craftsman, I thought back over my friendship with Rick, the awkward boy who was too big and bright to be gone so soon.

"You know, I hate this class. I can barely pass English and they want me to conjugate verbs in Spanish. You should be able to get second language credit for music. After all, music is a language, too," he said as he sat next to me in Spanish.

"It wouldn't do me any good if it was. I can't sing or play an instrument," I told him.

"Yeah, but you're passing this class," he responded with a huff of false irritation. "I can even speak redneck. Wanna head to the crick over yonder an' sit for a spell? See?" I just nodded; there was no use arguing with him.

And another memory.

"You can't not go to prom," he stated.

"I don't want to go. I don't dance. I'm not dating anyone, and I couldn't care less that Kelsey Dunlun is named Prom Queen. So why should I go to prom?" It was a rhetorical question, but he chose to answer anyway.

"Because it's Prom and one day we are going to look back on this with nostalgia and remember it as one of the best nights of our lives." He held his arms out and looked at me like this was a no-brainer.

We'd ended up going together. And he was right; I did look back on that night as one of the best, but not for the reasons he'd assumed. There had been a mix up with his tux order, and the pants had been way too big, so he'd tightened them as much as he possibly could. We'd gone with a group of friends to dinner. The food was awful. Then as we were getting ready to walk across Water Street to the Arthur R. Outlaw Convention Center, I noticed Rick wasn't walking beside me. I looked back to find Rick with his broken pants around his ankles. Never one to have any shame—thankfully, he was wearing boxers—he stood there and yelled across the parking garage, "My damn pants broke. Anybody got a safety pin?" Somehow, between all the girls we found a safety pin and pinned his pants. Unfortunately, the pin couldn't hold up to his enthusiastic dance moves and had broken while he was 'busting a move', causing him to lose his pants again.

He drove us back to my parents' house without his pants and walked in like there was nothing unusual about a boy walking into his best friend's house while holding his tuxedo jacket and pants over his arm. I immediately started laughing at the look on my parents' faces and haltingly told them the story through my laughter.

"Yuck it up," he'd said, "and remember to wash your hair, don't try to brush it. I'm going to bed."

And another memory.

"I think I'm going to apply to the Mobile College for music ministry. If you're going into ministry, they help with tuition." We were discussing applying to college. Rick was thinking of ways to assist with his tuition. His dad had to stop working because of his health and had been denied disability, so money for college was scarce.

"Isn't that a Baptist college?" I asked.

"Yeah, so? I go to a Baptist church," he'd retorted a little defensively.

I was unsure of what to say. We'd never discussed his sexuality, but it was obvious. "But…" I hesitated before continuing, "you're gay, right? Won't you have to hide who you are?" I'd said, and he'd started to cry.

"You don't hate me?" he'd asked through tears.

I hugged him and said, "Of course not, I love you. You're my best friend."

"You don't think I'm an abomination?"

"No, and nobody else does either."

"What do you mean nobody else does?" He'd lifted his head, and his voice had gone a little high pitched in despair at the thought of someone knowing.

"Your mom and I talked about it. She asked me if there was a boy you liked."

"SHE ASKED YOU IF THERE WAS A BOY I LIKED? HOW DID SHE KNOW?"

"Yes, she asked me. I mean, it's kind of obvious," I said unsure of how it was supposed to be such a secret.

"WHAT DO YOU MEAN IT'S OBVIOUS?" he'd screeched and began to pace the confines of my bedroom.

"Jeez and Petes, would you stop screeching and yelling? People know you're gay. Big deal. You can come out of the closet now. I'm just happy I don't have to share my clothes with you."

He huffed and gave me a haughty look. "I would never borrow your clothes. You have the fashion sense of a bag lady!"

We'd laugh, and that was that.

"Well, Candyland, it looks like you're not over the rainbow anymore. And you brought doughnuts. You know what those will do to my figure," snapped me out of my memories.

My vision cleared to find a shorter man with a beard, thick hair, and twinkling eyes.

"Wow, I never figured Rick would go for a bear," were the first words out of my mouth as I addressed my best friend's husband, who happened to have been a college friend of mine. We'd met during the first semester of our freshman year.

"Neither did he, honey," he replied with a laugh. "Come on in." He stepped back and held the door open for us to come inside.

Jason and I walked in and followed him back to a sun porch that was shaded by an oak tree. There, sitting on a glass end table, was a picture frame. It held two pictures. They were both of Rick and me. In the one on the left, Rick posed beside me in the tackiest Scarlett O'Hara bridesmaid's dress I'd ever seen. In the one on the right, I wore a lime green tux with a matching ruffled shirt, a paisley print cummerbund, and white wing tips.

Devon saw what I was looking at and said, "The two of you had a contest to see which of you could find the best wedding outfit. You had to wait a few years to get even, but I think you bested him on that occasion."

I knew he hadn't worn that in my wedding; I'd seen a few pictures, so I must have looked confused. It was a state of being for me. "He showed up to give his maid of honor speech in that," Jason filled in the blank. I wondered why I hadn't seen these pictures before.

"Then you did the same with your best bitch speech at our wedding," Devon added.

I laughed and wished I could remember it. The contest seemed like something Rick would get me to do. He always said I needed to come out of my shell.

Then I spent the next couple of hours getting to know the man who loved my best friend.

"Have you dated since the accident?" I asked, wanting to be supportive. I had no doubt that Rick would have wanted the person he loved to find happiness again.

"No. There hasn't been anyone that could match him," Devon said with a sadness in his voice and his eyes.

"I may not remember the two of you together, but I know he wouldn't want you to be alone." It was my effort to encourage him not to drown in grief.

"I'm not alone. I've got two of your mutts in the back yard that Melissa talked me into taking. They've already destroyed a couch, six feather pillows, two pairs of shoes, and eaten through a door." He laughed but then got serious again. "But I understand what you're saying. Maybe one day another prince will come," he said with another sad smile.

We talked for a little longer then Jason and I got up to leave, making sure Devon knew he was welcome any time and expected to show up for family dinners. I left feeling like I had a small piece of my best friend with me.

Once we were in the truck, I asked Jason why they didn't have a child. I knew Rick had wanted children. He'd talked about being a dad quite a bit.

"They had an adoption pending when the accident happened. She was really supposed to be a surrogate for them, but she got pregnant before that was finalized and asked if Rick and Devon would want to adopt the baby. They said yes, and that moved forward until the accident. The agency and the birth mother felt it would be better for the child to be placed in a two-parent home."

It made me sad to realize Devon not only lost his husband but a child at the same time. Once again, I realized how blessed I was even given the circumstances I was experiencing. At least I had the chance to experience them. I reached over and held Jason's hand as we drove home.

chapter eleven

We established a new routine over the next few weeks. Dawson had the hardest time with the changes. There were a few temper tantrums, but Jason or my parents or Bev or one of his siblings was always on hand to help diffuse the situations. It was a little odd to me that a five-year-old would be having such tantrums, but they ended once the routine stayed the same for a while. It helped that he got to spend a lot of time with Pappy.

The older kids had a multitude of activities along with being home-schooled, and I had therapy, which had been cut down to three days a week as of this past week. There were home exercises I had to do each day, but I could do them around our schedule. I hadn't been cleared to drive, so someone had to take the children and me wherever we needed to go. Jason did a lot, but he had tons of work to catch up on. His dad wasn't a young man anymore, and while they had a great staff, there were just some tasks Jason needed to handle. Thank goodness for Beverly and my mom and dad, they were practically at our beck and call.

Beverly was my right hand woman. She knew the ins and outs of how everything ran from the business to the kids' schedules. If I needed to know anything, I could ask Bev and she would know the answer. Usually she did more of the work around the house and helped with the business on the side. Since my accident, she'd stepped into a more hands-on role with our company, but Jason was still taking the brunt of the workload. It's hard to manage a company when you don't even remember having a company, much less how to run the damn thing.

Beverly and Mike were retired and working with us was a way they supplemented their income. They had a cottage on our property, so the commute to work was a snap, and the hours were flexible for the most part. Mike managed all of the maintenance and remodeling for the real estate business. He'd worked in construction, and there didn't seem to be anything he couldn't fix.

They had an adult son living with them. Brian had Down syndrome. He enjoyed living in the country and working with his dad. Part of the reason Beverly and Mike still worked was to put money away to care for Brian should something happen to either one of them. Brian also worked part-time as a greeter and pet liaison at The Dog On

It. He was very independent, but Bev and Mike knew there needed to be a care plan and finances available to help support Brian.

I worried that with Beverly taking on so much of the business workload, it would be too much for her long term. On top of that, I knew Jason was taking on way too much between our company, the shop with his dad, and the kids. Jason and I talked about it and decided to ask Melissa to take over the day-to-day operations for the company. Then she could hire someone to run The Dog On It.

Apparently, The Dog On It had been my brainchild. It started as a doggy day camp and extended stay boarding facility and morphed into a grooming salon, fashion boutiques, veterinary clinic, and pet friendly restaurants and hotel. Everything was themed around pets. Even though it was a for-profit business, half the profit went to support animal rescue. Learning that made me really happy. I'd always loved animals—well, some animals.

Devon was the head veterinarian. We'd met at Auburn as students and kept in touch over the years. Just about the time Jason and I were moving back to Mobile, Devon was looking to open his own clinic. So we pooled our resources, and the rest is history. He met Rick and they fell in love. It seems our building projects are a place to meet your future significant other. First Rick and Devon, and then Macy and Jeff.

Having trusted friends to help with our businesses was another thing that I could thank my lucky stars for during this time. It relieved a lot of the load from my shoulders and allowed me to focus on getting to know my family.

Over the last few days, my mom had come to tutor me on the family tree. There was going to be a 'small' family get together. Everyone wanted to see me and wish me well. They were polite enough not to camp out on my doorstep. I wished I could say the same for some of the so-called 'friends' and 'neighbors' who've dropped by unannounced pretty frequently.

Why did I need a tutorial on the family tree? Because it's massive. I've mentioned my ten aunts and uncles. All of them were alive and married with children, except for one aunt who'd become a nun, and some had grandchildren. One even had a great-grandchild. That's just my mom's side of the family, I'm not even adding in my dad's side of the family or Jason's. If I'd thought my kids had weird names, I was in for a shock.

"And Annette has two girls, Truly and Madly. They're sixteen and thirteen, and they—" my mom was explaining about my cousin's two daughters when I interrupted.

"Wait a second—she named her kids Truly and Madly?" I asked incredulously.

"Well, yeah. Why would I make that up?" Mom said, glancing up at me.

"I guess the potential third kid should be glad they stopped at just two." I laughed.

"Candy, what are you talking about? Are you having an episode?" she asked, slightly concerned for my wellbeing. Sometimes I said things that didn't quite make sense in the conversation, but I was getting better.

I laughed even harder. "No, Momma, it's the name of a song—'Truly Madly Deeply'." The third kid would've been named Deeply." By this time, my giggle box was turned over and I couldn't stop laughing, no matter how hard I tried.

"Candy, it's not nice to make fun of someone's name," she began to scold me, but even she couldn't keep a straight face, "but I guess we can be glad for small favors," she sputtered while trying not to laugh.

Making myself sober up, I asked, "Okay, who's next?"

We spent the rest of the afternoon going over the family tree, which was an Excel spreadsheet as tall as me. Mom and Meri had even gone through the trouble to make laminated cards with each person's information and picture. Each 'family' had their own color of paper. They'd stolen the idea from a movie, something about the devil and high-end fashion. Apparently, we weren't great at coming up with our own ideas, but we could adapt someone else's great idea to fit our needs. We laughed and shared some of the memories I had of growing up and the times we came back to visit before we moved back to Mobile.

Beverly had run out to pick up the girls from their respective practices. She left dinner cooking, since my mom was here it was safe. About an hour later, she was back with the girls in tow. They were chattering among themselves.

Damaris and Sybany walked over to give their grandmother and me a hug.

"Hey, Kitty," they both chimed. Neither was reserved with my mom, but when Sybany hugged me, it was very brief, and then she excused herself and went off to complete her chores. I'd never seen a kid so anxious to do chores.

Damaris sat down to catch up on what we were doing. It was funny to get her take on some of her cousins. Cousins is a generic term for anyone who isn't a grandparent, aunt, or uncle. It gets too confusing to keep all the relations straight.

Bev came in from the kitchen. "I'm gonna head home. We're taking Brian to see a movie this evening. Dinner's warming in the oven. I'll see y'all tomorrow." We all said goodbye, and Bev left for the day.

I sometimes had to remind myself not to stare, but I couldn't help watching Damaris as she spoke. Her face was so bright and open. She laughed easily and saw the littlest things.

"My whole body is sore. I'm beginning to think I should have focused on the piano, instead of choosing dance." She groaned as she slipped off her shoes.

"You should put that footbath to use," I told her. "No reason I should be the only one to enjoy it."

She perked up. "That would be nice, but I have to be careful not to soften my calluses. Don't want to get a blister while we are rehearsing for the show," Damaris explained when I gave her a questioning look.

"Oh I didn't think about that. Maybe we could take you for a massage. You have to take care of your body. Reward it for all its hard work."

"That's a great idea. I better go get my chores done before dinner." Then she was off to whatever task she had been assigned that week.

"I'll call Aunt Meri and see about getting us an appointment," I called after her.

I'd learned the kids had a rotating schedule of chores. For the most part, they seemed to stay on top of it without needing someone to tell them to get it done. There were a few times they slacked off and needed to be reminded, but I didn't find that unusual.

It was nice to be able to hold a conversation. My speech slurred slightly at times, and I had to think a little harder on occasion, but for the most part I spoke normally. The ability was a far cry from where I'd thought I would have been at this point. Deciding I'd had enough ancestry lessons, I suggested setting the table. I knew it was on Dawson's chore schedule, but I figured it might be nice to have it done when everyone else arrived. What kid doesn't like having their chore done for them? Dawson, that's who.

Dawson had been spending the day with Pappy. Lord only knew what they got up to, and I was too afraid to ask. My dad was going to be bringing him home and joining us for dinner.

When I crawled into bed that night, I thought over that evening. Things had ended well, but the start of dinner had been rough. Dawson was upset that I'd started setting the table when it was on his chore list, so I stepped back and let him complete the task. *What kid gets mad because someone else did their chore for them?* I'd asked myself again.

Dinner was lively. After his bath, I'd read a story to Dawson, finished his bedtime routine, and then I'd gone in to say good night to Xavier and Damaris. But when I went to Sybany's room, her light was turned off, and I'm pretty sure she pretended to be asleep. There was something going on with her that I couldn't quite put my finger on. I wanted to be patient and considerate of her feelings, but I wasn't a naturally patient person. It appeared that patience was not a skill I'd mastered in my adult life.

In the quiet of the house, I heard Jason walking down the hall toward the guest room, so I got out of bed and opened my bedroom door and startled him. "Umm hey…" I began and stopped, trying to come up with what to say.

"Hey. Do you need something?" he asked, a look of concern crossing his face as I hesitated.

"Uhh, would you mind coming in and talking for a few minutes?" I asked almost cautiously, as if inviting him into the room we'd once shared crossed the murky boundaries we'd established.

"Sure." I stepped back from the door and let him in. He walked over and sat on the end of the chaise by the fireplace.

Being blunt, I said, "I'm getting more worried about Sybany. I know there is something else going on. She avoids me. I'm trying not to invade her space, but I don't know how to reach her." Jason hung his head, looking at his clasped hands resting between his knees, and I paced in front of the fireplace. "Why was she the one to find me?" His head jerked, and I knew I'd hit on the heart of the matter. It seemed odd with so many people in and out of the house, that the two of us would be alone.

Jason took some steadying breaths before he spoke. "It was y'all's special time. The two of you were going to bake cookies to take to the adult day center where Brian likes to go on his days off. You said even if you burned the cookies or they tasted like ass, it was the time spent making them that was important." Obviously, I had the vocabulary of a well-heeled sailor.

"You'd picked her up from practice, so she went to take a shower while you got everything ready. We think you were on the step stool, trying to reach the container of cookie cutters, since they were found on the floor when your accident happened. The rest you know."

My heart broke for her even more. That was a lot to be on an eleven-year-old's conscience. "What do you think we should do? Do you think we should talk to Dr. Vermillion about some family sessions with us and Sybany?"

"That would probably be a good idea," he agreed. His shoulders were tense and he seemed to be waiting for something. It was hard to end the conversation. I didn't want to say he could leave now. And truth be told, I wasn't really ready for him to leave.

After a few moments, I asked, "Will you tell me about these pictures?" I pointed to the wall over the fireplace as I sat on the couch. "Some of them are self-explanatory, but some of them aren't."

"All right, let's see—this one," he said, pointing to the picture of the two of us in bed, "was when you flew up to surprise me for my birthday. I'd wanted to come home and couldn't, so you put this plan in motion to surprise me. You flew into Jacksonville and paid a ton for a cab to bring you all the way to my place.

"I had a roommate at the time, so we decided to rent a hotel room on the beach. The picture was taken the next morning when we woke up."

"Was that," I tripped over my words, "umm, our first time together?" Why did this have to be so damn awkward?

"Uhh, yeah, it was," he confirmed, blushing a little, and I wished like hell I could remember it.

"Was it any good?" As soon as I said it, I wanted to snatch the words back. My face must have been a thousand shades of red.

"Ugh…well, yeah. I'm smiling, aren't I?" And then he reached over and nudged my leg with his hand, giving me his trademark smirk framed by dimples. "Which one's next?"

I looked up at the wall and pointed to the one of us at our wedding. "What were we laughing about?"

His smile turned a little sad, which seemed odd since the picture was such a happy one. "We'd snuck away for a few minutes during the reception. You'd just told me we were going to have a baby. Somehow the photographer managed to get a picture of the moment."

I knew our wedding date and Rissa's birthday, and the dates didn't add up. "What happened?" Even though I knew what he would say, I wanted to know for certain.

Jason swallowed and said, "You miscarried a few weeks later. Then, not long after, we found out we were expecting Rissa. She's the one I was kissing in your belly. You were seven and a half months pregnant and I was deploying that day. I wanted her to know, even though I wasn't with her when she was born, I loved her from the moment I knew she was there."

His explanation brought tears to my eyes for a good reason this time. I was sad about the miscarriage, but it was like it happened to someone else; it still didn't connect with me.

"Missing her being born was a lot of the reason I decided to not stay in. I wanted to be with my family. Fortunately, I was there when Sybany was born," he explained then continued with his explanations of the pictures. "This one is the day we signed on our first house, and this one is when we broke ground on The Dog On It. That's our dog in the picture, Franz. He's where we got the name. We were always asking if the dog was on it. It being the couch, the bed, anything he wasn't supposed to be on." Jason laughed and shook his head at the memory.

"What happened to him?" I hadn't been allowed around the dogs because the doctors didn't want to chance me falling.

"He's back there with the rest of the herd. He's fifteen now. Not quite as spry as he once was, but you can't keep him down." He moved on to the next photo, the one of me in the window. "You were pregnant with Xavier and having a hard time sleeping. I woke up one morning and you were there, standing in front of the window. I knew I would never forget that moment, but I wanted you to see you as I saw you right then, so I grabbed my phone and took the picture.

"There's one of each of the kids as they took their first steps and lost their first tooth. A few other milestones they've hit. Rissa's first solo. Sybany's first somersault. Xavier playing his first complete song on the guitar. Dawson reading his first book." He'd smiled as he pointed each of them out, but it hadn't escaped my notice that he seemed to be avoiding one in particular.

I pointed to the photo of the baby in the pink hat. "Which of the girls is that?"

"That's Samarah Faith."

"Who's Samarah?" Once again, it was obvious, but I was trying to figure out where she fit.

"She was born between Xavier and Dawson." His voice now had a hint of sadness and melancholy. "They weren't sure why your water broke at twenty-one weeks. She didn't make it. We were sure we were done having kids, but apparently kids weren't done with us, and Dawson came along unexpectedly at just the right time. And that's the first picture of the six of us there." Jason pointed to the picture of all of us in the hospital bed.

We sat there in silence for a few minutes, maybe it was longer, before Jason got up and came to sit beside me. Wrapping his arm around me, he tucked my head under his chin, and said, "It's going to be okay."

"That's what everybody keeps telling me," I said. "It's so unreal.

I'm sad, but it's like the miscarriage and still birth happened to someone else, not me."

"There's no reason to feel bad about that. It's just the circumstances of what happened." He squeezed my shoulders. "I know how much you loved those babies, and I know you mourned them. You don't talk about them very much, but that's just the way you are. I was there when you lost both of them. I was there when you got your tattoos as your tribute to them. I would never question the impact their loss had on you, whether you remember it or not," he assured me while cradling me to his chest. My head fit snug under his chin, and my ear pressed to his firm chest. The steady beat of his heart soothed me.

chapter twelve

"I wish I could go back in time and talk to myself," I stated as I leaned against Jason. "The photo albums, scrapbooks, and home movies are great, but they don't tell me what was going on inside my head…or my heart."

"You can read your diary—"

I shoved up off of Jason's chest, cutting off the rest of his suggestion. "What diary?" came out as more of an indignant squeak than I would have liked. I'd kept a diary when I was younger, but I assumed I had abandoned it after the kids were born in favor of documenting their exploits in other ways, since I didn't find one in the bedside table, where it had always been kept in the past. I hadn't thought to ask about one.

"You've always kept a diary. It used to be handwritten, but once the kids were born, you started keeping it on the computer," he explained calmly, his demeanor the opposite of mine.

"Why hasn't anyone told me about this before now?" I threw my arms out to the side, as if to say 'what the hell'. "I've been struggling to figure out who I've become, and there's been a virtual guide all along!" Irritation evident in the tone of my voice.

Jason looked uncomfortable and somewhat chagrinned. "Dr. Vermillion suggested waiting until you asked before telling you most things. She thought you would naturally guide the discoveries as you grew stronger." He paused, appearing to consider what else he should divulge. "I would never purposefully keep things from you. I want you to know everything, but at the same time, I'm trying not to overwhelm you any more than you already are." The longer I went without saying anything, the more frustrated he appeared. "What would you do if you were me?" Exasperation evident in his voice. "There's no guide that says when your wife forgets you and everything about your life together, these are the steps you need to take. What would you have me do?" Jason stood up and started pacing back and forth. He pushed his hand over his tightly cropped hair.

I felt for him, but I didn't know what to say. I knew he was trying. He'd been patient, kind, understanding, and everything in between. Jason hadn't complained about anything since I'd woken up in the hospital. But there was no denying that having everyone else decide what I could handle was wearing on me. There was no doubt that Jason had done what he thought was best. He wasn't keeping information from me on purpose, and I needed to acknowledge his struggle as well. Even if I didn't want to, I empathized with his plight.

"The logical side of me knows that. But I have so many emotions, and I don't have control over them. It's like every time I think I've got a grasp on things, there's something else that's brought to light. I have no control over what I learn and when I learn it," I explained my reasoning. "Everybody else knows more about me than I do!"

The silence was tense as I sat on the couch with my arms folded across my chest, pouting like a petulant two-year-old. Jason mimicked my pose as he leaned against the fireplace. There was more to say, but I wasn't sure how to say it without sounding even bitchier than I already did. After five minutes of the silent standoff, Jason left the room.

My shoulders sagged in defeat. This was the closest Jason and I had come to arguing, and I hadn't a clue about how to handle it. With my out-of-whack emotions, I made mountains out of molehills and mountain ranges out of mountains. Knowing I needed to apologize for taking my frustration out on him was one thing; actually getting up to do it was another. The longer I sat there, the more difficult it became to rise up off the couch and say I was sorry.

I glanced up to see Jason walk back in the room carrying my open laptop. It looked like he was clicking buttons as he walked. He came to sit beside me on the couch and turned the screen to face me.

"This is the master file. Each year has a separate file. Then it's broken down into months, weeks, and days. You even went back and scanned all of your old handwritten diaries. I know the diaries are still around, but I'm not sure where they're stored at the moment. Beverly might know." He handed me the laptop and stood up.

"You aren't going to stay?" I wasn't sure why it surprised me, but it did.

Jason studied me for a moment before speaking. "Candice, I've never read your diary. Those are your private thoughts. You've never had a problem letting me know what you were thinking when you wanted me to know. Besides, you know where I am if you want to find me." He gave me another long look then turned and left the room, closing the door quietly behind him.

For a long time, I stared at the laptop screen. I stared so long the hard drive turned off. Now that the information was at hand, I wasn't sure I wanted to know. What if I found out something I didn't like? Maybe God had done me a favor by taking away some bad memories, but the price I had to pay was losing the good memories, too. Clicking open the file felt akin to opening Pandora's lunchbox—damn it—I meant, Pandora's Box. I'd been watching too much Sesame Street.

Finally, I clicked open the file. But I froze again as I stared at more files. Where should I start? Starting at the beginning seemed a little slow since the end was already there, but starting at the end felt like cheating.

After a bit of internal debate, I settled on the idea of choosing random occasions and days—whatever popped into mind. The first days I chose were the kids' birthdays.

July 19, 2004

On July 16, 2004 at 12:45pm I became a mom. Damaris Kathleen Woodruff joined our family. Hearing her cry for the first time caused my chest to feel like it was going to burst. I couldn't wait to see her. I had to have a C-section because she was face up and breech. The doctor didn't feel like she would turn this close to my due date. Not sure why but the idea of having a C-section was a lot less scary than pushing a baby out through my vagina.

My mom got to be in the room with me. The doctor broke the rules and let Jason stay on the phone until she was born and being checked out in the warmer. He got to hear her first cry and her stats as they were read off. She weighed 6 lbs. 5 oz. and was 20 and a quarter inches long. Mom held the phone up to my ear so Jason could talk to me, but I was sniffling so hard I could barely hear him, which makes me sad because I know the moment affected him just as much as it did me. I wish he could have been here to share it with me. I remember he told me he loved me and was proud of me and he couldn't wait to see pictures. I stuttered through tears to tell him Mom had taken tons of pictures, and I would email them as soon as I could, then he had to go.

They took Damaris to the nursery. I was very upset about that, but I told my mom to go with her so she wouldn't be alone. It's upsetting that because I had a C-section, even though it went great, my baby was taken away for hours. We didn't get to have those first few hours to bond. Once the doctors were finished with me, I was taken to my recovery room and left there by myself. I tried to close my eyes, but I wanted to hold my baby. It felt like eons went by instead of hours.

It took a few hours, but I finally broke down and paged the nurse to ask when I was going to get to see my baby. I'd given my mom strict instructions that nobody was to see the baby until I held her and Jason got to see her. The longer I waited, the more anxious I became.

Right about the time I was ready to get myself—morphine pump and all—out of bed and go find my baby, they brought her to me. I guess the nurses had the timing down to a science of how long they thought a new mom could be made to wait before she went in search of her baby.

When Rissa, as we had decided to call her, was in my arms, I felt so many different things. She had a head full of dark hair. I laid her down on the bed and unwrapped her blanket. I asked my mom to give me my camera. I took several pictures and then handed it back to her and asked her to use my laptop to upload them so I could get them to Jason as soon as possible. I counted Damaris's fingers and toes then swaddled her and cradled her to my chest.

A few minutes later, the nurse came in and said they were ready to move me to a room. I asked her if they could wait a bit until I sent the email and I could see if Jason replied. I really wanted to do my best to keep the promise that he got to see her first, and if they moved me, we would pass the waiting room, and I knew there were family members waiting. It took about another forty minutes to get the email sent. Not long after, he sent back a message saying she was beautiful like her mom and we would Skype later.

As we were moved to a room on the postpartum floor, we were descended upon by family. Everybody argued over who was going to hold her first. Macy was the first to ask her name. The reactions were varied, but they're shit out of luck if they don't like it. We named her in honor of Jason's grandmother, Melva, and my granny, Kathleen.

Once we were settled into the room, everybody took turns holding Damaris and telling her how beautiful she was and that they were going to be her favorite aunt, uncle, cousin, grandma, or whatever. I'm so thankful that I got to be near my family when she was born, but I would give anything to have Jason here.

When the nurse came in and announced it was time to try to feed the baby, people scattered like rats on a sinking ship to get out the door. I tried to breastfeed Rissa; it's a lot harder than it looks. I thought you put the baby up there and instinct takes over. Yeah, not so much. I was so scared I was going to hurt her, so I was being too timid. The nurse took over and just shoved Rissa at my boob. It felt like my boob was going to get pushed into my chest cavity. The nurse told me, "We haven't lost one at the breast yet," and pressed Rissa to my boob until she latched on. It worked out, and Rissa nursed and fell asleep. I listened to Mom and slept, too.

Rissa woke up every couple of hours, so I was awake when Jason *messaged to see if I could Skype.*

The rest of the entry detailed the first few days with Damaris. Reading about my first days as a mother made it more real, but it didn't jingle any memories. There was so much love, enthusiasm, and optimism in the words of a new mother. It was full of wonder. Part of me felt like voyeur looking in on someone else's life, almost like I was trespassing on sacred ground. I wanted to read more, but just didn't feel right about it. I closed the laptop and sat there contemplating what I'd read and what I should do next. There were no ready answers, so I went to bed, hoping I would have some understanding the next morning.

chapter thirteen

Over the next couple of days, I avoided the diary. I wasn't sure why, maybe I had an intuition about what was to come. I'd discovered what a pack rat I was about keeping 'memories'. Every email, card, note, art project, and any other piece of memorabilia that anybody from our family touched was kept and filed away. There were boxes of stuff from my years as a wife and mother. Each box was meticulously organized. I couldn't believe it. The amount of time it would have taken to keep this stuff had to be tremendous. I didn't remember being that organized or anal-retentive.

Until the day came that I was home alone and ran out of excuses. Everyone but me had somewhere else to be or something else to do. Laundry was done and put away. Bev kept the house cleaned and dinner made. I was free to focus on my recovery and reconnecting with my family. Working to learn to be a wife and mother was harder than any physical therapy I'd been assigned. With nothing pressing, I was at a loss for what to do with myself. An idle mind and hands can lead to unpleasant things, like cleaning behind the refrigerator or stove or deciding to delve back into your unremembered memories.

I spent all day reading, getting to know myself through my own words and thoughts. Pictures were dispersed throughout the journal entries. Visual memories to go with the words. These were the moments that stood out to me as a mother. But there were some things that just couldn't be captured, like the smell of my babies after their bath or a day playing out in the sun.

I picked up where I'd left off reading about the births of my children. Coincidentally, they were all born on a Friday, except for Samarah. Samarah was born on a Thursday. All of the details I could imagine faced me in black and white. No detail was too big or too small to have been documented.

November 22, 2005

Jason came home today. It was hard to decide how to introduce our daughter to him. In the end, I decided that their introduction should be private as it would have been had he been there when she was born.

Our mothers had flown back with me to California. They stayed with Rissa while I went to pick Jason up. I set up our video camera and left them with instructions to turn it on when I called. As we were coming in the door from the garage, they were to leave by the front door. I wanted the three of us to have those moments to ourselves.

Jason had to be exhausted from the traveling, but he was humming with excitement and nervousness. Rissa was sitting on a blanket in the middle of the living room floor. Jason knelt down beside her, slowly reaching his hand out to caress her hair. She babbled at him until she tipped over and cried from being startled. Jason looked terrified and asked what to do. I told him to pick her up, so he did. He was so timid. Watching this tough Marine, dressed in his cammis, looking frightened of a baby was hilarious. As soon as he picked her up, Damaris stopped crying, looked at him, and then tipped forward and gnawed on his nose. About two seconds later, she filled her diaper, and I told him welcome to parenthood.

That night when we put her to bed, he raised her ear close to his mouth and softly said, "I loved you before you were here, and I'll love you long after I'm gone." And I fell more in love with the man I married.

Then I skipped forward to the entry about Sybany's birthday. It was dated the day after she was born.

August 5, 2006

Sybany Leandra has made her appearance. Jason was fascinated by the experience. He started to give me a step-by-step commentary of what was happening until I yelled at him that I didn't want to know anything until she was born. I have way too vivid of an imagination to hear those details. Anyway, Jason bounced up and down on his little stool beside my head. I swear, if he could have stood beside the doctor as they sliced me open, he would have. He was completely in awe of every step of the process.

Once Sybany was held up for us to see, he was on his feet following her to the warmer. He called out all of her stats as if he was announcing the winner of a race. "SEVEN POUNDS, TEN OUNCES!" "TWENTY INCHES LONG!" "APGAR'S EIGHT!" His enthusiasm and excitement made me smile and distracted me from the rest of the C-section.

As he was allowed to bring her back over to me, he gazed at her with such adoration. When he glanced up at me, there were tears in his eyes. He'd missed those moments with Rissa. Lifting her until her ear was close to his mouth, he softly said, "I loved you before you were here, and I'll love you long after I'm gone." He'd whispered those same words to Damaris when he put her to bed his first night home. I didn't know it was physically possible to feel my heart expand again with love the same as it had the first time he made that promise to our child.

Next, I clicked through the entries until I came to the one detailing Xavier's arrival in our lives.

February 11, 2009

We're now a family of five. Jason Xavier Woodruff III made quite the appearance on February 6th. He came three days earlier than expected. Guess he didn't want to break the Friday tradition. We've decided to call him Xavier. It suits him. He weighed almost nine and a half pounds. Thank God, I didn't have to push him out. Nine-pounds six-ounces, twenty-one inches long is a big boy. Jason stayed with him, just like he did with Sybany. He whispered the same words again, "I loved you before you were here, and I'll love you long after I'm gone."

The girls are thrilled with him. I'm pretty sure Rissa thinks he's a doll. Life with three kids under five is crazy. What the hell were we thinking? I'm glad we've moved back home and have a ton of family to help out.

September 9, 2011

I got my second tattoo today, a small handprint over my heart. It's my way of keeping my baby girl with me. My heart is broken, as though a piece is missing. I haven't found any answers, but today I felt some semblance of peace.

Those moments will never leave me. The fear when my water broke at twenty-one weeks and knowing my baby's chances weren't good. Samarah Faith was born too early. She never drew a breath. Jason and I held her and told her how much we would miss her. The hospital chaplain came in to give a private blessing. He took a couple of pictures for us. I'm not sure I will ever be able to share those images. I don't know how to share her with anyone.

Learning the meaning of the tattoo brought tears to my eyes once again. I'd noticed the tiny, pale handprint the first time I was allowed to shower without someone with me. I'd taken the time to study myself and take in the changes that had taken place in the past almost two decades. Like most things, it hadn't felt right to ask someone else why it was there. I placed my hand over the tattoo resting over my heart and said a short prayer for my baby girl before I continued reading.

September 28, 2012

Dawson John was born this morning. He has to be the calmest baby I've ever met. His eyes already seemed focused and studying the world.

This is the lightest I've felt since we lost Samarah. He came as a surprise. I didn't think we would have any more children, but we weren't done. I worried throughout my entire pregnancy. I couldn't wait for his first cry, but he didn't cry. Dawson didn't cry until hours later when I woke him up. Lesson learned; let a sleeping baby sleep.

Jason rocked him and whispered the same words, "I loved you before you were here, and I'll love you long after I'm gone." Then he sang Guns N' Roses's "Sweet Child of Mine", which was just odd, but they each seemed to like it.

All of my babies have been special, but there's something about him.

The picture of the six of us in bed followed. Dawson was the balm that healed a broken heart. I continued to skip through entries, reading about each milestone. Even in the moments where it was obvious I was a frazzled mom, the love and pride for my children was vibrant. The littlest things were outlined in great detail. Every achievement was documented with pride.

I read for hours and hours, losing all track of time. My mind drifted, picturing all of the memories I no longer possessed. The more my mind wandered, the more tears began to fall. I was so wrapped up in my wandering thoughts that I didn't hear Jason and the kids come home. As I felt an arm come around me, I jerked my head up, my eyes meeting those of my four children. All of them uncertain of what to do. And I cried even more.

"Kids, go ahead and get ready for dinner. Mom will be all right. Remember what we talked about with her emotions?" They each nodded before walking away. Jason was the port in the storm as he sat next to me and pulled me into his arms. I clung to him as a babe clings to its mother. "What's wrong, Candy?" he asked gently. When I didn't answer, he continued to soothe me and seek the answer. "You can talk to me about anything." How he had so much compassion, I'll never understand.

"I'm just so mad!" I began, and once I began, there was no stopping the torrent of words that came pouring out. "Why don't I get to remember being their mother? Wouldn't anyone want to be their mother?" I jerked out of his arms and started pacing back and forth, my frustration too much to keep contained. "I read the diary of a woman that loved her children with her whole heart. They were her pride and joy. AND I CAN'T FUCKING REMEMBER ANY OF IT! WHAT THE HELL DID I DO TO DESERVE THIS? Is there something I don't know? Was I secretly a horrible person?" I looked at him, even knowing he couldn't answer those questions, I pleaded for the answers to be delivered.

Jason stood up and crossed the distance between us. He grabbed my arms to stop my pacing, looked me in the eye, and said, "I don't know why. But I do know you still have now. You still have a family that loves you and stands beside and behind you. You need to let go of the anger and embrace what you have now." At his words, I sagged into his embrace. He wrapped his arms around me and kissed the top of my head. "We'll make new memories." He held me in the safety of his arms, and before long, I felt four more sets of arms wrapped around me.

We stood there in the family room as a family for a long time. Once I brought myself under control, I leaned back and said, "Thank you." It was a thank you for so much more than holding me as I'd cried once again. "You're right, let's make the now count." Then realizing what time it was, I suggested it was time for dinner.

The look of worry that crossed all of their faces was quite funny, I began to chuckle and asked, "What's that look for?"

Jason recovered and answered, "Nothing. How about we go out for pizza?" There was a loud cheer and a mad dash for the door.

chapter fourteen

Another week had gone by, and we were so busy, but I was making the effort to appreciate what was happening then, not the missing past. Jason was still taking the brunt of the work for our business since Melissa was in the process of transitioning and looking for someone to take over The Dog On It. I was able to help a little, but I had to concentrate on everything I did, which took three times as long as it normally would. Life was hectic, and everyone was going in different directions. It made me think about the saying, *Life is what happens while you're busy making other plans.* John Lennon hit the nail on the head.

The kids loved it, though. They thrived, and it was clear, they were the focus of our life. But I worried that I couldn't keep up. Our lives had been building to this for the past fourteen years—well, seventeen years really. I'd had years to get to this point prior to my accident, and now I'd had only weeks. Thank God for Beverly. She kept everything running like clockwork around the house, reminding me which person needed to be where and when.

Since the big family cookout, our family and friends took turns stopping by. I tried to be friendly and welcoming to everyone who visited, but I swear every Tom, Dick, Mary Sue, and Jane who'd ever said hi to me wanted to come by, thinking they were going to get the 'scoop'. What scoop they thought they were going to get, I'm not sure. There were some people who believed I was faking the memory loss and thought they could trip me up. Others wanted to play the 'do you remember me' game. These things were no longer funny after the fifty-millionth time. It had begun to grate on my nerves, and I was getting pissy.

One Saturday morning, I went to the park with the intention to watch Xavier and Dawson's soccer games, but missed both games because of all the people wanting to talk to me. The final straw was when Xavier ran up to me all excited because he'd gotten his first hat-trick, and not only had I missed it but the person trying to pump me for information got irritated because he interrupted her.

"MOM! MOM! Did you see it? Did you see my hat-trick?" Xavier shouted, hopping from foot to foot, bouncing up and down.

"Excuse me, young man, I'm talking to your mom. You shouldn't interrupt adults when they are speaking," the woman said snidely, and Xavier shrank in on himself.

I saw red. Furious didn't begin to describe the emotion I felt. As I opened my mouth to unleash a verbal tirade, Jason stepped up and diffused the situation by saying, "Come on, we gotta get going." He swung one arm around my shoulders and the other around Xavier's, guiding us toward the parking lot. Damaris, Sybany, and Dawson trailed behind us. Jason's arm hugged me firmly to his side, and he kissed the side of my head, but he didn't say anything. The six of us were subdued on our way to the SUV.

After we were all settled in the car, Jason addressed Xavier, "Okay, champ, where are we heading for your celebration lunch?" Immediately his sisters and brother started throwing out suggestions.

Xavier wouldn't be swayed, his mind was made up. "Tres Amigos," he declared with certainty. The kid's love for tacos rivaled mine for Dr. Pepper.

"Tres Amigos it is," Jason agreed as he put the SUV in gear. Once we were on our way, he reached over and threaded his fingers through mine, raising my hand to his lips to press a kiss to the back of my hand before squeezing it and lowering our joined hands to rest on his thigh.

Twenty minutes later, we were seated in a huge family booth, waiting on our lunch. The kids had abandoned us for the small arcade. My anger had turned to frustration and disappointment. I was working so hard to recover, but the one thing I couldn't recover was my memory. It felt like without my memory, my ability to be a mother had been severed.

"You need to let it go, babe. Things will get easier," Jason said, as if he read my mind.

"I shouldn't have to fucking let it go! People, who probably never spoke to me before, are vying to find out the gossip. Like I'm a fucking freak show or something! I'm not here for their personal amusement. They should stick with the real housewives of whatever fucking town," I ranted. Jason didn't say anything while I verbally expunged my anger.

"Let's go camping," Jason suggested.

"Camping?" I questioned, sure I misheard him. I wasn't a camping type.

He nodded his head. "Yeah, we love camping. Let's get away, just you, me, and the kids. We'll unplug, relax, and recharge. Camping is a great way to get away from it all."

I was skeptical. However, the kids walked up and heard camping, and that was all it took. They were so excited, I couldn't possibly not agree. So, that was how I found myself in the middle of the woods the next day, setting up a tent.

Jason firmly believed that everyone had a part to do. No one was excused from helping set up camp. He was in his element with nature.

Me...not so much. I was not in my comfort zone. Even if I'd come to love camping over our years together, I didn't remember it, and I didn't feel any latent desire to commune with the animal kingdom. On the inside, I was freaking out. I love nature. It's beautiful when I'm looking at it through a piece of glass while sitting in my favorite chair inside my air-conditioned house. Now that I was up close and personal with the great outdoors, I was busy trying to keep from becoming a wilderness snack.

When Jason was satisfied that our 'camp' was set up as it should be, he announced it was time to catch dinner. To which I stammered, "C–c–catch dinner?"

"Yeah," Jason replied, "it's the rules; we have to catch dinner."

"But didn't we bring hot dogs and stuff?" I pointed out.

"That's just back up," he informed me.

Off to the lake we went. The kids knew the routine and spaced themselves out over the bank after getting their bait. Jason was setting me up for success until he pulled out the worms.

"You want *me* to put a worm on a hook?" I asked incredulously. The horror of even the thought was enough to make me nauseous.

"Yes, everybody has to bait their own hook," he replied calmly with a straight face.

"I'm *not* putting a worm on a hook," I asserted with firm

conviction.

"It's okay, I brought you some fake bait." He started, chuckling at my discomfort. "I just wanted to see if you would do it."

"That was mean!" But even the kids were laughing.

Soon everyone was settled down and quiet, waiting for the fish to bite. We didn't have to wait long. The kids started reeling the fish in. Secretly, I was wishing the fish steered clear of my hook. I got my wish for a while, but as Sybany was reeling in her third fish, there was a tug on my line. I was so shocked, I jerked the pole and swung around. How the poor fish stayed on the line, I'm not sure, but it did—much to my dismay. It landed about fifteen feet away, flopping all over the ground. I clutched the pole and hopped around like I was the fish on the line. Thank God the fish didn't make as much noise as I did.

Jason came over and took the pole from my hands, reeling the line in a bit. Then he handed the pole to Xavier and took the fish off the hook, dropping it in the bucket with the other fish.

"Now that Mom's caught a fish and we got a show, we can go get ready for dinner," Jason told the kids, who all laughed, as he picked up the bucket and started back to the campsite.

He instructed Damaris to start the fire while everyone else started cleaning fish. The kids went about their assigned duties. When he pulled out the knife, my head started to swim.

"I'm not doing that. I don't care if I go hungry, I'm not cleaning a fish." I was very serious. There was no way in hell I was doing it. He couldn't make me.

"It's okay, babe. Can you go help Rissa get everything else ready?" I happily agreed to that.

The rest of my first night of camping was uneventful. We ate fish and vegetables cooked over a fire. Everyone munched on smores as the kids told stories. It was a great night, until we settled into our sleeping bags and I began to worry that a bear was coming to eat me. Nobody else had a problem sleeping.

As the sun began to light the morning sky, I crept out of the tent and walked down to the lake to watch the sunrise. Sitting there, I could understand someone's desire to experience nature. It wasn't long before a blanket was placed around my shoulders, and Jason sat down next to me.

"Mind if I join you?" he asked. We sat there for a few minutes before he said, "I've always liked watching the sunrise with you."

"Really," I said.

"Yeah, it reminds me of our beginning. There's always hope." He spoke quietly, reverently as he remembered our time together. I was jealous he could relive those times and I couldn't.

There's something about the early morning stillness that causes people to slow down. It wasn't long before, one by one, the kids joined us, and we watched the day begin as a family. I reminded myself it was about the now. As wrong as the rest of the camping trip would go, that moment would be one of my favorite memories. It was a precious gem. Maybe even more so because I'd lost so many.

We ate fish for breakfast. I didn't think I would ever want to see a fish again. After breakfast, Jason suggested we go for a hike. We'd walked for a good ways when nature called. Jason told me to go a few feet off of the trail. I was trying to be a good sport and not complain, but peeing in the great outdoors is not easy when you're a female.

But my biggest worry was getting bit on the ass by a snake. So I had a long stick, which I used to sweep around the area to make sure there were no slithery serpents lurking. I didn't stop to think about the other wildlife I could potentially piss off. During my sweeping of the area, I startled a skunk. I screamed, it screamed, and its defense mechanism kicked in as it scurried in the opposite direction.

Jason rushed over and upon smelling the scene he uttered, "Oh shit!"

We hurried back to camp with everyone walking as far away from me as possible. I immediately went to the lake and stripped off my clothes, walking into the lake when I was down to my bra and panties until I was submerged.

"Here's some soap and a towel and some clothes," I heard from the bank. I turned to see Sybany there and told her thanks. She laid the towel and clothes down and tossed me the bar of soap. "We're going to be packing up camp so we can head home."

"Okay, I'll be up there soon."

"Dad said take your time," she told me before turning to head back to the camp.

After spending an hour scrubbing to no avail, I got dressed for the ride home. I didn't care that Jason said I'd loved camping over the last seventeen years: I fucking hated camping with a passion.

They'd already hauled everything back to the SUV when I stopped trying to wash the smell off.

"Um, babe, it would be better for you to sit in the back," Jason suggested.

I sat in the back by myself with every window rolled down. I'm surprised I didn't get blown out the back window from all the wind.

Fortunately, Beverly had a treatment ready when we got home. She'd looked it up on the Internet. I took three more showers in the outdoor shower. It worked reasonably well to get rid of the smell.

Then I went in and soaked in the deep claw footed tub. And I was certain that I absolutely loathed and despised camping!

A couple of afternoons later, I was in the kitchen doing my best to follow the recipes to make dinner. Jason walked in the back door followed by Dawson and Xavier. They'd gone over to help Jason's dad with a project at Jason's parents' house.

"Hi, guys! How'd it go with J.W.?" I asked Jason.

"It was good. We got a lot done. Boys, go get cleaned up," Jason told them.

The boys charged out of the room as I'd learned boys are apt to do. There wasn't a slow speed in their genetics.

"Watcha doing, babe?" he asked me.

"I'm making dinner," I replied with confidence. He worked hard to keep the look of panic off his face, I'll give him that.

"Great!" he said with forced enthusiasm. "Where are the girls?" He changed the subject as he glanced across the living room.

"Umm, Sybany is stretching, and Damaris is on the phone with a friend."

"Where is she?" There was a tick in his cheek.

"In her room, I guess." I didn't think anything of it, but I knew he wasn't happy. I had no idea why, though.

He walked out of the kitchen, and I heard, "Damaris, get down here now."

"Yeah, Daddy?" came less than a minute later.

"Why were you on the phone in your bedroom?" he asked her. I stepped into the family room to find out what was going on.

"Because Mom said okay," she replied. Which I had.

"You know the rules, young lady. If you can't discuss it in the family room, you don't need to talk about it. One week, no phone or computer except for schoolwork or to talk to us."

"Yes, sir," she mumbled with her head down, staring at the floor.

"Go sit down. We're going to have a family meeting. Dawson, Xavier, Sybany, get down here, we're having a family meeting," he yelled up the stairs. The boys came running down the stairs, and Sybany came from down the hall by the staircase. "Have a seat, everyone. We need to talk."

I sat just like all the kids, who looked like they may be facing lock-down.

Jason started by asking, "Sybany, have you done your chores today?"

"No, sir," she answered.

"That's what I thought," he said. "All right, this has gone on long enough. We have rules in this family, and just because Mom had an accident and doesn't remember all of them, doesn't mean y'all get to take advantage. We give y'all a lot of freedom, but y'all have to hold up your end of the bargain. That means doing your chores and following the rules. No more using Mom's condition to do stuff you know you aren't supposed to. No more telling your Mom you're allowed to do stuff you aren't. Even if you do it by letting her assume, it's still a lie—"

Dawson chose this moment to chime into the conversation. "But jou tol' Mommy she wiked camping, and she hates camping." My head swung around to Jason, and my eyes were about to bulge out of my head. I KNEW IT!

"That was different—"

"But jou said a wie is a wie," Dawson continued, "and den jou told her she wiked to fish, and Mommy never fishes."

"I knew it!" I proclaimed, my eyes narrowing at my confirmed suspicions. "I knew I hated camping."

"Okay," Jason conceded, "I shouldn't have made Mom believe she liked camping, even though I did it for the right reasons." I just raised an eyebrow. He was going to be groveling for a long time to come in order to make up for the camping trip from hell. "We need to focus. We have to get back to being a family. We need to stick together."

"We should do like they did in that movie," Xavier suggested. "You know the one where the guy dates the chick who can't remember."

"*50 First Dates,*" Damaris piped up.

"Yeah, we could each take Mommy on dates," Dawson said. His excitement was infectious.

"We can't date Mom, Dawson," Sybany said, "'cause people who date kiss and hold hands."

"We could do like that one family and court Mom," Damaris suggested. She was the obvious problem solver.

"But I want to hold Mommy's hand and kiss her," Dawson protested in earnest. He was very affectionate when he wanted to be.

"That's a good idea, kids. What do you think, Candy?" Jason asked while looking at me for an answer.

"Sounds like it could be fun, and I don't mind hugs and kisses." I smiled at Dawson, hoping he would continue to be open with me. He was the least reserved of the kids when it came to interacting with me.

"We should all plan surprises for our dates with Mom," Damaris added. I think she took after me when it came to adding the small details to an occasion or event.

"Yeah!" All of the kids started getting excited as they talked about the plans they could make. It was decided they would draw numbers to see who got the first date.

"Is something burning?" Jason asked. He sniffed the air, causing his brow to wrinkle with worry.

"OH SHIT! I FORGOT DINNER ON THE STOVE!" I exclaimed as I jumped up off the couch and ran into the kitchen. Sure enough, one of the pots had boiled dry and was beginning to smoke. I jerked the pan off the stove and tossed it in the sink, turning the water on. I guess I had my answer about whether or not I had learned to cook without requiring the fire department to stop by.

I looked up to find everyone staring at me. Tears formed in my eyes. Jason wrapped me in a hug and said, "Don't worry, we learned long ago not to let you cook unsupervised." He laughed when I tried to push him away. "It's nice that some things don't change."

chapter
fifteen

$\mathcal{L}$ater on that week, Dr. V greeted me with her usual smile as I walked into her office. "How are things going?" she asked her usual opening question.

"All right for the most part. I've been released from physical therapy, and I can drive now. It's easier to think clearly. I'm working with a personal trainer to work on my endurance, so I feel like I'm making some progress." I listed off the easy positives.

She nodded her head and said, "That's a good accomplishment. What else has been going on?"

I wanted to be honest to her prodding, but part of me was hesitant to give voice to some of my less pleasant thoughts. It didn't matter how much privacy was assured, I didn't want to feel judged. But I wasn't going to be sitting across from Dr. V at dinner, and she wouldn't share my thoughts with anyone, so if there was anyone I could be open with about my doubts, it would be her.

"I've started reading my diaries." She nodded her head to encourage me to continue. "Reading the entries made me angry. I don't connect to those memories as mine, but I can feel the emotion and love in them. They're the words of a woman who loved her life, loved her children, loved her husband, and had a great network of family and friends. It makes me angry that I've been robbed of that. In some ways, I'm glad some of the pain is gone, but if I'd been given the choice, I'd keep those hard memories in order to keep the good ones, as well.

"My emotions are still crazy. Well, really, just the emotions that spur crying. I can't control it once it gets started."

"That's understandable. How are you relating to the kids and Jason?"

I nervously laughed. "Ummm, well, the kids and I are going to start dating."

"Dating?"

"Yeah, the kids came up with the idea that they should court me so I can get to know them. They got the idea from a movie. They're very excited about it."

"It's a novel approach. How are you all going to go about it?" she asked.

"The kids drew numbers, and they each get to plan their date. I'm kind of excited to see what they plan. They're each so different." I smiled as I thought about the possibilities we had ahead for us.

We talked about the kids, and then she asked, "Those are some great positives. What are some of the negatives?" There was the hard question.

"Well...I'm mad that I'm not in control of what I'm told and when I'm told." I pinned her with a somewhat accusatory look.

"You are in control because all you have to do is ask—"

"How the hell am I supposed to know what to ask?" I interrupted her, irritated at the way my feelings were being brushed aside.

"When you're curious and want to know something, you ask," was her simple explanation. "You and the children are moving forward, which is a big positive. How are you and Jason?"

I thought about it before answering. "We're okay. I'm not sure what else to say."

"Well, that's your assignment before we meet next."

I nodded, and we wrapped up the appointment. I'd gone in on kind of a high of expectation that things were moving forward in a positive way, and I left feeling like I'd had my legs knocked out from under me.

chapter sixteen

$\mathcal{I}$ was thinking about my assignment the next day, but I couldn't quite figure out what Dr. V was getting at by telling me to consider my relationship with Jason. I'd been trying to figure out how to help take care of the helpless, the ones who have no control over anything. Like most things people don't want to deal with, I shoved it to the back of my mind.

Tonight was my first kid 'date'. The nervousness in my stomach was something different than any other date I'd ever been on, at least the ones I remembered. All I'd been told was to dress in something comfortable that I didn't mind getting messy. My excitement built all day. I'd been cleared to drive, so I didn't have to depend on others to get us wherever we were going.

Damaris had drawn the winning number for the first 'date'. Once we got in the car, she started giving me directions. Jason had turned the GPS off because it flustered me. There had been no such thing as GPS seventeen years ago, and having some disembodied voice yelling at me to turn this way or that caused unnecessary anxiety. I had a general idea of where we were going, but I had no idea what was there. Damaris chattered away about dance, music, books, and gossip interspersed with giving directions. The anticipation compounded the closer we got to our destination.

We pulled up to an industrial looking building. As we approached the door, I saw the sign for The Experimental Kitchen. I looked over at Rissa. She had a huge grin splashed across her face. I notice she had one of her dad's dimples. "Don't worry, they won't leave us unattended. It's a cooking class. I figured we could learn to cook something together, a brand new memory that we've never had before."

"That's a great idea, Rissa. But to be on the safe side, we should probably make a note of where the fire extinguishers are," I jokingly said, but we both knew it was the truth.

"Hi, ladies! Welcome to The Experimental Kitchen. Have y'all joined us before?" I looked at Damaris—yes, I looked at the thirteen-year-old—for the answer.

"No, ma'am, but we have reservations for tonight's class. Candice and Damaris Woodruff," Damaris politely answered.

The enthusiastic greeter did a little clap and said, "Wonderful! I'm Suzette. We're so excited to have you join us. We'll need the two of you to fill out some information for us. The first page is general information, and the second page is the waiver. Fill these out and bring them back over when you're done." She pointed to a group of chairs situated in a semicircle in front of a table.

Damaris and I took our seats and began to fill out the forms. They were very basic, so it didn't take very long, and soon we were handing them back in to Suzette. "Help yourselves to some refreshments. We'll be starting the presentation soon, then we'll move on to the lesson."

We picked out a couple of things to nibble on and a drink then sat back down in the chairs to wait for the presentation to begin. "How does this work?" I asked Rissa.

"First, they give a class. Then we go to our assigned kitchen to make the dishes. After we make the dishes, we get to eat the dinner we made. It sounded like a lot of fun when Aunt Meri talked about it." She was upbeat and excited about what was to come. I was trepidatious. The last two meals I'd attempted had turned into disasters. During the first, I fell and lost my memory, and the second I'd burned beyond recognition.

"Sounds like fun. Do you know what we're making?" I wanted to sound more upbeat than I felt. I sincerely hoped I didn't let her down. "How are your rehearsals going?" After I asked the second question, I realized I hadn't given her the chance to answer my first question.

She exhaled. "Good. Mrs. Martha is a really good teacher, but she expects a lot. If you aren't giving it your all, she'll call you out on it. I think it's coming together. It's hard to take a ballet that everyone is familiar with and make it your own somehow."

"I can't wait to see it. I'm very proud of how dedicated you are to your goal." Damaris had been scheduled to take a summer intensive with a ballet company in New York, but had withdrawn after my accident. The guilt for what my accident had cost my family added up.

"Thank you, Momma." She smiled to herself. "I remember the first time you took me and Sybany to see a ballet. It was The Nutcracker. Watching the ballerinas, I just knew I wanted to be one. Every time I step on a stage, I get that same feeling." As she talked, I could hear the wonder in her voice, and she got a dreamy look like she was transported into the ballet.

"You really love ballet. I hope dance always give you that feeling."

"People don't realize how much work it is besides just the dancing. There's a lot of conditioning and technique. If I want to dance professionally, I have to be conscious of taking care of my body so it can hold up to the demands. It's a constant learning process." The dedication and determination these kids had was incredible. But part of me worried that they would feel pigeonholed and constrained in the future. Having a goal was a good thing, but people, especially adolescents, grow and change so much. I wanted them to know as long as they were happy, giving it their all, and being productive in some manner, whatever they choose to pursue would be okay.

"What are you studying in school?"

"I'm working on my book report for this month." At my questioning look, she filled in the blank. "You and Dad require us to read one book a month and prepare a report as part of our schoolwork. This month I'm reading Misty Copeland's autobiography. She's so inspirational. I know I'm very lucky to have access to the training and information, but seeing her accomplishments reminds me that I have to love ballet to be successful."

"Do you have interests outside of ballet?" I was so uninformed at that point of how dedicated she had to be, even at her age, to achieve her goals.

"I love ballet. I love everything about it. But if I chose something else, I'd be a vet, like Devon. Although, it's really hard to see an animal in pain."

Each facet of my children's personalities that I discovered made me proud and connected me to them. "I could never stand to see an animal in pain, but I didn't have the stomach to be a veterinarian."

"Yeah, that's why you did the rescue," she grinned, "but it can still be really messy," she finished with a laugh.

"I noticed that today." I grimaced. Today I had been helping out with the dogs at the house. When I'd entered the room, the dogs became excited. My equilibrium was kind of wonky at rare times, causing me to be somewhat unsteady on my feet, so I'd sat down on the floor and let the dogs climb all over me in search of a pet or rub. My tonsils were swabbed more than once.

A lady wearing a pink apron bearing The Experimental Kitchen logo stepped up behind the table. "Hello, everyone. I'm Darlene. Thank you for joining us for this evening's class. We have a fun and fabulous menu planned for y'all. We're going to get started with some explanations about the ingredients y'all will be using and how they come together in the menu." Darlene went on to talk about how spices compliment and play off each other and how using unlikely ingredients can set a dish apart. After about thirty minutes, Darlene introduced the kitchen assistants, who would be walking around to help us amateur chefs as we worked in our individual kitchens. Then we were assigned our kitchens.

As soon as we entered our kitchen, it was readily apparent that Rissa would be the head chef. She picked up the recipes and began naming off everything we needed to gather. Each step was labeled to make dinner flow smoothly. We began by making the main course. Once it was in the oven, we made the sides then assembled dessert. After everything was either baking in the oven or warming in the warming drawer, we put together a colorful spinach salad with mandarin oranges, strawberries, blueberries, and precooked eggs, bacon, and chicken, and topped with a raspberry vinaigrette and feta cheese. It was surprisingly delicious, and since it didn't require cooking, I successfully helped make our meal without burning it.

Rissa cracked me up with her impressions of famous chefs while we prepared dinner. She did Julia Child, Justin Wilson, Emeril Lagasse, Bobby Flay, the Iron Chef, and the chef from The Muppets. Then she switched to her impression of a food critic as we ate dinner. It was hard to eat while laughing at her antics. We had a great time. By the time we'd finished dessert, which were these individual blueberry cobblers in a small mason jar, my sides ached from laughing so hard.

As we were getting in the SUV, Rissa suggested stopping and picking up doughnuts as a treat for everybody who hadn't had the chance to enjoy our scrumptious meal. We drove to the same Krispy Kreme on Hillcrest that Jason and I had gone to the day we went to Devon's house.

Standing at the counter, I offered my suggestion. "How about a mixed dozen? What does everybody like?" When I glanced over at Rissa for her answer, I was once again greeted with *that* look, the one that said, 'You poor pitiful soul, you have no clue.' "What? How many doughnuts can one family eat?"

"A lot," was her response. "Xavier can eat a dozen in one sitting by himself. Plus, we'll need some for in the morning."

"Won't they be stale by morning?"

"No, Momma, you just put it in the microwave with a cup of water for about ten seconds," she patiently explained. Once she said it, I remembered doing that lots of times.

Nodding my head in understanding, I deferred to her for the family doughnut eating habits and asked, "Okay. What do we get?"

We arrived home with four-dozen assorted doughnuts. I'd begun to worry my family had an addiction to these doughnuts. But I had to admit, it was nice to see the splurge. Our family meals were designed to meet the needs of growing athletes, so there wasn't much junk food to be had. Everybody converged on the kitchen table when we set the boxes down. The kids all got chocolate milk, and Jason asked if I wanted coffee.

"Not this late at night," I said. I wasn't a coffee drinker. I'd forgotten my addiction to Starbucks, which might be considered a positive since they're so expensive.

"It's decaf," he offered to tempt me to imbibe.

"I'd rather have a Dr. Pepper," I replied, catching his headshake.

"This late at night," he mimicked me as I reached into the fridge.

"Nobody likes a wiseass, you know," I joked.

"Better a wiseass than a dumbass."

"Can I be a wise-ass, too?" Dawson asked. Children have an innate ability to point out your parental flaws.

Jason replied, "I hope you'll be wise, but not an ass, and don't say the word ass."

"Why'd can jou say'd it?" Couldn't deny it was a valid question.

"Because we're older and have more insurance." I channeled my inner Towanda. "Now, eat your doughnut," I answered. Jason quirked an eyebrow at me. I looked at him and said, "He dropped it, didn't he?"

"For now," Jason murmured, and I had a feeling this would resurface at the most inopportune moment.

"Yeah, well, at least I didn't lie to him about liking camping *and* fishing," I returned without any anger in my voice.

Jason had the grace to appear chagrinned. "Come on, you can't hold that against me forever." I quirked my eyebrow at him, in a *'you really believe that'* manner. "You do like camping as long as we stay in one of the cabins. But all of the family cabins were occupied that weekend. I knew you needed to get away, and I didn't want to tell everyone we were up there, since that would defeat the purpose because then people would be stopping by." Poor guy, his heart was in the right place, but I'd been sprayed by a damn skunk. He was going to be paying for that transgression for years to come.

chapter
seventeen

*I*t was later on that night—the wee hours of the morning, actually—when it happened. I'd been reading on my Kindle, which was amazing. I could take my books everywhere. There were so many new technologies. I felt like I had stepped on to the deck of the U.S.S. Enterprise—the star ship, not the aircraft carrier. It was mind-blowing. Jason had commented that one great thing about my memory loss was I could reread all the books I already had and we'd save a ton on one-click charges. I wasn't quite sure what he was talking about at the time, but certainly, I was being disparaged.

So, there I was, nice and relaxed, curled up under my covers, reading a book. Then at sixty percent through the book, BAM! The author might as well have shot me in the chest. I began to cry. I cried to the point of being on the verge of hyperventilating. One of the side effects of the accident had been my emotions were easily triggered, mainly crying. No matter what I tried to make myself think about, I couldn't calm down.

When all else failed, I decided on a brilliant course of action; I got out of bed and stumbled my way to the guest room, in which Jason was sleeping. I opened the door, tears streaming down my face, making gasping noises as I attempted to inhale around the sobbing.

Jason sprang upright in the bed. "What's wrong?" he asked obviously concerned. I was trying to get the words out, but all that came out was another sob. "Are the kids okay?" Throwing the covers off, he climbed out of bed and began to cross the floor as he slipped into boxers. If I hadn't been so upset, I would have enjoyed the view. Instead, I met him halfway between the bed and the door. I wrapped my arms around him and continued to cry into his chest, but I managed to nod that the kids were all right. "Is it one of the dogs?" He was alarmed, but remained calm enough to attempt to extract answers from me, the crying psycho that had barged into his room at one-thirty.

"He died," I wailed, another round of sobbing and crying commencing.

"Who died?" The concern and alarm in his voice grew.

"ChChaaaase."

"Your cousin Chase died?" Wasn't sure about cousin Chase's breathing status, but I wasn't talking about him.

"Noooooo. Chaaase Graaayson," I managed to get out in between sobs. It was very hard to talk when I couldn't breathe.

"Who's Chase Grayson?" Jason asked confused, not knowing who the hell I was crying over.

"He's a boy in," sob, "the book," sob, sniffle, "I'm reading," sob, "and she killed him." Sniffle, sob, sniffle. "He'll never," sob' "get to–to," sob, "meet his son." Wail, sniffle, repeat. "It's n–not faaair."

"You're crying over a fictional character in a book?" Jason said this as if he couldn't believe what he was hearing. "You do realize it's just a story and he isn't real?" Normally, that would have resulted in him getting a kick in the balls, but I had to give him some leeway. I mean, I was quite hysterical—and not in the funny way—so he wanted to bring me back to reality. I continued to cry no matter what reassurances he gave me. "Come on, let's lie down. Everything will be better when you get some sleep."

Jason guided me to the bed, and we lay down. He lay flat on his back with me cradled to his side, my head resting on his shoulder. I fell asleep crying over a fictional character.

I awoke the next morning unsure of where I was for a split second. It didn't take me long to realize my firm pillow was rhythmically moving up and down. Cracking open one eye, I surveyed my bedfellow as much as possible without lifting my head. The view was nice. Jason might be forty-one, but he was fit and solid. Right about the time that thought crossed my mind, another realization surfaced; my thigh was pressed to Jason's groin. The phrase 'morning wood' did *not* do him justice; more like morning granite. Or maybe I'd just been reading one too many trashy sex novels detailing glorious members and velvet-covered steel rods. Desire flared and flowed through my veins, and I had no idea what to do, so I did nothing.

I lay there and pretended to be asleep, hoping Jason would wake up and leave the bed first. I was keenly aware of our bodies pressed together and carefully maneuvered my crotch away from his leg. Yeah, that would be embarrassing. Forever and a half later, I wasn't sure how much longer I could stay unmoving against him. Feeling him next to me did nothing to squash the fantasies flashing on the lids of my closed eyes. I was stiffer than a board, but I thought I was playing it cool and getting away with my Sleeping Beauty act.

"I know you're awake." A sleep-roughened voice caused my eyes to pop open, and I pushed my head back to look at him.

"How'd you know?" I asked, showing my dumbness to how well two individuals could come to know each other over seventeen years together.

"Babe, I've slept next to you for over fifteen years. I know your body language," he asserted, grinning at me with those damn dimples.

MOTHER FUCKER! He knew what he was doing. "That's kind of unfair and one-sided," I said, doing my best to deflect the attention.

"How so," he asked with a knowing smirk slashed across his way-too-good-looking-for-first-thing-in-the-morning-when-I-was-all-hot-and-bothered face, "seems like my arousal is fairly obvious."

Did he just say arousal? Really? And why did it feel like the temperature spiked another ten degrees. It had to be hot flashes. Yeah, that was it. I was the right age for menopause, so I'm going with hot flashes, I attempted to convince myself. That's all this was, hormones out of whack. I wasn't practically dry—or not so dry—humping the husband-I-can't-remember's leg in my sleep. We'd barely had a conversation that didn't revolve around business or the kids.

Next thing I knew, I was flipped onto my back, a muscled chest pressing me firmly into the mattress. We were torso to torso; our legs tangled together. As I gasped from shock, Jason's mouth landed on mine. I hesitated to call it a kiss because it was more like a possession. He knew just how to get a response from me. His hands slid into my hair to cradle my head while his forearms squeezed my shoulders and upper arms. My arms raised of their own accord and wrapped around his broad shoulders, clutching and searching to bring the heat closer. I felt the world shift, and the only thought I had was, *HOLY HELL FIRE AND BRIMSTONE!* Why that expression, I hadn't the foggiest notion, but fairly sure I was trying not to take the Lord's name in vain.

Jason didn't endeavor to take it any further than a kiss, but aroused bodies have a mind of their own. Mine was fully engaged; however, my brain had shut off. I clutched at Jason's back like I wanted to crawl inside him. Well, I wanted something inside, and it definitely wasn't me in him. His caress stoked the fires within me. I couldn't remember ever being this turned on in my life, not that I had much experience to draw from.

"God, Candice, I've missed you." Those words were all it took to snap me out of my momentary insanity. My eyes flew open, and my hands stalled in their journey over the contours of his back.

I said the first thing that came to mind. "I gotta pee." Okay, Forrest Gump. Then I scrambled out from under him. Jason didn't try to stop me, but he called my name in plea that entreated more than a simple physical need. I didn't look back as I rushed through the bedroom door and down the hall. If I turned around to respond to him, things were going to go too far.

I rushed back to the master bedroom and into the bathroom, not stopping until I was standing in front of the sink. Spinning to look in the mirror, I saw the reflection of a woman flushed with desire. I took note of her swollen lips, the slight redness around her mouth from his early morning stubble, the rapidly rising and falling breast peaked by hardened nipples, the fists clenched tightly, as if trying to hold her in place and keep her from running back to make a mistake.

"How would it be a mistake?" I asked the woman's reflection.

"Because I don't know him, and having a physical relationship isn't a good basis for a long lasting relationship," she replied in a prim manner.

"AHH! What the hell do you know?" I yelled back and turned to go back into the bedroom, thinking that my body knew him. Obvious-fucking-ly.

When I entered the bedroom, there he stood. Shirtless. Molded by form fitting boxers, which left nothing to the imagination. And my imagination was already working overtime. Amazingly there wasn't smoke billowing from my vagina. Aww fuck me sideways! No, you idiot, that's part of the problem. "Umm," was all I could utter.

"Are you all right?" he asked, concern clouding his face.

"Could you put on a shirt," I deflected once again. "And some pants." Cause those damn boxer briefs weren't hiding a mother fucking thing, and it made it soooo hard—no pun intended—to be good. Just then the thought *If you can't be good, at least be good at it* speed walked its way across my mind. I groaned, because I had no doubt he would be very, very, very good at it.

He walked past me into the bathroom; I assumed going to the closet to fulfill my request. Although half of me wanted him to ignore it and just stand there in the early morning sunlight, which filtered into the room from the curtains I had neglected to close the night before.

I walked over to the couch and tried to get my raging hormones under control. *You need to reign yourself in,* I lectured myself, *there's no need to complicate this situation even more by getting physically intimate with him. There's enough going on as you learn to be a mother. They're the ones who need your attention. Stop focusing on what you desire, and think about the defenseless kids. They need you, so keep your act together.*

Jason walked back into the bedroom clothed in athletic shorts and a T-shirt and sat beside me, slightly angled in my direction, snapping me out of my thoughts.

"I'm sorry if you didn't want what happened to happen and it made you uncomfortable—"

"No, don't apologize," I interrupted him and then went blank on what to say next.

The silence stretched as I tried to think of what else to say, but Jason beat me to it. "Candice, I would never be unfaithful to you, but we've always had a very active sex life, and it's been weeks—months—since we made love. I'm not trying to make excuses, but I want to be with you. I'm just as attracted to you now as I was seventeen years ago. I miss being close to you." He appeared to be considering what to say next. "We've become glorified fucking—or non-fucking, as the case may be—roommates. And we aren't making any progress forward. I understand why you've focused on the kids, but I'm here too. We don't have to jump into sex, but can't we at least make an effort to get our relationship back? Get to know each other again," he said the words so sincerely it brought tears to my eyes…again. Damn emotions!

"You mean like date," I asked in a shaky voice.

"Okay, yeah, let's call it dating. I don't care what we call it as long as we're giving it a shot." Jason was already a little less weighed down by the emotional baggage. His shoulders were a little less stooped. I hadn't paid attention to how my decision to focus on the children had affected him.

Watching him sitting there, asking me to give him a chance, made me realize how much I had pushed him to the back burner as I paid attention to everything else around me. Unintentionally, I'd alienated him by not taking into consideration his needs or feelings. Selfishness wasn't something I was used to feeling, but I felt it then. He—*we*—deserved a chance to rebuild our relationship. Without it, the rest of our life would crumble.

"When?" I asked. Curiosity was already getting the better of me.

Jason thought for a moment and then said, "Tonight; be ready at six."

"Okay, it's a date," I said.

"It's a date," he agreed. He stood up, leaned over, and kissed my cheek. I watched as he walked out of the room with a little more bounce in his step.

chapter eighteen

The cold shower I'd taken did nothing to curb my libido. On top of everything else, I could add sexual frustration. The moment I set foot in Meri's spa, she knew and gave me a knowing once-over. Thankfully, she held her tongue since the girls were with me. The three of us were having a mom and daughter spa day.

Both girls put their bodies through rigorous training. It was important to make sure they were given the tools to keep their bodies healthy. They had trainers and chiropractors, but there was no denying that they continually pushed their bodies to perform. It was simply the nature of the sports they pursued. They couldn't progress in their chosen sports if they didn't work at it. There was way more to gymnastics than walking into a gym and turning a few flips. The same was true of ballet. Most people saw the elaborate costumes and shiny satin shoes, not the blisters, fatigue, and injuries.

If either of the girls decided they didn't want to maintain the level of training necessary to compete or perform at their current level, they would have the option to quit, but once the decision was made, there would be no turning back. They both loved what they did; at least that was what they said based on my diary. We never had to force them to be up and ready to go to the gym or the studio.

"All right, ladies, we have y'all scheduled for the whole shebang. Come on back to the ladies' dressing room, get changed into a robe, and then we'll get y'all settled in the lounge," Meri instructed, and we set off to switch into robes. Meri had done a great job with the spa. The atmosphere was serene and tranquil. You'd never have a clue that it was on one of the busiest streets in town.

The girls and I got changed and made our way to the lounge. The lounge was a big room they used for spa parties. Who'd ever heard of such a thing? A spa party? They had apparently become popular during the time of my forgotten memories, along with reality TV, bridezillas, Brazilian waxing, iPods, iPads, and other stuff I couldn't fathom.

Once we were each seated in a spa chair, Meri and the techs got started; securing our hair in wraps, putting some concoction on our faces, then pointing steam machines at our faces. They removed all of our fingernail and toenail polish. Feet were submerged in the hot water, then our hands were slathered with a cream and wrapped in warm moist towels. Each foot was scrubbed, massaged, buffed, and polished in turn. Both girls made a point to tell their tech not to remove the calluses, even though the girls came here regularly.

"Bunny, what're you going to do for the summer showcase?" Rissa questioned her sister. In addition to their names, they each had a nickname. Damaris was Rissa Roo. Sybany was CinnaBunny, which had been shortened to Bunny. Xavier was Tree Frog, which became Frogger, and at times, was now shortened to Frog. And Dawson was Duckson, which had been shortened to Duck. Jason had coined each of the names, and so far no one objected.

The summer showcase was a talent show arranged by our homeschool group. The showcase gave the children a chance to demonstrate their talents to a different audience than they were usually exposed to in the activities to which they were affiliated. No prizes were awarded, but admission was charged and went to help supplement educational funds for materials for courses such as science, home economics, or any class that needed extra materials. They'd even bought an old car to teach about basic maintenance. Jason offered apprenticeships to a couple of kids who were interested in working on cars. Not every person is cut out for college, and we were lucky to be a part of a homeschool group that valued teaching to a kid's abilities and interest.

"Don't know. Not like I can do double handsprings or somersaults on the stage," Sybany grumbled.

Excited, Rissa suddenly leaned forward and clapped her hands. "Why don't you and me team up and do The Maestro?"

Sybany considered the suggestion for a moment before she replied, "Which one would I do, the maestro or the puppet? I'm okay at dance but not great. I don't know if I could do anything complicated."

"Both!" Her enthusiasm filled her voice as she practically bounced in her spa chair. "I'll start out as the maestro with you as the puppet. I'll be demanding, making you do a dance and get frustrated when you mess up, and then, as I sleep, a fairy comes to grant your wish to be the maestro. When I wake up, I discover I'm the puppet and you've taken over as the maestro, making me do more complicated routines as revenge."

"That sounds like a lovely idea," I encouraged their planning. It was nice to see Sybany coming out of her shell around me, even though she wasn't interacting directly with me.

"We can make it work, Bunny. I know we can." Rissa wasn't going to be swayed from the idea. I think Sybany was just as excited, but more reserved about showing her feelings.

Sybany had met with Dr. V a couple of times on her own, but nothing had really come of those meetings. The next session was supposed to include Jason and me. I'd hoped the more I recovered physically, the less worried she would be. However, she stayed reserved, which was very unlike the way she'd been described prior to my accident.

The girls continued to discuss their ideas for the performance until it was time to get our massages. They were both used to it. They'd had to lose a lot of modesty in the changing rooms. Even though we did not allow the high cut gymnastics attire, they were still quite revealing. Sybany wore a leotard with short legs, albeit really short shorts, but at least it provided a little more coverage. When she was older, she could decide which leotard she wanted to wear.

Meri had been giving me *the* eye the entire time we were in the lounge, so I knew as soon as she could get me alone the inquisition would commence. You know *the* eye, the one that says, *I know you've been up to shenanigans, and I'm going to find out all your secrets.* The CIA had nothing on an older sister. At least, I didn't have to worry about her telling Mom. I girded my loins for her interrogation. A grown, married woman shouldn't be embarrassed that she made out with her husband. It's a completely natural phenomena that occurs every day between couples all over the world. Of course, most of those couples remembered their history together.

"Okay, spill it!" Meri commanded as soon as the door shut. I should've been happy that she let me keep my robe on while she questioned me.

When all else fails, play dumb; it'll buy you a few seconds. "I don't know what you're talking about."

She snickered and said, "Don't play coy with me. I know you've been up to some monkey business, 'cause you look guilty as homemade sin. So give me some details," she paused and then added, "but not too many. I have to look at Jason across the dinner table with a straight face."

It was no use avoiding. She was going to pester me until I caved in, and I needed someone to talk to about these mixed up emotions. "We ended up in bed together." As I was formulating how to relay the rest of the story, she let out a whoop. "Don't get too excited. I broke it up by telling him I had to pee—"

"Okay, Forrest." Sometimes we thought too much alike.

"—and ran out of the room," I finished in spite of her interruption.

"So you're telling me that you made out with your husband, who you've been madly in love with for almost two decades, then you announced you had to pee, ran out of the room, and you feel guilty. Do I have that right?" She stood with her arms crossed and an eyebrow cocked. It was obvious she thought I was dumb as a lamppost.

I gave a swift nod and confirmed her summary of the events. "Pretty much."

"Have you lost your damn mind?" I just looked at her like she was the idiot and the village was looking for her. "Okay, bad example," she conceded. "Why do you feel guilty? You're married to the man you're hot for. What's the big deal?" She waited for an answer with an expectant look upon her face, but I was having trouble putting it into words.

She wouldn't be deterred, so I told it like I saw it. "I don't remember him. I don't remember loving him. And now I have children, whom I'm supposed to set an example for when it comes to how to conduct themselves and what to expect in a relationship. I know I wasn't pure as freshly fallen snow, but I had sex with people I was involved with and knew before taking that step. I don't know if I regretted not waiting, but I know that I want to set an example to my children that physical intimacy should be with someone you love and respect. I respect and like Jason, but I'm not in love with him.

"Yeah, it's every high school fantasy I had come to life, but I'm not in high school anymore. My actions affect more than me and Jason. Jason has been great. I couldn't ask for a more supportive husband, but I don't know how to be his wife. I'm barely hanging on being a mom, and that's only because I have a tremendous amount of help. Should I just step into this role of wife and mother when I don't have the experience? I know in my head that I obviously made a commitment to my family the day Jason and I said our vows, but I don't fucking remember! How can I be everything for everyone instantly?" I didn't expect an answer, it was a rhetorical question, but she gave me one anyway.

"Then get to know him. Figure out where your common ground is outside of the kids and the business. The two of you need to connect." She made it sound so simple.

We faced each other, as if we were on opposing teams when, in fact, we wanted the same thing—my happiness. "It's not that easy—"

"Yes, it is," she huffed. "Go out to dinner. Send the kids to Mom and Dad's or my house. You can't fool the kids into thinking everything is fine when it's not. If you and Jason end up not making it, the world won't end, but you can't give up before you even try. You owe it to not only the kids but more importantly, to yourselves."

"He said the same thing," I admitted as I chewed nervously on my lip.

"I knew he was my favorite brother-in-law for a reason." Her face broke into a huge smile.

"He's your only brother-in-law," I asserted with enough sarcasm to peel the paint on the walls. Then I sighed deeply and said, "We're going on a date tonight."

"Ohh where are y'all going?" She was definitely gonna want the details tomorrow. I made a note not to answer my phone.

I shrugged, attempting to be nonchalant. "I don't know. He told me to be ready at six."

Meri rubbed her hands together with unadulterated glee and squealed. "Oh, honey, we gotta get you fixed up. Jason's gonna have to up his game to keep up with you."

I did my best to rein her in. "Don't get ahead of yourself. I don't even know where we're going. He could be taking me to the Dairy Queen for all I know." Not that my attempts did any good. My efforts had no effect on dimming her enthusiasm.

"Well, if he's dumb enough to take you to Dairy Queen on your first date, you'll be the most well-groomed woman in the place." Meri sniggered as if she didn't think Jason would be that stupid.

Next thing I knew, I was face down on the massage table and being treated like a piece of meat to be tenderized by the masseuse. By the time the girls and I were ready to go, I was polished from head to toe. A new dress adorned my body. Meri had sent one of her techs over to a boutique owned by a friend of hers to pick up my new outfit. The dress was dressy enough for fine dining, but casual enough not to be out of place in a less formal setting unless he did, in fact, take me to Dairy Queen.

Rissa sighed. She had a romantic soul. "Oh, Mommy, Daddy's gonna be knocked on his butt." Sybany nodded in agreement, but didn't speak to add to the sentiment.

I hoped the feeling would be mutual…for all of our sakes. More than one prayer silently crossed my lips as we made our way home. Nerves weren't going to get the best of me, I knew that much. I was going to be calm and collected and put in the effort to make my marriage what I'd been told it had been before my accident. I had no clue what the night would hold, but it was going to be a positive step in a new direction. I could only hope it would circle back to where I had come from.

Kitty and Paw Paw were already at the house when we pulled in. They were preparing dinner for the kids. Smelled like my mom's sloppy joes and homemade onion rings. "Are you making homemade onion rings?" I asked, my mouth already watering at the thought.

"Yes, I am. Xavier made a request," Mom confirmed what my nose smelled.

I was already reaching for one. Kitty's onion rings were not to be missed. "MOMMA, YOU CAN'T EAT ONION RINGS!" Rissa exclaimed, causing me to jump. "What if Daddy wants to kiss you? You'll have onion breath."

There had been a few moments since I had woken up from my

coma that I'd wanted the floor to open up and swallow me. My thirteen-year-old daughter giving me dating advice about what to do to prepare for kissing her father ranked at the top of the list.

I looked around and asked, "Where is Jason?"

"He'll be here soon," my mom told me, giving me an amused smile.

Dawson and Xavier came into the kitchen. "You wook boooootiful, Momma," Dawson exclaimed.

I fought an internal battle, but the proonion ring side won. I shoved an onion ring in my mouth. "I'll make sure he eats one, so it won't matter if I have onion breath." Heaven exploded in my mouth as the doorbell rang. Anticipating it was Jason, I quickly grabbed a paper towel, put an onion ring on it, then headed for the front door.

As I walked to the door, I had an entourage following in my wake. Opening the door to find Jason standing there dressed in button down, relaxed jeans, and flip flops. When he opened his mouth to say something, I shoved the onion ring in his mouth. He was a bit taken aback, but chewed and swallowed.

"Well, that wasn't the greeting I was expecting." He grinned as he chewed, dimples in full force.

"Umm I couldn't resist Mom's onion rings, and Rissa was worried you wouldn't want to kiss me if I had onion breath," I divulged truthfully and then thought better of it, but I couldn't take the words back, so there was no use worrying about it.

He laughed and smirked. "A little onion breath wouldn't have stopped me. Ready to go?" He held his hand out to me.

"Yeah, let me grab my purse." I turned to get it, and Rissa held it out to me. There would be no delaying. I stepped out the door onto the porch. Jason placed his hand on the small of my back. I was more nervous for this date than I had been on my first date in high school.

We took our first step down the porch stairs when a young voice rang out across the evening. "'Member, be a wiseass, Daddy, not a dumbass."

Jason looked back over his shoulder and said, "Thanks for the advice, Duck." Then, almost as an afterthought, added, "And don't say ass."

I could just imagine what my parents thought about that.

chapter nineteen

$\mathcal{J}$ason opened my door and helped me into the truck, waiting until I was settled before shutting the door and making his way around the truck. Manners are always important. My dad still opens my mom's door when she gets in and out of the car. Pappy does the same for Little Granny. Hell will freeze over before one of my daughters ever walks out the door because a boy honked the car horn. This isn't a drive thru. Lord help my boys if I ever found out they tried such a stunt when picking up a date. Good manners never go out of style, and being respectful goes a long way.

We were quiet for several minutes. The radio was turned off, so silence abounded in the truck cab. I desperately wanted to turn on the radio, but I didn't want to be rude, so I kept my hands tightly clasped together on my lap. I couldn't take the silence anymore, so I asked Jason how his day was.

He glanced over at me then turned his back to the road as he answered. "Not too bad. I had a few arrangements to make. Then Mike, Steven, and I spent the better part of a day looking at potential properties."

"What kind of properties," I inquired, genuinely interested in what the 'business' entailed beyond the pet stuff. Running the business didn't really interest me, but I knew it was time I took an active role in learning about our finances.

"A few houses that we would flip and then a couple of pieces of land to develop for commercial use—"

"What do you mean flip the houses?" That was a new phrase for me, and it made no sense whatsoever. I began to pick at my newly manicured fingernails, since I no longer had any cuticles.

Jason reached over, grabbed one of my hands, threaded his fingers through mine, and then rested our joined hands on the center console. My heart sped up and sweat was beading across my body. Damn hot flashes! They picked the most inopportune times to appear; always when Jason was near. My physical response had nothing to do with being excited because Jason was holding my hand. Jason, the boy I'd dreamed about for two years straight, had no effect on me at all. And if I told myself that enough, I just might start to believe it.

I could fool myself better than anybody. There's a great line in the movie *Secondhand Lions* that I had watched with Dawson the other day. When the character of Hub, the wise and grouchy great-uncle, gives part of his *'everything you need to know about being a man speech'*, he tells Walter, 'Just because something isn't true doesn't mean you can't believe in it.' The line hit home for me because there are a lot of things I didn't know as true, but I had to believe in them to get through each day. Or else I might go crazy; I had enough shit on my mental plate to deal with without adding a nervous breakdown. So, if I chose to believe I was having a hot flash instead of lusting after the married man I was dating, so be it. That fact that the married man was married to me didn't dissuade me from my attempts to convince myself.

"We buy a house that's in need of repair for significantly below market value. Then we repair and refurbish the house. Some we keep on as rental properties. Others we sell at an improved value for a profit. Selling it for a profit is called flipping a house." Jason's explanation made sense, but didn't sound like anything I would have chosen to do as a business venture.

"How did we get into that? Last I remember I was going to start my masters in Library Science, and from what I'd been told, you were in the military. Those careers seemed like an awful big leap to real estate."

"When we got married," he glanced at me, "I intended to stay in for my full career. But we knew we wanted to move back here when that was done, so we bought property here before we got married. I had already purchased a commercial piece after my first deployment. I'd planned to take over my dad's shop and expand it once I retired." That made sense. Jason worked with his dad now. "Then we bought the land where we planned to build a house." I wondered if that was the property our house sat on now, but it seemed unlikely we would have been able to afford that much land just starting out. "A couple of years after we got married, we were approached by a company wanting to purchase the commercial land, and then we got a second offer. Our property had an old convenience store on it, but every other corner had already been redeveloped as more people moved into the area. On the other three corners, there was a pharmacy, a grocery store with a pharmacy, and a gas station. Turned out that the two offers came from a local oil company, who wanted to build a gas station, and a pharmacy chain. Well, the pharmacy chain had deeper pockets, and they really wanted that corner, because there was nowhere else to build within a quarter mile. Our property sat right before a hill in the road that you couldn't see what was on the other side of it, so people were more likely to stop at a business before the hill. They went back and forth with bids a couple of times until the pharmacy chain came back with an amount the oil company couldn't match.

"We took part of that money and invested it over a couple of years. The other part we used to build a few duplex complexes. Once I got out of the Corps, we moved back and began flipping properties, investing in commercial real estate, and we started The Dog On It, in addition to the duplex complexes. Things have just continued to grow. We've been very lucky," Jason concluded his explanation of our business.

"How many properties do we own?" I asked.

Jason thought about it for a second before responding. "About a hundred and twenty houses and duplexes and seventeen commercial properties, not including The Dog On It."

That seemed like a lot. Curious, I asked my next question, "How do we afford all that?"

He seemed a little chagrinned. Most people don't like to talk about money. "Well, we built up over thirteen years. Once we received the money from the initial sale of the commercial property, we paid off what was left of the loans and used the rest to invest and started building duplexes, which are relatively cheap for the return. Everything just grew from there."

Those answers lead me to the hardest question. "So," I paused to gather my courage, "how much money do we have?" It shouldn't be difficult to ask, but it's hard to ask about money. Jason didn't hesitate.

"Personally we're worth close to two million, and the business, which we own, is worth several million," he said steadily, as if that wasn't a shocking number. Yeah, I was going to need to pay more attention to those accounts and financial papers.

It wasn't long before we were pulling into a parking lot downtown and walking over to LoDa. LoDa stood for lower Dauphin Street, which was pronounced Dahfin, not dolphin. Pronounce it dolphin, and we'd know you were not from around here. On Friday nights during the spring and summer, Artwalk vendors filled the area. There was a great crowd milling around the booths as they enjoyed the live music. Jason and I joined the crowd, and I started browsing as we made our way to an unknown destination. I stopped to look at some beautiful pottery made by a local artist named Lisa Warren. Pointing out a piece to Jason, I mentioned that might be a nice gift for Macy's upcoming birthday. He agreed, and we waited for the artist to finish another transaction.

Lisa, a tall woman with dark red hair, finished with her other customer and stepped over to us. "Are y'all interested in a particular piece?"

"Yes, ma'am," I said, showing her the ceramic jewelry organizer I thought Macy would like. "Wonderful, let me get this wrapped up for you." She took a few minutes to wrap the organizer and slip it into a bag. "Your total is sixty-two dollars and eighty-five cents. Will that be cash or charge?" she asked, smiling at us. Jason handed over his debit card. She completed the transaction and thanked us for our purchase.

"Let's go eat. We have a reservation later on." Jason guided me to the LoDa Bier Garten. "They serve some great German dishes and of course, beer," Jason explained as we walked in and took a seat at a long, wooden table.

A waitress walked over and handed us menus. "What can I get y'all to drink?" Jason ordered a Hefeweizen for himself and a Woodchuck for me. "I'll go put your drink orders in while y'all look over the menu."

Unsure if I'd been here before or what I might like, I asked Jason, "What's good here?"

He glanced up from studying his menu. "You normally get the pork schnitzel with the potatoes."

I nodded my head. My decision was made. When the waitress returned with our drinks, we placed our order.

"What do you do at the auto shop?" I asked, not just wanting to make conversation; I really wanted to get to know Jason. I was going to do my best not to mention the kids.

"I design and build custom engines." He reached across the table to take one of my hands in his.

"What kind of motors," I inanely asked then winced at my dumbness.

Jason grinned. "Car engines, but specifically antique and classic cars. We try to keep it as authentic as possible. A lot of times we have to make replicas based on the original design."

"Is that something you really like?"

"Yeah. I mean, it helps that I can do what I love and make money at it without having to take a lot of crap work to make ends meet, ya know?" He started going into detail about the type of work he did, what he was working on now, his favorite car he ever got to work on, the car—or owner, rather—that he hated, and his dream car. For the most part, I had no clue. The extent of my automotive knowledge was you put gas in a car and that's how it ran. There wasn't a mechanical bone in my body. My dad tried the 'you must know how to change a tire and all that jazz' until I almost dropped a car on him because I put the jack on wrong.

Watching Jason as he talked about cars was great. He was very animated and serious as he detailed his work. Doing what he was passionate about showed in the way he spoke.

"Sounds really detailed—," I was interrupted by our food being delivered.

"Can I get another beer, a water, and a Dr. Pepper?" Jason said to the waitress.

She nodded her head and said, "Sure thing, darlin'." No, she wasn't flirting. Calling someone darling, sweetie, sugar, or any other numerous terms of endearment was a cultural thing.

Jason turned back to me. "You usually don't like to drink alcohol with your meal," he said to my bemused look. Sometimes I wondered if he was a mind reader.

I smiled at how well he knew me, even when I didn't know myself. "Thank you. I was going to ask for something else to drink."

We both began eating the dishes we'd chosen. "Oh my God, this is delicious. It's almost like a fried pork chop but better," I said around a moan. When I glanced at Jason, he looked sort of pained before he straightened his expression.

"Glad you're enjoying it, but save room for dessert."

"Oh, there's dessert?" I knew I loved sweets.

"Yes, but we won't be eating it here." I wasn't sure how I was going to have room for his promised dessert. The portions the bier garten served were huge.

"Trust me, you'll love it," he said with confidence. I had no doubt, since he hadn't made a wrong choice yet. I felt so fortunate… and loved that he was so thoughtful and concerned with my wants and needs. I didn't think I'd ever even considered that side of him in high school. Not that I really could have, considering I never said more than two words to him. I'd been content to merely stare at him and dream.

We kept up the conversation throughout our meal, flowing easily from topic to topic. I had a great time getting to know him out of our family setting. We clicked with each other. I imagined the butterflies in my stomach were similar to those I felt the first time we got to know each other. They were more pronounced than even the ones I'd had as I dreamed of him in Geometry.

As we exited the restaurant, he reached for my hand. It felt completely natural, so I relaxed and enjoyed the moment as we made our way down the sidewalk to a custard shop.

"Colonel Custard," I said in a slightly amused tone as I read the sign above the door.

"Yes," he grinned like a kid getting ready to walk into a candy store, "they have a lemon custard that you love, and they make great milkshakes."

"All right, let's try this deliciousness you've promised me." I reached for the door, but Jason beat me to it. He held the door so I could step through with his hand resting on the small of my back. His thoughtfulness wouldn't surprise me on a normal first date, but he did this kind of thing whenever the opportunity presented itself.

Strolling down the street with our treats in hand, I had to admit this custard was as good as Ben and Jerry's. The bonus was the fresh waffle cone housing my lemon custard with blueberries mixed in to give it the perfect balance of sweet and tart. It also helped stave off the humidity, although not by much. It was a good thing Meri had used all of those concoctions in my hair, or else it would have become a frizzy mess.

I loved looking in all the shop windows. There were several art shops I wanted to come back and browse through when time permitted.

Jason stopped us in front of a local art house theater named Crescent Theater. I knew that because I read the sign as we walked past the marquee, not because I remembered. Jason knocked on the door. It didn't take long before friendly guy answered the door. "Hey, Jason, Candice. Good to see y'all again. It's been a while. Come on in," he said without letting us get a word in edgewise as he stepped back from the doorway so we could pass. I walked in first with Jason's hand on the small of my back. The feeling of his hand on my back caused more sensation and feeling than I wanted to identify at the moment. "Go ahead and have a seat in the theater. I have the movie set up, and I'll be going up to get it started. Help yourself to the snacks. See y'all after the show," the movie theater guy called over his shoulder.

Smiling at Jason, I remarked, "He's a bit—hyper."

"Yeah, that's Max, but he's a great guy and huge supporter of the local film community," Jason filled in some of the details as we entered the little theater. There was a row of black recliners. I glanced over my shoulder to Jason. "Keep going. Nowhere else to sit—"

"But midways up and directly in the middle of the screen." It was a quirk I'd had since I saw my first movie. My heart did a little flip, well more like a swan dive off the highest platform, and I was having a stern talk with my 'hot flashes' about their appearances. Their response was, 'You're a moron.' "This has been a great date so far. I can't wait to see what you have lined up next," I told him.

"During the months we lived in different places, we would have phone dates. One of the easy things we could do together was watch a movie. So, tonight, I have a movie lined up." His explanation of our movie date, along with those damn dimples accompanying his sheepish smile, did absolutely nothing to calm the 'hot flashes'.

The movie began, and I settled in to enjoy the show. We were going to be watching *Bandits*. "Is *Bandits* a movie we liked?" I asked

Jason, since I wondered what the significance of this movie was for us. I was sure there must be one, considering all the attention to detail he'd put into the rest of our date.

"Not really." He shook his head. "It's the first movie we ever watched on a phone date. I hated it, but you thought it was great," he explained.

"Oh, then I can't wait to see if I still like it." Enthusiasm peppered my statement. Taking in the fact that the armrest between the seats was raised and that we were all alone in the theater, filled my head with a few thoughts of the not so innocent date variety. I paid more attention to those thoughts than I did the movie, until about halfway through, I muttered, "Fuck it," and leaned my head against his shoulder. His arm slipped down from the back of the chair to conform around my shoulder, and I snuggled in closer to his side. And I must say, the movie got a hell of a lot better. Jason made a very comfy pillow.

chapter twenty

$\mathcal{D}$uring the rest of the movie, I'd been very aware of Jason's fingers trailing a feather light path up and down my bare upper arm. Each stroke of his fingers fed my growing desire. Even I couldn't convince myself these were 'hot flashes' anymore. The plot of the movie had been completely lost on me. My concentration on anything but Jason had flown out the theater door. Our walk back to the truck had been much quicker than our walk to the restaurant and theater. The thought, '*You're getting closer,*' cracked like singsong thunder with each step.

As we pulled into the garage, end-of-the-first-date jitters felt like a swarm of butterflies in my abdomen.

There were a few lowlight lamps on throughout the house. I'd always hated a dark house, but I wanted my bedroom pitch black when I slept. Everyone else was already asleep. Mom and Dad were in another guest room. I slipped my shoes off when we stepped into the kitchen. My mouth felt as if I had spent a month in the Sahara, so I went over to the cabinet, retrieved a glass, and then filled it with filtered water from the fridge. Ice cold water tasted better than room temperature tap water any day. I took a couple of big gulps then asked Jason if he wanted a drink. He nodded yes, so I handed him the half full glass. Once he'd downed the rest of the water, he sat the glass in the sink and extended his hand to me. As our fingers connected, the swarm of butterflies became a tornado.

Jason held my hand until we reached the master bedroom door. I contemplated inviting him in and wondered if he would accept. He squeezed my hand to bring my attention to him. "I had a great time. I hope we get to do it again sometime," he said, showing no sign of feeling the same nervousness coursing through me.

"I had a wonderful time. Thank you for being so thoughtful. We'll definitely have to do it again soon."

He leaned down and kissed my cheek. "Sweet dreams, Candy. I love you." One last squeeze of my hand then he turned and went to the guest room.

I stood there dumbstruck for a minute before I opened the bedroom door. Not really paying attention when I walked in the room, I didn't notice the lights were on until I bumped into a floral arrangement.

Then I looked up and saw a garden brought to life. There were flowers on every flat surface. Flowers in vases. Kissing balls in various sizes hung from the ceiling. Pale rose petals carpeted the hardwood floor in a thick blanket.

Without thinking, I spun around and rushed to the guest room. Not bothering to knock on the door, I barged in on a shirtless Jason. Unable to stop, at the risk of losing my courage, I rushed forward until I stood directly in front of him. I reached up and grabbed his face, bringing his lips to mine.

He was frozen in surprise at first, but it didn't take him long to get with the program. His arms came around me, pressing me to his firm chest. Then his mouth and tongue reinvigorated our kiss to a level I'd only experienced that morning. Unsure of how long our kiss continued, I melted into the embrace, until Jason drew back and said, "That was a much better goodnight. Let me walk you back to your room."

My brain muddled, I followed his lead without saying anything. At the bedroom door, he kissed me again briefly. Jason opened the door and gently directed me inside before shutting the door. I stared at the door dumbfounded and confused. Why had he turned me down? Isn't sex what he wanted? Ugh, why did this shit have to be so fucking confusing?

In a daze, I walked to the bathroom to remove my makeup and brush my teeth. Once I completed that task, I went into the closet to retrieve my pajamas. Closet didn't do it justice. The room was three stories. The first floor housed every day clothes, shoes, and accessories. There was a staircase leading to the second floor. The bottom of the staircase flared out and faced a three-sided mirror. The second floor kept dress clothes, formal wear, and accessories. A beautiful, black, wrought iron, spiral staircase led to the third floor reading loft. Each floor had a door, which led to the corresponding floor of the house. I had to admit I loved the closet, but the third floor was my favorite.

The third floor contained floor to ceiling bookshelves, a desk, and a daybed filled with assorted pillows. It wasn't long before I headed up to my personal idea of heaven. My reading nook was an escape from the world and my never-ending worries about everything I'd forgotten.

However, tonight it wasn't a book I wanted to escape into. On my way to the daybed, I retrieved my laptop from the desk, pushing the power button as I walked. The log on screen popped up, and I typed in my credentials. Quickly, I got myself settled on the daybed.

I wasn't sure of the exact date, but I had a good idea of when the event I was looking for occurred. It didn't take me long to find the entry.

December 16, 2000

Macy's parents hosted a Christmas party tonight. I'd promised Macy I would stop by, so I did. Who's the first person I run into? Jason Woodruff. It wasn't a surprise he was there, but did he have to be the first fucking person I met? And did I really have to blush like a tenth grader with a crush? So fucking embarrassing. I spent my time trying to avoid him until I could politely excuse myself and leave. If anything, he's gotten better looking since high school. He's definitely more muscular, and he still has those damn dimples. I could see the laughter in his eyes at my awkwardness when Macy introduced us. I'm gonna go bury my head under my pillow.

December 17, 2000

I think I've awoken in some alternative dimension. Jason emailed me with some bullshit excuse about needing help picking a gift for Macy. I know he's full of shit because Macy already told me that he always gets her a gift card. But after a few emails back and forth, I have to admit I'm curious. I can't figure out what his game is, but I agreed to go shopping with him tomorrow.

December 18, 2000

Dear Lord in Heaven! A flirty Jason is a dangerous Jason. I always knew he was charming, but if he set his mind to it, he could get blood from a turnip. Speaking of turnips, he must think I fell off the turnip truck yesterday. He showed up at the mall with a shopping list longer than Santa's. I think he even invented a few relatives. We spent hours shopping. He'd flirt; I tried to act aloof and unaffected by his charm and his mother fucking dimples. He tried to ask for my number after dinner, but I shot him down. I'm not sure why he suddenly has the desire to get to know me. The last time we saw each other before the party, I'd said hello and he looked at me like he had no clue that I sat behind him in class for months, which he didn't. I never had the courage to speak to him again.

I have to admit, it was a bit of a power trip to spend the day watching him do his best to win me over and then walking away after telling him I wasn't interested.

Was that what I was doing now? Controlling how I interacted with Jason because it was one thing I could control? Maybe that was what Dr. V had been alluding to during our last session. It was time to do some soul searching on my part. I continued reading.

I'm sure we'll have to see each other again. I'm not going to give up my friendship with Macy because I can't handle being around him. I can control my reaction to him. That's why God invented vibrators and batteries. Note to self; buy batteries, a lot of fucking batteries. It's not like he and I will see each other all that often. I don't anticipate seeing him again until Macy gets married, and since she claims she's never getting married, I have nothing to worry about.

January 1, 2001

It's 2:38, and if it hadn't been for the fact no camera crew popped out of hiding, I would have thought I was on Candid Camera. JASON-MOTHER-FUCKING-WOODRUFF KISSED ME! HE KISSED ME! My New Years' kiss came from Jason Woodruff. What the fuck parallel universe have I landed in? Simply because I turned down his offer of a date, he kisses me? Who does that? Although the better question is what kind of idiot would enjoy a kiss given because of that reason? Well, put me at the head of the class with a dunce hat, because JUMPING JESUS ON A POGO STICK can he kiss. I think the world must have shifted on its axis. But I played it cool and acted like it did nothing for me. Saying something to the effect of it hadn't been what I thought it would be. I can't remember for sure because my brain was scrambled. Then I turned and hightailed it away to find Rick and we left. I didn't even bother to say goodbye to Macy. I'll have to call her later.

Why am I being tortured?

Jason sent me an email at 4:17 this morning apologizing for his behavior, stating that he didn't know what came over him and he was very sorry for kissing me against my wishes. It wasn't like he asked and I said no. He didn't force me to do anything. When I drew back, he didn't pursue it any further. I don't know what to do. He feels guilty but for the wrong reason. What should I say to him? Nobody says I have to do it right now, so I'll think on it for a bit.

chapter twenty-one

$\mathcal{S}$aturday, Jason and I spent the morning at the soccer fields for the boys' games. We dropped Rissa off at the dance studio for class and Sybany at the gym for practice on our way to the park. Jason's mom and dad came to cheer the boys on. Luckily, it seemed some of the novelty of my situation had worn off. Everybody and their mother wasn't stopping by to ask inane questions.

The younger kids played first, so Xavier kept me clued in to what was happening on the field, or what was supposed to be happening on the field. Honestly, it looked like each player's primary objective was to chase the ball no matter which way it was going, unless he or she wanted to stop and pick a flower or watch a bird or run off the field to get a drink. It was a three-ring circus with Jason, the opposing coach, and the referee sharing the duties of ringmaster. The players' antics were very entertaining. By the end of the game, my sides hurt from laughing.

"Good game, buddy," I congratulated Dawson as he ran up to us.

He seriously replied, "I know'ed. I ran and ran. Did jou see how much I ran, Momma?" The kid never stopped bouncing.

"I saw you, buddy. I can't believe how much you ran." I left out the flower picking, bird watching, and drink fetching that interspersed all of the running.

Squatting down, he rolled his socks down. He discovered his forgotten treasure tucked in his shin guard. "Momma, here, I picked jou a flower," Dawson told me as he held up a squashed a slightly slimy yellow dandelion.

"Aww thank you, Dawson. I love it," I declared sincerely.

"I know," he replied, "all wadies wike ta get fowers. I made sure Daddy knew dat ta pwan for y'all's date wast night."

I laughed at his assertion. "Thank you, buddy. The flowers were a great surprise." I hadn't a clue how Jason managed to accomplish getting all of those flowers on short notice.

There's a lot I was still unclear on, but I pushed all of that to the back of my mind as Xavier's team ran onto the field to start their game. Dawson sat next to me the entire game. About ten minutes into the game, Dawson reached over and took my hand. I smiled down at him, and he looked back at me and gave an exaggerated wink. He was a total flirt. I saw so much of Pappy in him.

We finished watching Xavier's game and then went to lunch at McAlister's. Jason picked my order again, just like I would have ordered it. He'd really been paying attention all these years. He knew down to the smallest detail what I would like. It was a good thing one of us did.

Putting on my brave face, I decided to ask how Jason accomplished the garden in my room.

A chagrinned expression filled his face, and he kind of shrugged his shoulders in an 'it was nothing' kind of way, but he answered, even when the details weren't fluffy and nice. "Well, after Dawson mentioned every lady likes flowers," Jason winked at Dawson, and Dawson gave him an exaggerated wink back, "I knew it would have to be big to get my feelings across. So I called your Aunt Nancy and threw myself at her mercy. She told me I was crazy and there was no way in hell she could accomplish that in a few hours' notice, but she would call around and see what she could come up with. An hour later, she called me back and said I was in luck that someone else's misfortune was going to save my ass. I asked her if she robbed a funeral home. She assured me she had not, but a friend of hers had a wedding that canceled at the last minute.

"The bride's parents were more than happy not to have to pay for the flowers. But the florist was three hours away." Southerners tell distance by the time it would take to get to or from the destination. "I sent a couple of guys from the shop up there to pick everything up. Then your mom, the kids, Meri, and Macy all pitched in to decorate the room."

My heart did that little pitter-patter flip thing, and I said, "I'll have to tell everyone thank you. I can't believe how much effort y'all put into that. It was like sleeping in my very own garden."

"I'm glad you liked it. Seeing you smile was worth the effort, not to mention the thank you." He paused for a moment, then continued, "But I'm not done yet."

"I don't know how you are going to top that," I joked in all seriousness.

"Oh there are ways," was all he said. A mischievous smile graced his lips.

We finished up lunch and took the smelly boys home for a shower. The boys had another idea, a dip in the backyard pool. So we spent the afternoon diving for rings, playing pool basketball, and Marco Polo. The four of us played until it was time to pick up the girls. Jason left to bring them home. He was also going to pick up dinner because Sybany and I had our date that night.

Sybany had asked her dad if she could use our season tickets to the local university's student dinner theater. I anxiously awaited the chance to talk with Sybany one on one. After the boys settled in the game room to watch some random sporting event on the T.V., I went to shower and readied myself for my evening out.

Sybany and I settled into our chairs with a long stretch of silence. Sybany was beautiful with her hair in perfect loose rolled curls pulled up and pinned on one side and an adorable rockabilly dress. A student waitress walked up and asked what we would like to drink. We both asked for sweet tea. There was a limited amount of time the two of us would have to talk due to the performance of "The 25th Annual Putnam County Spelling Bee". I had to give her credit, she'd put a lot of thought into how to not have to interact with me, but I wasn't giving up.

I broached a topic I knew she was passionate about–gymnastics. "How was practice today?"

"Good. I'm working on a new floor routine." She kept her eyes averted as she gave her brief answer.

"I can't wait to see it." Genuine enthusiasm laced my voice. She smiled and briefly met my eyes but quickly looked away. "How'd you decide you wanted to pursue gymnastics?"

"I took classes with Rissa and liked it. Turns out, I'm good at it." Okay, she wasn't going to be as easy as I thought.

"What's your favorite part?" I probed. Persistence was a trait I still had in spades.

"Floor." She continued to look off at anything but me.

"Oh what do you like about floor?" Pulling teeth might have been easier than getting a preteen to talk. Where was Meri with her interrogation techniques when I needed her?

"I get to create a performance. Kind of like in dance."

I wasn't making much headway on the gymnastics topic, so I switched to books. "What book are you reading for this month's report?"

Guilt filled her eyes. "I haven't started one yet," she confessed, glancing at me but looking away before I could engage her.

Not wanting to alienate her by chastising her, I asked if there was something she might have been interested in. "What sort of books do you like?"

"Fantasy books are good. I like adventure, too," she said after thinking for a moment.

"Have you read the Harry Potter series, yet?" I asked, doing my best not to let my excitement show, thinking this might be a way for us to connect.

"Not yet." She shook her head as she answered.

"How about we read it together? It's been so long since I read them, and I've forgot how it ended." She frowned a little at that last bit, and I mentally kicked myself in the fucking ass for reminding her that I'd lost my memory. "That'll get you through seven months of book reports," I added to sweeten the deal. You may not be able to buy love and forgiveness, but I wasn't above ingratiating myself for the cause.

She didn't have a chance to reply before the show started and dinner was served. We didn't talk much during the rest of the show, and she nodded off soon after we got in the SUV to drive home.

When we pulled in the driveway, I called Jason to ask him to come carry her in to the house. He met us in the garage and asked how it went when I opened my door.

"Okay, not as good as I hoped, but I think we made a little progress. I'm trying not to be disappointed."

He wrapped his arms around me, cradling my head against his

solid chest. "Don't get too discouraged, she's a tough nut to crack—like someone else I know."

"Hardy har har, aren't you a comedian," I said without any heat to the words.

He chuckled. "Come on, let's put Sleeping Beauty to bed before she turns into a pumpkin."

"You're mixin' up fairy tales." I playfully poked him in the chest.

"Either way, the results are the same if she gets woken up." Then he walked around the SUV and retrieved our daughter, carrying her to her room.

He laid her on the bed as I gazed around the darkened room. Writing filled the walls. I wanted to read all of the words, hoping for a clue to my youngest daughter, but to do so felt like I would be prying into her diary.

chapter twenty-two

$\mathcal{S}$unday was a normal day. It was quite refreshing. Jason's family came over, and we grilled and spent time in the pool. Watching the kids act like carefree kids made my heart skip a few beats. We forgot that I'd forgotten, and we were just a regular family if only for a few hours.

The next morning, I was killing time by helping with some of the household chores. I carried handfuls of hanging clothes to the kids' rooms. Rissa's clothes were laid on her bed to be hung up in her closet later. In our house, once you became a teenager, you were responsible for putting your clothes away. Then I continued on through the Jack and Jill bathroom that connected the girls' rooms. I laid the boys' clothes on Sybany's bed so my hands would be free to hang her clothes.

Opening her closet door, I noticed everything was meticulously organized by style and color. Nothing was out of place in her closet. I began hanging up clothes in the appropriate spots. As I pushed clothes to one side to make room on the bar for a skirt, I noticed writing on the wall. This writing stood out because it was the only writing in the closet, unlike her bedroom walls, which had writing all over. Moving the clothes farther to the side, I read what she'd written. The writing appeared to have been written with a shaky hand by someone sitting in the corner.

Mom died

Pain fills a broken heart

Leaving cracks deep inside

Unanswered questions

Forgotten possibility

Abandoned to half a life

Scared of the unknown

Too brave to show

Until I'm alone

Part of me is gone

Mom lived

Brokenhearted my pain lingers

Unanswered questions

Forgotten possibility

A whole life missing

Scared of the unknown

Must be brave

Can't let my fears show

Until I'm alone

My mom died

My mom lived

Life changed forever

No way to make it right

Can't understand how good

Intentions went so wrong

My heart broke into a thousand more pieces. I stared at the words, struggling to understand how to help my daughter accept that there was no fault to be found. Getting myself together, I left the closet to retrieve my cell phone.

Overall, the phone with its touchscreen and apps befuddled me, but the kids had endeavored to teach me how to use modern technology. *Back To The Future* had not prepared me for reality in the twenty-first century. One 'app' I'd mastered was the camera.

I found my phone on a console table in the family room. Retrieving it, I went back to the closet to take a picture of the poem. My plan was to show it to Jason and Dr. V. Being a responsible mother was more important than allowing Sybany her privacy. We'd tried giving her space to come to terms with the events of the day I lost my memory. Obviously, that plan wasn't working one damn bit. It was time to change tactics.

I went about finishing hanging up the rest of the clothes then picked up my laptop. Browsing through pictures, I studied each, hoping the spark of recognition would rekindle my memory. Nothing. Nada. Nil. I recognized the pictures, but not the feelings of the moment it captured.

"Wacha doin'?" Xavier asked as he collapsed on the couch beside me.

Meeting his gaze, I smiled and answered, "Going through our family photos," hesitating for a moment before I continued, "seeing if anything jogs my memory." I wanted the kids to know it was okay to have worries and fear, but that we couldn't let it define our lives.

He looked unimpressed. "Did you find any pictures of me?"

"There are tons of pictures of you. Let's see what we have here," I said as I opened the first file folder with his name. The first picture caption read, Mommy and Xavier meeting for the first time. "Seems this is the first time we met face-to-face." He was swaddled in a blanket as Jason held him up next to my face.

"But you don't remember it anymore, right?" he questioned, a curious look on his face.

"That's right," I replied, doing my best to keep the regret out of my voice.

His lips pressed together, and he hmphed. Then he spoke some of the most important words I'd heard. "Well, I don't remember it either, so that's okay 'cause I know you love me."

"Oh, how do you know?"

"'Cause good moms love their kids. And you're a great mom. And you always told me you loved me." He looked pensive and then said, "Why would you say it if it wasn't true?"

Thinking of the right words was important. "I don't think I would have said them if they weren't true. I know right now everything is mixed up, but I'm getting stronger each day. And even though I don't remember what happened before, I remember what's happened since. And it makes me more grateful every day for the time I have with each of you. I may not be the exact same kind of mom I was before my accident, but I hope I'll be just as good of a mom as I was before." I bumped his shoulder. "Well, as long as I don't attempt to cook anything. Then all bets are off."

He grimaced. "Please, don't try to cook. You're a good mom without cooking." Xavier did his best to reassure me.

"I bet I could handle a snack."

"As long as you don't use anything sharp."

"Pretty sure ice cream doesn't require anything sharp."

"But we haven't had lunch yet." This was said with obvious concern.

I stood up and began to make my way to the kitchen, calling over my shoulder, "I won't tell if you won't." There was an immediate scrambling of feet rushing toward the kitchen.

Xavier joined me as I pulled the carton from the freezer then waited patiently for me to fill out bowls.

"Chocolate sauce," I asked.

His eyes were getting bigger. "Yeah," he said in amazement. This was definitely a treat.

He and I settled down at the table to enjoy our midday treat. Xavier was done with his before I'd made a dent in mine. "Can I still have lunch?" he asked, and fear we were going to go broke feeding him before he was grown became a little more real.

We were rushing to get out the door for our appointment, but I pulled Jason aside anyway. I didn't want him to be blindsided with something I knew was important about our kids. Even though we slept in separate rooms, we'd made a conscious effort to present a united front for the kids since the come Jesus meeting about fibbing.

"What's this?" Jason asked as I handed him my phone.

"I found it in the back of Sybany's closet when I was hanging up her clothes," I told him around gnawing on my lip.

He read it before meeting my gaze. "No use chewing a hole in your lip," he said as he pulled my lip from between my teeth. "We'll talk to the doctor about it. That's the reason we're going to see Dr. Vermillion." How he remained so calm during all of this upheaval, I'll never understand. His low-key demeanor definitely balanced my worrywart tendencies. "Come on, let's get this show on the road."

"Sybany, it's time to go," Jason yelled across the house.

It wasn't long before she trudged down the stairs. You'd have thought we were taking her for a root canal, or worse, by the way she was dragging her feet.

Our arrival at the doctor's office brought my nerves to the surface. I'd been striving to appear more in control than I felt. But sitting in the waiting room, I began to chew on the corner of my thumbnail and bounce my knee. Jason reached over and lightly patted my knee then tugged my thumb from between my teeth. He wrapped my hand in his, squeezing it reassuringly while wrapping his free arm around Sybany's shoulders. Sybany leaned until her head rested on his chest. Jason bent his head down to kiss the top of her head, and my heart did a funny little thing—similar to what I imagined the Grinch felt when his heart grew. I'd never thought seeing a man as a father would be sexy. I'd been wrong.

"Hi, guys, good to see y'all. Are you ready?" Dr. Vermillion said from her doorway.

I leaned forward to catch Sybany's gaze. "Do you mind if Daddy and I talk to Dr. Vermillion first, then you can go in and talk to her?" She nodded her head.

"Bunny, your head's not full of rocks, so we can't hear it rattling," Jason said. I was being the good cop, so I let the little things slide a lot more than her dad did.

"Yes, sir." It was barely above a whisper.

"May I have your phone?" I asked Jason, and then I handed her Jason's phone. "You can play the mean birds game, but don't go online. *I* don't want to get in trouble for breaking the rules again." At that, she finally gave me a little smile. That smile was more hardearned than a fucking World Championship.

Jason and I took a seat on the couch. Dr. V's office was very comfortable and relaxed. It didn't make me feel like I was in a doctor's office to have my head examined.

Dr. V opened with, "How's it going, guys?"

Our responses came at the same time. "Good," was all Jason had to say.

"Better than expected in some ways, but not so good in others," I replied and handed her my phone containing the writing from Sybany's closet.

The doctor took her time reading before she said, "She's definitely internalized a lot of responsibility for what happened. Have you talked with her about this yet?"

I shook my head. "Not yet. I just found that this morning, and we wanted to talk with you first. I thought maybe if you spoke with her alone, she might open up a little more and maybe discuss some of the things she's feeling without revealing we've seen what she wrote. She's be—"

"Why don't you want her to know you saw it?"

I thought about how to put my concerns. "She wrote this where it was unlikely to be seen." Dr. V nodded her head. "Normally, she writes out in the open. There are writings and doodles all over her bedroom walls. Anybody can see them when they walk in. But this, she hid. I don't want her to feel like she's not entitled to private thoughts and feelings. I would prefer that she be given the chance to confide in someone in a safe, nonjudgmental environment. Then, if she doesn't, we reveal what we know."

"Do you agree with that, Jason?" she asked.

"Yes, I do. They're—Candice and Sybany—are a lot alike.

They'll confide when they are ready. I think Sybany knew eventually somebody would see what she wrote, and she knows we're here today to help her deal with some of her feelings. I think she'll take the opportunity to speak with you because there's no one there who 'has' to tell her she didn't do anything wrong."

"So the two of you would like me to talk to her alone and see if she will open up to me and then bring the two of you back in, correct?" We both said yes. "And what if that doesn't work and she doesn't open up to me, since she hasn't confided in me during our previous sessions?"

"Then we'll approach her together with you as someone to help her express her feelings," Jason explained with confidence.

"Okay. Let's bring Sybany in," Dr. V said. I don't think she disagreed with our course of action, but wanted to make sure we acknowledged this might not go as planned.

Jason and I stood in the doorway as he called her name. "Your mom and I are going to sit out here for a few minutes while you talk with Dr. Vermillion, but anytime you're ready for us to come in, you just let her know, okay?"

Sybany nodded her head. I didn't mention Jason letting her slide on the head nod.

"I'm looking forward to chatting with you again, Sybany. Would you like any juice or water before we get started?" Dr. V inquired.

"No, thank you," Sybany replied without looking up from where she was scuffing her Chuck on the floor.

"Then come on in and have a seat," she instructed Sybany before giving us a reassuring smile and closing the door.

I trusted Dr. V. She'd been great with me, but this was my fragile child we were dealing with. Instincts to protect her had sprung to life, and there would be no denying I would gladly sacrifice my life for hers. It was that realization that made me recognize that I was, in fact, feeling motherly, and I was no longer going through the motions, trying to fake it until I made it. I'd always cared about the kids, but I'd doubted myself tremendously as a mother.

Over the course of the thirty minutes Sybany and Dr. V spent in the office, I wore a path from the front door to the office door and back again. Jason sat there as placid as ever. I did ponder the thought of what it would take to make him lose his calm, cool, and collected demeanor. When the door finally opened, I wanted to barrel past the good doctor and wrap my arms around my daughter; however, I remained reserved as to not overwhelm Sybany.

Once we were all seated in the office, Dr. V began. "Sybany's been explaining to me how she feels about your accident, and she has something she wants to tell you. Go ahead, Sybany, it's okay." When Sybany hesitated, Dr. V spoke again. "Remember what we talked about."

Sybany swallowed and took a deep breath before speaking in a low voice. "I'm sorry for what happened—" As I began to interrupt to assure Sybany she was in no way at fault for my accident, Dr. V subtly shook her head. "—and I'm sorry I wasn't in the kitchen helping like I was supposed to be," she drew in a shaky breath before she continued, "because I was on the computer playing The Crystal Secret game, since I wanted to make it to the next level before Alexis did. I'm sorry I broke the rules and wasn't doing what I was told to. I didn't mean for you to get hurt." By this time, tears had started to fall off her cheeks and her voice was quivering.

I felt horrible that she'd been dealing with this kind of guilt for so long. Kids make mistakes, and I had no doubt, given the situation, Jason would have understood that as well. I got up off the couch and walked over to the chair she sat in. My hands firmly clasped around her arms, pulling her up to me. I tucked her head under my chin and wrapped my arms around her. "Shhhh, don't cry, baby girl. I need you to calm down and listen to me." It took a couple of minutes, but her tears lessened, and I began to reiterate how my accident was not her fault. "Sybany, honey, you being on the computer didn't cause my accident, and it didn't make it any worse. We can't second-guess the circumstances, because things could have happened any number of ways. But I do know, without a shadow of a doubt, that you are not to blame for anything that happened. What you are responsible for is coming as soon as you heard me fall and calling the ambulance and calling Bev and Mike since they were the closest. You stayed calm and levelheaded throughout the whole thing, and I'm so proud that you knew what to do and did it. I want you to look at me." She slowly raised her head. "We all do things we shouldn't from time to time, but you playing a game on the computer isn't anything that you need to feel this guilty for. I think you've punished yourself enough, and now we need to move forward and not let the 'what ifs' weigh us down anymore, okay?" She gave a small nod, but at least it was something. I glanced over to Jason to see if he had anything to say.

Looking at his face, I realized he felt just as guilty as Sybany did at that moment. His face was ashen and he looked grief stricken. Jason was the rule enforcer, and she'd been afraid because she broke the rules; therefore, afraid of him and the consequences he would impose. In just seconds, he further amazed me. Jason pushed aside those emotions and spoke to Sybany as he walked over to be near her, "Sybany, I don't want you to ever be scared to tell us what you're thinking and feeling because you're afraid of the consequences. I know we have rules, and some of those rules are more stringent than others, but I promise you the world isn't going to end because you broke one. But, please, don't tell the boys that or they may never take a bath again, and that would be worse than anything." She smiled at his joke and gave a little laugh. He rubbed his hand over her hair.

In spite of the heaviness of the afternoon's revelations, I felt lighter as the three of us left Dr. V's office. That was until she called after me, "I'm still waiting on the answer to my question, Candice. I hope you'll have an answer for me next time."

I frowned because I was pretty damn sure I knew the answer, and I didn't like it one damn iota.

chapter twenty-three

My advice to Sybany to stop dwelling on the 'what ifs' and second-guessing everything reverberated through my mind. Knowing I needed to let things go was one thing; doing it was another. I needed to take my own advice and start living in the present. Easier said than done, but I made a commitment to myself to try harder to live and enjoy the life with which I'd been blessed.

We had a great family dinner that night. The six of us were finding a groove. Sybany and I letting our walls down appeared to give everyone permission to relax. It's strange how I didn't notice the tension that had filled the house until it started to dissipate.

Laughter rang out more than it had since I had woken up in the hospital. I didn't want the night to end. "Let's have a movie night!" I suggested to keep the fun times going. "We can make popcorn and eat junk food—"

"Mom, I can't eat junk, I'm preparing for a performance," Rissa reminded me.

"Yeah, Rissa's right, I can't eat junk food either. Coach says you are what you eat," Sybany agreed with her sister.

I wasn't giving up, though. "No problem. We can have healthy snacks. I'll make a platter of veggies and fruits to snack on."

"But I wan' popcorn an' treats an' stuff, not veg-a-ta-bles," Dawson chimed in his disagreement to his sisters' choices.

"Yeah, we just had vegetables and stuff for dinner. It's time for dessert," Xavier exclaimed.

"Okay, okay. How about everybody picks two snacks to have during the movie, does that work for everyone?" There was a round of yeahs and wohoos. "All right, let's get the kitchen cleaned up, then we can pop a movie in."

"What movie are we gonna watch?" Dawson asked.

My mind whirled as I tried to think of a movie that everyone in the family could watch and enjoy. I didn't have a clue about recent movies. The first movie that came to mind was the one I picked. "We're going to watch The Lion King. Have you seen that one?"

Dawson and Xavier shook their heads, but Damaris said, "I think you watched it with Bunny and me a long time ago."

"It's a really old movie now, but it's really funny." I had their attention, so I continued. "It's a cartoon about a lion cub and how he grows up to be king because lions are king of the jungle. Hurry up so we can get watching."

Everything was going great until King Mufasa got trampled by the herd of wildebeest.

Dawson gasped and looked at Jason and me with big, round eyes. "Did he die?"

"Yeah, buddy, he died," Jason answered.

"But why did he die?" he cried. "Simba needs his dad."

"Duck, sometimes bad things happen to people—I mean, lions, and I'm sure Mufasa went to heaven, so he can always be with Simba."

Jason's reasoning didn't sit well with our youngest child.

"But wha' if Mommy had gone ta heaven? I don' wan' Mommy or jou ta go ta heaven." Anxiety filled his voice. His anxiety was palpable.

"Mommy's okay, bud," Jason reassured Dawson, trying to keep him from completely flipping out.

"I'm okay, buddy," I attempted to give my own reassurances at the same time.

"But what if you got trampled in a stampede?" His hands began to flap.

I was really unsure of what to say to that question. "Ummm, buddy, I think the likelihood that I would get trampled in a stampede is highly unlikely."

"But we habe cows. More people get killed by cows dan by sharks." At that point, I was really confused because I had no idea what sharks and stampeding cows had to do with my accident. "What if jou fawl out in da pasture and da cows trample jou?"

"Dawson, have you been watching that shark show again?" Jason asked while giving him a knowing look.

"Xavier was watching it first." Dawson used the old 'throw your sibling under the bus to deflect attention and save yourself' defense.

"Xavier is older, and it doesn't give him nightmares—" Jason began, but Dawson wasn't letting go.

"Dey doesn't gibed me nightmares no more, Daddy. Fwogga showed me how dey made Jaws and stuff. Sharks don' wike eatin' peoples 'cause we don' taste good." Pride that he faced his fears laced his voice, and a smile spread across his face. He'd been distracted from his upsetting thoughts of me being trampled in a stampede of cattle.

"Buddy, I'm glad you faced your fear of sharks and learned more about them. That was very smart and brave of you," I told him, "and I don't plan on spending much time out in the pasture, so the chances of me being trampled are very low. Besides, cows are easy going." Wrong thing to say.

"If cows are so nice, why can't I go in the pasture?" he asked. I drew a blank. This was a parental catch twenty-two. The kid had undeniably caught me with the unexpected.

Jason answered, "Cows are generally calm, but we never know what might happen, which is why you aren't allowed in the pasture with the cows or the barn with the other animals by yourself."

"Can we watch the rest of the movie now that we know all about cows?" Xavier asked, clearly frustrated by the interruption. The girls nodded in agreement.

Note to self; watching a movie, where a parent dies, with your kids after having a life threatening accident is not a smart move. So far, my living in the now wasn't going so well.

chapter twenty-four

$\mathcal{A}$ few nights later, it was time for my 'date' with Dawson. He had a definite plan for every part of our date. He'd even gone so far as to pick out the outfit he wanted me to wear; a Kelly-green sleeveless dress, strappy gold sandals, large hoop earrings, and a gold cuff bracelet. For a kid, who just a few days ago worried I was going to stumble and be trampled by cows, he had no qualms about putting me in four-inch heels. The outfit had me quite curious about our intended destination.

At about quarter to six that evening, I walked into the family room. Nobody was there, so I continued on into the kitchen. Beverly stood at the stove, finishing dinner.

"Where's Jason?" I asked her.

"He had to run out. He'll be back in a bit," she filled me in on Jason's whereabouts. "Do you want a glass of wine? You look like you could use a little liquid courage."

"Is it that obvious how nervous I am?" Dawson's idea of a date did have me a little concerned. His unique view of life had to translate into an interesting date.

"Other than the fact you're wringing your hands?" She nodded toward my hands clasped in front of me. "Not at all."

Unclenching my hands, I made a concerted effort to relax my body. Dawson was a five-year-old little boy. It was highly unlikely he'd have us doing something crazy. "I'll pass on the wine, thanks. Umm, what are you making for dinner?"

"Glazed salmon, fried corn, and a spinach salad." The meal sounded delicious.

"Sounds yummy. I'm sure the girls will be pleased."

Bev laughed and said, "Xavier won't starve, but I'm sure he'll be raiding the kitchen for a 'snack' later."

The doorbell rang, drawing my attention. "I bet that's my date. Don't want to keep him waiting. See you tomorrow." I headed for the front door, opening it to a handsome and debonair young man dressed in a three-piece-suit and wing tips. Who knew they made wing tips for boys.

Extending his hand, which held a bouquet of flowers, and giving a little bow. "For'd jou, my wady."

"Oh, well, thank you, young sir. Let me just put these in water." Keeping in line with the way Dawson acted, I asked, "Would you like to step inside?" I stepped back, opening the door a little wider.

"Thank jou, ma'am." He stepped inside. "I'll wait here." His posture was very stiff.

"I'll be right back." Turning, I walked back across the family room to the kitchen. "Bev, do you know where we keep the vases?"

"Oh, I'll put those in water for you." She smiled, reaching for the bouquet. "You go have fun with that handsome young man."

"I will. Good night." I waved my hand and made my way back to my date for the evening. "Okay, I'm all set."

"Yay," he exclaimed then seemed to remember he was being more sophisticated. He straightened his back, put one hand on his stomach, and crooked his other arm, raising it higher than normal. I placed my hand in the crook of his elbow, and he opened the door.

As we descended the stairs, I noticed Jason standing by the back passenger side door. I quirked my eyebrow at him in silent questions as to why he was there. Jason just smiled and reached to open the rear door.

Dawson addressed Jason. "Mr. Woodruff, are all da arrangedments in order?"

Jason nodded his head and replied, "Yes, sir, everything is in order, per your request."

The dialog between the two of them had the ring of a script being performed.

"Thank you, Mr. Woodruff," Dawson stated then looked at me. "My dear, wet me assist jou inta da car." He reached for my hand and held it as I stepped up into the back seat of the SUV. Then he stepped back, allowing Jason to shut the door. Their voices were muffled, but I could make out the conversation. "How'd I do, Daddy?" Dawson's voice returned to his typical five-year-old self.

"You did great, Duck, but we don't want to keep Mommy waiting." Then the pounding of feet sounded as Dawson ran around the SUV. I watched as Jason followed at a normal pace. The footsteps stopped at the driver's side rear door. Even though I couldn't see him, I could picture Dawson resuming his refined persona. Jason caught up with him and opened the door. As Dawson scrambled up to the back seat, Jason met my gaze and winked. I knew there was going to be a lot of back-story for this date.

As Jason began driving down the driveway, Dawson asked, "Mommy, would jou wike ta wisten ta some music?" His question was very earnest. He was trying very hard to act grown up.

"That would be great, Dawson." I gave him an encouraging smile.

"Mr. Woodruff, pwease turn da radio on," Dawson requested very politely. Soon the upbeat tones of big band music filled the SUV.

"Did you have a good day, Dawson?" Making small talk to pass the time as we made our way to the surprise destination.

We chatted the rest of the way to the restaurant, which turned out to be a little hole-in-the-wall Italian place. Jason parked and got out to open Dawson's door. We'd each undone our seat belts. As Dawson went to climb down, he stopped and held his hand out in a stop motion, even though I hadn't moved, saying, "Just wait dere, Mommy. I'll come 'scort jou."

I smiled and agreed, "Okay, I'll wait right here."

When my door opened, Dawson extended his hand to assist me from the back seat. I loved his gentlemanly manners. He was adorable. Once again, he crooked his arm and placed my hand on his arm. We walked slowly across the parking lot. Dawson's chest was puffed out with pride. At the door to the restaurant, he stepped up to hold the door open for me and made a dramatic flourish with his arm for me to enter the restaurant.

There was a smiling young woman standing at the hostess stand. As we drew closer, she greeted us. "Good evening, Mr. Woodruff, we have your table ready. Please, follow me."

Without a doubt, I was a part of a large production.

We were led to a small table topped with a linen tablecloth and napkins and a small flower arrangement of orchids. The restaurant was nice, but this table stood out as different.

Dawson stepped around me, pulling my chair out for me. I sat, attempting to be graceful, and said, "Thank you, Dawson." Once I was settled in my chair, he walked around to the other side of the table and climbed up in his chair. Based on how high he sat, there was a booster seat.

Jennifer handed us our menus. "Sir, would you prefer the red or white vintage this evening?" she inquired.

Dawson appeared to contemplate for a second. "We would wike ta sample da white dis eb'ning, pwease, Jennifer." I was pretty sure they were discussing wine, but I couldn't imagine that Jason would have let this production go so far as to include wine; no matter how grown up Dawson wanted to pretend to be.

As she left, we studied our menus. "Do you have a suggestion for dinner?" I asked him.

"Da spaghetti and meatballs is yummy," he said, slipping back into an excited five-year-old.

"Oh that does sound good," I agreed as I read the description. Actually, everything sounded delicious, but red sauce didn't seem like a good idea, considering my outfit.

Jennifer returned to our table. She held a bottle of sparkling white grape juice out to Dawson, who nodded his head. Jennifer poured a sample in the wine glass. Dawson picked up the goblet, gently swirled the liquid, brought the glass close to his nose and inhaled, then he took a sip, paused a moment and took another sip. He pondered for a moment and then said to Jennifer, "Dat will do nicewy, Jennifer." And she poured each of us a glass of sparkling grape juice. I did my best not to giggle at his antics, but there was a huge smile on my lips.

"Are the two of you ready to order, or do you need a minute or two?" she asked.

Dawson looked at me. "Mommy, do jou know'd what you wan'?"

"I believe so."

"What would jou wan'?" he asked me then corrected himself. "I meaned, what would jou wike?"

"I'll have the chicken alfredo and a Caesar salad," I told him.

He then relayed my order to Jennifer along with his order of spaghetti and meatballs. Jennifer left to place our order with the kitchen.

He and I chatted as we waited for our food. Dawson never ran out of things to discuss. He talked in depth about catching tadpoles to watch them sprout legs and turn into frogs. Maybe my pet ban should be expanded to include amphibians as well.

Covertly, I glanced over to Jason, who was sitting at the bar. He was talking with the bartender. The bartender, who happened to be an attractive female, was unmistakably flirting given her body language. The fact that she was fucking flirting with *my* husband didn't sit too well. A full-fledged desire to snatch a bitch bald headed began to take root. But as if he could sense my eyes on him, Jason turned his head toward me and gave me a heart stopping smile, featuring full-on dimples. Damn those dimples were going to get me in trouble. I returned his smile and put my focus back on Dawson, who had moved on to describing the time he got bucked off a horse.

Jennifer delivered our salads, and we began eating as we continued chatting. It wasn't long before the main course was brought to the table. Dawson's plate had a tall pile of noodles and three fist-sized meatballs. Dawson's appetite might have rivaled Xavier's.

Before digging into his plate of spaghetti and meatballs, he pulled his napkin from his lap, tucked it in his collar, and smoothed it across his chest. He seemed to be reconsidering tucking his napkin in and looked at me, so I smiled, reached down, pulled my napkin up, and tucked it in the low neckline of my dress. "There, now we match!" I proclaimed. He smiled and began to eat, sucking in the noodles like a five-year-old normally would, letting it whip up and pop him on the nose.

After dinner, Jennifer brought over the bill. She held it out to him. He concentrated then said to her, "Dis is thwee-seben dot four-eight, so dat means I pay jou thirdy-seben dowars and fowdy-eight cents, wight?"

"That's right," she agreed with a smile.

"Fowdy dowars is more dan dat, so I gibed jou two tweny dowar biwills, cause dat makes fowdy. And den Daddy said use da ten dowars fo' da tip." He handed her two twenties and a ten, then he said, "Did I ged it wight?"

"You got it exactly right, little dude," she confirmed with a smile. She walked away and gave a discreet thumbs up to Jason, who smiled and nodded his head.

"Awe jou weady fo' da nex' pawt of ou' ebening?" Dawson drew my attention.

"Of course. I can't wait to see what you have planned next," I said, enthusiastic to find out what he had planned next.

"I's gonna be fun—I meaned, we will hab a stewpendus time." He slipped back and forth between himself and the persona he was portraying. He came around the table to hold my chair. As I stood and took his arm he paused. "Mommy, I need ta go ta da potty," he whispered.

"Okay, buddy. Do you know where it is?"

"Yeah, i's wight downed da hall."

"All right," I said, and he scrambled down the hall. I decided to take the opportunity to do the same.

We met back in the foyer of the restaurant. "Weady?" he asked, and I said yes. As we began to walk, I noticed he looked over at his dad, smiled, and gave a thumbs up. Jason smiled back at Dawson and returned the thumbs up. Jason's and my eyes met, and we shared a smile and knowing glance. And I fell a little more at that moment.

Dawson and I didn't go far when we exited the restaurant. We walked past a few storefronts until we arrived at a dance studio. Dawson opened the door in the same manner as before, and I entered the air-conditioned studio. Even though the walk had been brief, the humidity formed a sticky film on my skin.

"Y'all must be Dawson and Candice Woodruff," a friendly voice called. I found it belonged to a friendly woman wearing a sparkly costume used in ballroom dancing. She crossed the studio to us and extended her hand to shake ours. "I'm Charlotte, and I'll be your instructor this evening. Now, do either of you have any prior dance experience?"

"No, I don't believe I do," I answered, but I had no idea if I did or not.

"I go ta dance cwass. I'm da bes' at tap an' jazz," Dawson supplied, but he didn't make eye contact with her, instead he looked past her shoulder.

"Great! We'll let's get started on the basics." She brought us out to the dance floor and began talking to us about form and steps. A few minutes into her talk, I noticed Jason enter the studio and sit in a chair against the wall. He leaned forward with his elbows resting on his thighs, hands clasped between his knees.

I concentrated on the instructions Charlotte was relaying to Dawson and me. No matter how many times I told myself to stop sneaking furtive glances at Jason, my eyes wouldn't obey.

Soon, Charlotte turned on the music and began having Dawson and me follow the basic box step movements of her and her partner Michael as they danced beside us. Dawson paid close attention to his feet. His brow was creased with concentration. I did my best to keep up, but putting me in four-inch heels for the first time in months wasn't his best idea, even if I did feel like a million bucks.

Charlotte thought we'd progressed enough that we could manage a dance by ourselves. He and I danced a few, laughing at all of our missteps. Left foot slide left, feet together, left foot slide back, feet together, right foot slide right, feet together, right foot slide forward, feet together, and repeat as we moved around the dance floor. We were having a great time making our basic box step. I didn't notice Jason had walked over to us until he bent down to whisper in Dawson's ear. Dawson grinned, nodded his head, and stepped back, passing my hand to his dad's.

Jason smiled at me and asked, "May I have this dance?"

"Yes," I answered automatically in a breathless voice I didn't recognize.

Jason turned to face me, putting his other hand on my waist to draw me closer. His fingers spread across my lower back, the pinky resting on the crest of my ass. Our bodies weren't pressed together that tightly, but my body's response was undeniable. My heart began to pound in a nervous rhythm as we waited for the music to start. The sound of a guitar filled the studio, and Jason began to move us around the dance floor.

HOLY HELL! He's gorgeous. He's sweet. He's caring. He's charming. He's thoughtful. He's observant. He has the patience of a saint. He's a great father. His ability to knock all sane thought from my mind with a kiss was undisputed. And to top it all off, he could dance. I don't mean swaying from side to side. No, we covered the entire dance floor to a fast-paced song about losing one's self. I made a mental note to look it up later, because I couldn't focus on the music. I was too wrapped up in the man holding me in his arms as he led me around the dance floor. Guess what they say is true; if you have a good dance partner leading you, you can dance no matter how uncoordinated you are. In Jason's arms, I felt like I was floating and my feet barely grazed the floor. Good thing or I might have broken an ankle.

By the time the song ended, I was breathing so heavily I was practically panting. There was no way I could deny it was in response to the man whose arms I'd just spent the past four and a half minutes. As we drew apart, he raised my hand; flipping it over, he placed a brief kiss to my wrist. If it hadn't been for the little voice interrupting us, it would have turned into a much steamier affair.

"Daaaaaaad, don' steal my mobes," Dawson complained. "Mommy's my date. Jou can hab her back waiter."

Jason grinned, unrepentant in his actions. "Sorry, Duck, I couldn't help myself. She's all yours…for now." He winked at me and walked back across the studio to the chair he'd been sitting in. I stood there with my mouth agape at the man's audacity.

"Momma, jou gonna catch fwies if jou don' cwose jou mouf," Dawson claimed and snapped me from my runaway, hormone-filled, mental train ride to X-ratedville.

"Oh, right, how about we get a drink of water? I'm parched," I suggested.

"Okay, jou can sit down, I'll ge' it." He started to turn away but thought of something else, so he turned back to me. "But don' sit nex' ta Daddy. Y'all are giben each udder da googly eyes y'all make before you start huggin' an' stuff."

Oh dear Lord, did the kid have to call me out? "No problem, bud, I'm just going to go sit over here at the table and rest my feet." That seemed to satisfy him, so he left to retrieve the water.

I proceeded to the nearest table and collapsed in unladylike fashion in the chair, exhaling my frustration. I glanced across the room at Jason, who just grinned and sat back with his arms folded across his chest. The rat bastard knew exactly what he'd done with that dance, not to mention the way his shirt was stretched across his shoulders at the moment. I narrowed my eyes and glared at him. Before I thought better of it, I stuck my tongue out at him like a petulant two-year-old.

"Why you sticking jou tongue out at Daddy?" Dawson's voice broke me from my childish actions.

I jerked my tongue back and licked my lips. "Oh, I was just wetting my lips. They're really dry." Based on the look he gave me, it wasn't a believable excuse.

"I was dinking," he began, "jou shoud be my pardner fo' da summer show."

"How would I be your partner?" I was confused again. Nothing new there. Confusion had become a state of being for me.

"My dance partner, siwee," he explained like it should have been obvious.

"Umm, buddy, I don't dance that well."

"I dhought about dat, too. Jou can be da boy, and I'll be da gurl. Pappy says Ginge' Wogers did eberyfing Fwed Astaire did, 'cept she did it backwards an' in high heels."

"Why would that work? Why don't you just perform by yourself?"

"Id woked in Da Wion King. Timon wore a skirt ta dance fo' da hyendas," he explained. I wasn't sure I liked being the gaseous warthog in that scenario.

"Okay, but why can't you dance by yourself?"

"I'd wook pwetty siwee dancing by'd mysef, Mommy." Then

233

he gave me the eyes. Those pitiful, pleading eyes that would make the hardest heart melt, and I found myself saying yes.

We danced a few more, and Dawson started planning our routine. I had a feeling this was not going to be a fun endeavor. He took his performance seriously.

Jason drove us home and pulled in front of the house. Dawson walked me to the front door and kissed my hand. "I had a spwendid ebening, my dear. I hope we can do'd it again soon," he declared as he straightened to stand tall.

"I had a lovely evening, as well, and hope to do it again soon." I leaned down and kissed his cheek. Then I went inside and shut the door. Peeking through the sidelight window, I watched as Dawson ran down the steps and gave Jason a high five and some sort of hand explosion gesture. I chuckled to myself at their antics. Slipping my shoes off, I hobbled into the family room, where Bev was sitting on the couch, reading a paperback book.

Bev stood as I entered the family room. "Hey," I greeted her, "how did it go tonight?"

"Oh, easy as usual. The kids are already settled down in their rooms. They said they all have early mornings tomorrow."

"Okay, thanks for hanging out with them tonight. I'm going to check on them and head to bed."

She waved and said, "I'll see y'all tomorrow." Then she headed for the kitchen door.

I checked on all of the kids, but as Bev said, they were all out. It was hard to believe. I never wanted to go to bed when I was their age. Shrugging my shoulders, I headed to my room. I wasn't sure what else to do since Dawson and Jason hadn't come inside yet.

Sitting on the chaise, I rubbed my throbbing feet. I thought about the night. I'd thoroughly enjoyed my time with Dawson, but it was Jason whom dominated my thoughts. The lengths he would go through for our kids was amazing. Seeing him as a father was a turn on, which was still weird to me, became another facet to consider. I'd dated one guy with a child, and I'd decided that wasn't for me. At twenty-one, I hadn't been ready to be a mother figure, and I wasn't ready to take second place to anyone, even a kid, when it came to a relationship. But with Jason, it was different. Practically everything about the man turned me on, but seeing how much he loved his family brought it to a whole other level. And let's not mention the dancing and the kiss on my wrist, which still tingled like a pleasant burn on my skin. I was so wrapped up in my thoughts the knock on my door startled me. I stood up and began to make my way to the bedroom door.

Opening the door, Jason stepped into the room, and my back was pressed against the wall and his lips were on mine before I knew what was happening. It didn't take me long to get with the program, and I kissed him back with vengeance. My arms wrapped around his neck, fingers digging into his shoulder muscles.

There was no part of my mouth left untouched. Our tongues dueled in an age-old mating dance, until he gently bit down on mine and then sucked on it to soothe the slight sting. Moisture pooled in my thong. If his body hadn't been pressing me to the wall, I would've melted into a puddle at his feet. I'd thought my reaction to him before had been strong; it had been just a small, kindling spark compared to the inferno that engulfed me now. I didn't remember ever being kissed so thoroughly. The pressure of his body leaning into mine caused a wonderful friction. My nipples beaded into painful nubs that sufficed to stoke the heat inside me.

I had no idea how long we stayed like this, but all too soon, he drew back slightly and left a trail of kisses across my jaw. His tongue lightly teased my skin. The closer he got to his destination, the more my body heated. I feared I might spontaneously combust, or I would have if I could form a coherent thought. Jason kissed the spot just below my ear before grabbing my earlobe between his teeth and biting with just enough pressure to cause me to hiss and then soothing the sting, just as he had with my tongue. A shiver coursed over my body.

"Nice to know some things don't change." His warm breath caressed my ear. "Next time you decide to do something with that tongue of yours, put it to better use," he drawled in my ear, and then he was gone. My eyes were still unfocused, and I was panting as if I'd just run a race. As he walked out the door he called, "Sweet dreams."

Oh, that jackass! That was just plain fucking mean!

chapter twenty-five

My curiosity was roused, and it wouldn't be satisfied until I had answers. Various scenarios wove through my mind. Anxiety gnawed at my stomach. Sometimes my imagination got the better of me.

I made my way to the auto shop, hoping to have Jason join me for lunch. Stepping inside the office, I was greeted by the clerk. "Hey, Candy! How's it going?"

"Good. How are you?" I returned her greeting. She must've caught the bemused expression that made a frequent appearance on my face. I could see the moment the she recalled that I didn't know who the hell she was any longer.

"Oh, shoot, I forgot. I'm Jules," she introduced herself. "I've worked here almost four years."

I smiled to put her at ease. People sometimes had a hard time figuring out the balance of how to deal with me. It was hard to get the mix of treating me as if nothing had changed and acting like I had trouble understanding English correctly. "Don't worry about it." I laughed. "I'm sure we'll get to know each other again.

"You here to see Macy or Jason?" she inquired.

"Jason."

She angled her head and looked through a large Plexiglas window. "He's in his office. Down the hall, around the corner, second door on the right. Just go on in. He doesn't have anybody in there."

I said thanks and carefully limped my way down the hall. My feet burned from wearing the heels last night, but the discomfort was totally worth it to see the smile lighting Dawson's face.

Macy's office door was closed, which I was grateful for since I didn't want to make small talk while I had something weighing on my mind. I knew it was hers because of the nameplate beside the door that read Macy Strom, not because I remembered. Not letting that get me down, I pushed it to the back of my mind. There was no point in dwelling on what I couldn't change. Living in the now relieved a lot of my worries.

Jason's office door was open, so I knocked as I entered. Sitting at a drafting table, his back had been to the door. He turned around, and a smile lit his face when he saw it was me. "Hey," he said with shock filling his face as he tossed the pencil down on the table. "This is a nice surprise."

"Hi, I was wondering if you might want to go to lunch with me if you aren't too busy." Nervousness whirled in my stomach. I felt like I was approaching a boy to ask him to be my date for my first Sadie Hawkins dance. If my hands hadn't been clutched together, my knuckles white from the pressure, I would've been wringing them.

"Absolutely," he said, rising from his stool and walking toward me. "Anywhere in particular you would like to go?"

"Umm, I'm not sure what all is close by. I don't want to keep you from working." Unsure if coming here was the right move made me prone to ramble, so I bit my lip to stop my mouth from getting away with itself.

He smiled and said, "It's never an interruption when it's you. How 'bout we go down to the café just down the road?"

Nodding my head in agreement, I turned to leave the office. As I stepped out into the hall, a hand clasped mine, and my heart skipped a beat. It was a pattern I was becoming familiar with any time Jason touched me. I looked down at our joined hands and then up into Jason's blue eyes and smiled, reveling in the feelings I wasn't prepared to identify just yet.

We walked outside—well, I limped while he kept pace with me—and he directed me to his truck. He opened my door and helped me up into the cab. Then he hurried around the front of the truck and climbed in the cab. Immediately he cranked the truck and turned the air conditioner on full blast. I fought the urge to lean toward the air vent and fan my shirt. Midsummer heat turns any closed-up vehicle into an oven.

It didn't take us long to make it to the café. He repeated his actions from a few minutes ago in reverse and came back around the truck to open my door. We made our way to the door holding hands. Reaching for his hand when he was near was becoming second nature to me. At the door, he released my hand and opened the door. As I stepped through the doorway, Jason's hand came to rest on my lower back, and it stayed there until I was seated in a booth. The position of his hand resurrected memories of that hand's activities from the night before, not that they were buried very far from the surface.

After we'd made our order with the friendly waitress, Jason broached the topic of why I'd come to have lunch with him. "So, what's up?" he asked in his straightforward manner.

"First, I want to say that last night was great and I had a lot of fun with Dawson." He nodded his head, and I continued, "But it just doesn't seem natural for a kid his age. And given some of his other behaviors I've noticed," I hesitated as I tried to find the right words, "he…just… seems different than I would expect a five-year-old to be." I felt horrible for talking negatively about a child—my child—but I wanted to know, and I felt better about asking Jason than searching my diaries for the answer. I looked down, watching as I picked at my cuticles.

"Hey," he reached over, stopping me from destroying my nail beds, and threaded his fingers through mine, "it's okay to ask." He paused and gathered his thoughts. He exhaled heavily and continued. "You're right, Dawson is different. Just after he turned four he was placed on the Autism spectrum. He's very high functioning, but he has quirks—for lack of a better word—mostly in social interactions. You probably remember the term Asperger's Syndrome," he paused, looking at me for confirmation, so I nodded my head, "that's what his diagnosis would have been years ago, but that term was done away with when it comes to diagnosis. Now, it's all spectrum; it's just a matter of if and where someone with Autism falls on the spectrum.

"It's why he gets so into character and is particular about how things are done. If it's done this way one time, that's the way it will always be done. He can deal with change; it's just slightly more difficult for him. He likes kids his age, but he prefers adults. He and Pappy spend a lot of time together. They watch a lot of old movies. That's where Dawson gets a lot of his ideas. Like the date last night, in the old movies, the couples always dressed up and went out to dinner and dancing.

"We—Dawson, Pappy, Little Granny, and me—practiced for days so he could get the routine down. He's a great mimic and rarely forgets. We go to that restaurant a lot, so they were happy to help with Dawson's plan." I nodded my head encouraging him to continue.

"For the most part, Dawson is like a lot of other little kids; he just has some unique needs. It took a while for the professionals to agree on a diagnosis because he doesn't exhibit some of the characteristics normally associated with Autism. People are surprised because he is so loving, but they don't notice that it's on his terms. If you hug him, he's quick to pull away. He'll talk to any and everybody, but he doesn't look them in the eye. These things are subtle. Once we settled on a routine and knew how to recognize his triggers, we were able to help him deal with changes a lot better.

"Why didn't you tell me?"

He contemplated my question then said, "I... I guess I didn't want you to treat him differently. I thought you'd pick up on how we treat him and emulate us and things would just...work out."

"Oh," was my response. I began to pose questions, and Jason answered them with patience, without sparing any detail.

We talked about Dawson and then moved on to other topics. It was so nice to hear our life from Jason's point of view that I got caught up in his memories and didn't realize two hours had gone by until my phone alarm beeped.

"Goodness, I'm sorry for keeping you from work for so long," I apologized, gathering my purse to get ready to leave.

"No apologies needed. Any time you want to come distract me, feel free. It's not often I get to have lunch with a beautiful lady while I'm at work." Jason's grin was as affecting as always, and I scrambled to think of something to say in response. I came up blank. "Come on, let's get back, so I can wrap things up and get home."

When we made it back to the shop, Jason walked me to my car, settling a quick kiss on my lips before I fumbled my way into the SUV. He stood there waiting for me until I left the parking lot. I didn't realize he hadn't moved until I looked in the rear-view mirror before I pulled out onto the road to return home.

I thought back over my conversation with Jason and a piece of the puzzle started to fall into place. The times Dawson insisted that certain clothes had to go together or a certain pair of shoes had to be worn. Why he wanted to wear long sleeves, even when it was ninety degrees outside. In the three months since my accident, he'd gotten agitated on occasion, but usually someone was around to intervene and help him deal with what was happening. I guess I'd picked up on some of those techniques to deal with his agitation and stop it from progressing into a downward spiral.

Part of me was upset that I hadn't been told, but another wondered if I would have looked at him differently if I had known as Jason had worried.

By the time Jason came home from work, I'd gotten mad. I'd thought back over not being told about Dawson, and it brought back the irritation of things being withheld from me. It was once again someone else's decision what I was allowed to know and when. I'd worked myself into a state.

Dinner was a bit frigid. I ignored Jason and talked with the kids. After dinner, I avoided him as we went about the kids' nighttime routine. I recognized Dawson's insistence that the shower knob be turned to a certain spot and the books be read, prayers said in, and songs sang in a specific order with new insight. I kissed him goodnight and then stopped by everyone else's rooms. Rissa was reading, and Bunny and Xavier were playing a video game.

"Ten more minutes, guys, and then y'all need to get ready for bed."

"Yes, ma'am." They both answered without looking up from the game.

I made my way to my room, but before I closed the door, Jason put his hand on it and walked in after me.

"What's wrong?" he asked without beating around the bush.

I admired his forthright nature, but I wasn't in the mood. "Nothing." Nothing–the equivalent of waving a red flag in front of a bull. I continued into the room, set on ignoring him.

"Come on, Candice, I know you're upset about something. I don't know what changed between this afternoon and when I got home, but you might as well tell me and let's work whatever it is out." He pushed the issue. Then he walked past me and sat on the couch, settling in for the duration.

I contemplated leaving the room, but he put an end to that idea. "Don't bother walking out. I'll just follow you." I glared at him. It annoyed the hell out of me that he knew me well enough to predict my next move. "I know you're mad at me about something; you might as well tell me."

I stewed in my anger a little longer, huffing at his calm demeanor, before I began to rant. "I've told you how much I don't like having information withheld from me, yet you purposefully kept Dawson's diagnosis to yourself." I paced around the room, talking with my hands as I was prone to do. "Did you really think I would love him less because he has a fucking disability?" Coming to a stop directly in front of him, I waited. My hands clenched on my hips, and my foot tapped to the rhythm of my anger.

He hung his head and rubbed both hands over it, like he wanted to erase bad thoughts. When he looked up, his eyes were filled with sadness, regret, and guilt.

"I had a harder time accepting the diagnosis than you did. At the time, I worried it was going to limit him in what he could do. I didn't want to admit there was something 'wrong' with him." He shook his head as he spoke.

"You, on the other hand," his eyes met mine, "were determined that he just needed the tools to deal with his issues and he would still be able to accomplish anything. He has Autism, he isn't Autism, and it wasn't going to be the defining characteristic of his life. You moved forward with implementing the changes to help him. You worked with a therapist and developed a treatment plan. I was resistant.

"After seeing the positive changes with him and realizing it had nothing to do with something being wrong with him, I came around. We did a lot of work to get to an even keel. It's not something we talk about a lot now. I didn't think about sitting you down and telling you if it wasn't causing an issue." He stopped and then said something I really wasn't expecting. "In truth, I'm ashamed of the way I reacted when we received the diagnosis—that I thought he would be less for some reason. I guess, in some way, I projected that reaction on to you. I'm thankful that Dawson doesn't remember my reaction," pausing again,

244

his eyes flickered with pain, "and there's a part of me that's glad you don't remember it either because it made you look at me differently. It took a while for you to forgive me. I'd be lying if I didn't say I hadn't been tempted to delete those diary entries before you had a chance to read them."

"What did you think would happen if I read them?" I wondered aloud.

"I don't know, but I guess that we would've dealt with it then. Maybe you would see how well he does in day-to-day life, and it wouldn't be so hard to forgive me the second time."

I sat on the other end of the couch. Nothing was said for the longest time. Finally, I broke the silence and said, "I understand how you felt. But I have to be honest and admit that you not trusting me with something so vital about our son is very hurtful. Since I woke up in the hospital, I've trusted you and your intentions. I know you didn't intend to hurt me, but you did—"

"I'm very sorry for that, Candy. It's not that I didn't trust you," he swallowed deeply, "so much as regret about my actions in the past." He reached for my hand. "It's the way you're looking at me right now, like you've lost faith in me."

"That's not it at all. I'm hurt, but I'm not angry anymore. I think I've displayed a lot of faith in you. I know it seems like I only came home to our house for the kids, but on some level, I must have felt safe and secure being in your care." It felt good to be providing comfort to him for a change. If I was honest with myself, it was nice to have him mess up and not be so damn perfect all the time. This time it was me squeezing his hand reassuringly, conveying that things would be okay. The connection between the two of us grew stronger. "But you can't keep things from me."

"I know," he agreed wholeheartedly. His eyes met mine unflinchingly.

Striving to lighten the mood, I said, "Is there anything else? Secret wives? Love child?"

"No and nooo." He laughed. "The four we have are plenty."

"Addicted to gambling or porn or whatever?"

"Umm, no and I have no need for it; I have you." To which a spiff sound escaped my lips.

"Have you been raiding my ice cream stash?"

"Not if my life depended on it." His assertion was serious.

"Okay, then I think we're good. But don't keep things from me anymore."

"I promise I won't keep anything else from you, Candice." He kissed my hand and pulled me across the couch until I was next to him, then he lifted me onto his lap. Framing my face with his hands, he looked me in the eye. "I swear to you, I'll never intentionally keep anything from you." When I nodded my head, he leaned forward and placed a gentle kiss on my lips.

As the heat once again flared to life within me, I deepened the kiss and his hands slid back into my hair to cradle my head. A fireworks display accompanied by the Philharmonic played in my mind. My response to Jason was growing beyond my control. Desire flowed through my body. My back arched to push my breasts closer to the source of their need.

chapter twenty-six

*J*ust as I contemplated taking our make out session to the next level, raising my hands to unfasten the buttons of Jason's shirt, there was a knock at the door.

"Momma, my stomach doesn't feel so good," Xavier yelled through the door.

I jumped off of Jason's lap faster than a teenager getting caught making out by her parents. "I'll be right there, bud," I called out and set about straightening my clothes. Not sure why I straightened my clothes, since nothing was out of place, but it gave me something to do with my hands while I brought my raging hormones under control.

Inhaling a deep calming breath, I walked over to the door and opened it, letting Xavier in. "What's wrong, buddy?"

"I don't feel good," he whined in a pathetic voice. His face was scrunched up and he was holding his stomach.

Feeling his forehead, I remarked, "You feel a little warm. Go sit by Daddy while I get the thermometer. Do you feel like you need to throw up?"

He wobbled his head in what I think was supposed to mean yes and sort-of stumbled over to the couch and lay down. I noticed Jason had strategically placed a throw pillow on his lap. The ice water effect of a kid's voice on the other side of the door must not produce the same passion dousing reaction on men as it did on women.

I headed for the medicine closet in the bathroom and pulled out a bucket, thermometer, children's Pepto Bismal, and Tylenol before heading back to the bedroom and my ailing little boy.

Setting the bucket down, I said, "Here's a bucket if you feel like you're going to throw up. I want to take your temperature first." He just kind of grumbled what I think was okay. I stuck the thermometer in his ear while Jason rubbed his leg and said, "It'll be all right, Frogger."

BEEP The thermometer read, 101.3. So he had a bit of a fever. I finished reading the directions on the medicine bottles and dispensed each into its cup. "Okay, buddy, I want you to sit up and take these for me." He did as instructed and then flopped back down with his eyes closed. I rubbed my hand over his hair and leaned down and kissed his head before going back to the bathroom to rinse the cups and put the medicine away.

I came back in and sat on the arm of the couch next to Jason and stared at my little boy. Helplessness filled me and my heart ached for him. I'd never dealt with a sick kid before. I avoided them like the plague—avoided sick people in general. I wasn't cut out to be a nurse. But now that it was my child who was sick, I'd do anything to relieve his suffering. After a couple of minutes, I whispered to Jason that I was going to check on the other kids.

Sound asleep, Dawson's mouth was wide open with his thumb barely hanging from the corner. I straightened the covers and moved on to Sybany's room.

Her bedside lamp was on. She'd fallen asleep while reading if the Kindle lying beside her was any clue. I put the Kindle on the nightstand, pulled up her blankets, kissed her forehead, and turned off the light.

Damaris lay in her bead reading. Her eyes looked heavy. "Hey, sweetie, just wanted to check on you."

"I'm just trying to finish this chapter and then go to sleep." She yawned. "But I say that every chapter, and then when it ends, I have to read the next one."

I laughed at her familiar conundrum. "I know that feeling. Don't stay up too late. You don't want to be too tired tomorrow."

"I know," she groaned, "Mistress Martha doesn't take it easy on anyone."

"Well, I just wanted to see how you were feeling. Xavier is complaining of a tummy ache," I explained.

She looked sympathetic. "Oh yuck, but I feel fine. Hope he feels better soon."

"I'm sure he will. Get some sleep." Kissing her forehead before I left the room and headed back to the master suite.

Two of my boys—the biggest one of all and the biggest little one—were still huddled on the couch. Xavier had settled into sleep while lying down. Jason had done the same thing, but he'd slouched down in a sitting position with his head thrown back on the edge of the couch. His hand rested on Xavier's leg. Standing there, watching the two of them and thinking about my interactions with my other children, my heart swelled again.

Placing a throw blanket over the two of them, I decided to curl up on the chaise and read for a bit. I wanted to be awake if Xavier needed me.

Just over an hour later, I heard a faint cry of, "Mommy." The voice sounded pitiful and frightened, so I rushed from the room and up the stairs to Dawson's room.

Flipping on the light, I asked, "What's the matter, baby?"

"I don' fewel good," he whined as more tears pooled in his eyes.

I picked him up and rested my hand against his forehead. "Where do you feel bad?"

"My tummy huuurts." I turned to head downstairs with him in my arms, legs wrapped around my waist and his head resting on my shoulder. "I fink I'm gonna be siiiiick." His little voice broke my heart all over again, but I was about to learn a valuable lesson.

"Do you think you need to throw up or poopoo?" I asked as if I had all the time in the world to prepare for what was to come.

"Dro—" he began and then puked down the front of me. I shrieked out of shock and then spun for the nearest bathroom. "I sowwy, Maaahmeee," he cried while still gagging.

"It's all right, buddy. Mommy was just surprised, that's all," I tried to soothe him. Lesson learned; by the time the kid says they are going to be sick, it's going to be immediate and there isn't time to narrow down which end it will come from.

He was sobbing in earnest now. "I sow—," puke. And more crying.

We made it to the bathroom, and I leaned him over the commode while rubbing his back. His arms were wrapped tightly around me, refusing to let go as we stood over the bowl. He didn't have much left in his stomach.

A couple of seconds later, Jason came rushing into the bathroom. "What's wrong?" he panted.

I looked up and turned toward him while saying, "Dawson's sick now, too."

"Ooooooh," was his understated reply as he recoiled. He recovered quickly. "I'll take care of him. You go get cleaned up and bring up the medicine."

"Okay," I agreed then said to Dawson as I went to lower his feet to the floor, "Daddy's here. Mommy's gonna go get cleaned up and bring you some medicine."

His panic-stricken eyes looked up at me, and he clung to me tighter and cried, "NOOOOO don' weave me."

"Buddy, it's okay. Daddy's here, and Mommy will be right back. All right?"

"Yeah, Duck, I'm here. You'll be okay." Jason took Dawson, supported him to stand and then looked at me and said, "Go ahead. He'll be okay."

I nodded my head. "I'll be right back."

As I left the bathroom, I heard, "Wanna take a bath, bud? It'll help you feel better. Maybe even have some bubbles."

"Bubbles?" the little voice responded with a sad enthusiasm.

"Yeah, I think this calls for some feel better bubbles," Jason replied.

"Dey make me fweel bedder?"

"I bet they will."

"Okay," Dawson said weakly.

I sighed at the sweetness and then remembered I needed to get a move on and get back upstairs.

Hurrying down the stairs, I entered my room and checked on Xavier. He was fast asleep, and his face seemed a little more relaxed. I sighed and continued into the bathroom, pulling off my clothes as I went, desperately trying not to smear vomit on my face. Once my top was over my head, I tossed it in the sink and ran some water. My pants and undergarments soon followed, landing haphazardly on the floor.

Not even bothering to let the water get warm, I stepped in the shower and soaped up and washed off in less than a minute. In less than ten minutes, I was on my way back up the stairs with the medicine.

I found them in the bathroom with Dawson in the tub filled with bubbles while Jason pouring cups full of water over Dawson's shoulders and talking to him in a soft, soothing tone. "Doesn't that feel good, buddy? Rinsing all the yucky stuff away."

I made my way over to the tub with the medicine cups. "Here you go, buddy. These will make you feel better." Extending my hand to hold one to his mouth for him to drink, I was shocked when he started shaking his head no and using his hands to push mine away.

"No, I don' wan' it. It tase bad!" he vehemently exclaimed, starting to kick his legs and bang his feet against the bottom of the tub.

"I promise it will make you feel better," I persuaded, and he resisted, his body shaking.

It didn't take long before Jason stepped in. "Dawson, you have to take the medicine. It will make you feel better." His tone was stern, no room for arguing. I was okay with him being the bad cop.

"But —," Dawson started.

"No buts. Take the medicine."

There was a bit more whining and crying without any tears, but he took the first one then smiled and said, "Tha' wasn' so bad," while giggling. He was happy again, as if a switch flipped.

I smiled, relieved that he hadn't gotten more upset. "See, I told ya. Now take this one," I instructed holding up the medicine cup filled with Pepto Bismal.

He took the medicine cup and swallowed the contents without a whimper. "Tha' one tased so good."

"You'll feel better soon. Ready to get out of the tub and get in some fresh jammies?"

"Yeah."

"Okay, let Daddy get you out and dried off, and I'll get you some jammies."

I glanced over at Jason. He had his hand on Dawson's back and was telling him to get ready to get out of the tub. Jason looked up at me and our eyes locked briefly. In that glance, I realized, without a doubt, I was falling in love with Jason. There was no denying it any longer.

But I didn't have time to contemplate that discovery; I needed to get my boy his PJs, so I hightailed it out of the bathroom. By the time I returned, my breathing had returned to normal, but nervousness to be near Jason was back in full force.

Dawson dressed in his PJs, and then looked up at me—it was obvious I was the weak link—with these big, blue eyes and said in the most woeful voice, "Can I sweep wid jou?" His bottom lip may have even quivered.

There was no way I could resist. "Okay, buddy, let's go downstairs. But you have to be really quiet. Your brother's asleep on the couch."

"Okay, I be quite," he said. Yes, he said, changing the et sound to a te.

Jason carried him down the stairs to the master bedroom. I detoured to the kitchen to get a large bowl, since Xavier had the bucket from the medicine closet and I didn't know where another bucket was located off the top of my head.

Walking into the bedroom, I crossed the room to the bed and set the bowl on my bedside table. Dawson was already snuggled in the middle of the bed with Jason sitting next to him, rubbing Dawson's back.

"I'll be right back. I need to use the bathroom," I told them.

It wasn't long until I was back in the room. I checked on Xavier. He was fine, so I made my way back to the bed. I climbed under the covers.

"Okay, I'm gonna go to bed, too," Jason said and rose to leave.

"Where jou goin', Daddy?" Dawson asked in a slightly panicked voice.

Jason glanced at me and replied, "I'm going to bed in the guest room. Remember, that's where Daddy sleeps right now."

That was not what Dawson wanted to hear. He immediately started flailing, crying, and yelling, "No, jou suepose ta sweep here wid Mommy. Jou said I couwd sweep wid jou."

He was ramping up into a full-on fit. "Buddy, calm down. It's okay. Shhh. You don't want to wake Xavier." I made a spilt-second decision. Was I giving in? Hell yes. But the end result was I wanted it, too; this just made it easier. "Daddy can sleep in here with us." Jason's head popped up with shock filling his face. I nodded, signaling I knew what I was doing. "Calm down. Daddy just needs to go get ready for bed and then he'll be back."

"Jou pwomise jou come back?" Dawson entreated tearfully.

Jason broke eye contact with me and looked at Dawson. "Yes, Duck, I'll be right back."

He left the room and was back within five minutes, turning off lights as he came to bed. He pulled the covers back and lay down in our bed for the first time in months.

Probably about ten minutes later, I heard, "Goodnight, I love you," and felt him turning over.

I awoke to an aching back. Lying on my side, I'd been pushed to the edge of the bed with Dawson's head and shoulders wedged against my back. Glancing over my should I saw Jason lying on his side, facing me, with one of Dawson's feet propped on his face and the other just below Jason's chin. Hopefully Dawson didn't kick because that was sure to hurt.

Getting out of bed, I went to the bathroom. It was just after six, so I decided to lie back down. For such a small little fellow, Dawson was hard to move, and he'd crept even farther across my side of the bed. Finally I gave up on moving him and walked around to Jason's side of the bed. There was just enough room for me to lay on my right side if I snuggled against his back, so I did and threaded my left arm over his waist. Feeling his warmth permeating my chest as it pressed to his back, it wasn't long before I dozed back off into the best sleep I'd had up to that point.

chapter twenty-seven

"Momma, I'm hungry." I heard a voice say as I was shaken awake.

Popping my eyes open, I was greeted with the blurry vision of Xavier's face an inch from mine as he leaned over me. I jerked back in surprise.

"You feeling better, buddy?" I whispered with a sleep raspy voice.

He nodded his head enthusiastically. "Yeah," then added, "I'm hungry."

Less than twelve hours ago, he was moaning about how horrible he felt, and now he wanted food. This befuddled me, but I would later learn kids recover much quicker than adults.

Carefully tossing off the covers and sliding out of bed so I didn't wake Jason or Dawson, I asked, "What do you want to eat?"

Xavier didn't blink. "Maybe Dad can make breakfast burritos."

Directing him away from the bed. "Let's let him sleep a few more minutes. Your brother got sick last night, too, so they could use the rest. We'll take care of it."

Confidence filled me. I knew I'd rocked being a mom last night. It was as if I'd become a full-fledged mom after getting puked on and hanging in to take care of my kids. Now I was ready to tackle breakfast. Breakfast burritos weren't going to be any match for me. After my triumph of the night before, I could conquer the world of breakfast. Instead of wallowing in my self-congratulation, I should've paid attention to Xavier staring longingly back at the bed, where his father and brother slept unaware of the travesty that was about to occur.

It should be impossible to char sausage on one side while the other remains raw. How can scrambled eggs be dry? The tortillas became as hard as Frisbees. Disaster stared back at me, and I no longer felt triumphant. But admitting defeat was not in my plan.

"Just a few more minutes," I called over my shoulder, imitating the peppiness of a cheerleader.

"DAD, YOU'RE AWAKE!" Xavier yelled as if a knight in shining armor had charged in to save the day.

Relief caused my shoulders to relax. Turning to say good morning, I heard the whispered, "You gotta do somethin'. She burned the sausage and the eggs and the tortillas." I turned off the burners. So much for my not admitting defeat plan.

Avoiding the two sets of eyes, I confessed, "Breakfast seems to be a bust." My lip did a great imitation of Dawson's from the night before.

"Gives us an excuse to go out for breakfast," he said as if there was nothing he'd rather do than herd everyone to a restaurant first thing in the morning.

Cooking was definitely my Achilles heel. The emotional high I'd been riding had vanished in the wake of burned sausage, overcooked eggs, and petrified tortillas. "I really can't cook, can I?"

He grinned and shook his head. "No, not really."

"Then how did we eat before we had someone to cook for us?"

"A lot of macaroni and cheese and prepackaged meals."

I grimaced. "That sounds awful."

"Go tell your brother and sisters to get dressed so we can go grab something to eat," Jason told Xavier, who sped from the room as if he'd been launched, and then he walked over to me and said with all sincerity, "It could be worse—we could have had to eat it and pretend it was good and then figure out a way to sneak something to eat without you finding out. At least this way, it's all out in the open."

"I wanted to make everybody breakfast and prove I could do it."

"You can do lots of other stuff. Now, you might want to go get changed, or at least put on a robe." A pointed look at my chest accompanied his statement. I looked down and discovered that, even when I wasn't paying attention, my body reacted to his closeness.

"Right, I'll go get dressed. We wouldn't want Xavier to starve."

My mad dash from the kitchen made Xavier's look like he had the speed of a turtle.

In my bedroom, I fired off a text to my girlfriends. I need to talk. Anybody available?

What's up? Macy responded.

When? Came from Meri.

I'm in. Tonya replied.

Everybody want to meet at 7 at Butch's? Macy suggested.

Setting my phone down, I finished getting ready to go to breakfast.

When I entered the kitchen, Jason asked, "Everything okay?"

Surprised, I replied, "Oh, yeah. Umm Macy suggested all of the girls getting together tonight at seven."

"You should go out and relax with the girls," he encouraged. "You haven't gone out to do anything just for fun since you came home."

"All right, I'll let them know I'll be there."

"Good. Now let's see if we can round the kids up and get out the door."

By seven-fifteen that evening, all the ladies were settled into a big booth at Butch's, a little bar with a limited menu. Drink and food orders were placed, then they all turned to look at me expectantly.

I was center stage and boy did I feel the pressure. "Okay, I need y'all to be painfully honest with me. Think y'all can do that?"

Various affirmatives and headshakes gave me permission to continue.

Taking a steadying breath, I blurted it out. "Ricky Martin's gay?" Doing my best to keep my expression straight-faced.

Just as seriously Macy said, "Yes." Then she patted my hand.

"WHAT THE HELL! Do they have to get all the good-looking guys? Rick always claimed he was gay. No straight man could shake his bonbons that good and be straight, but Rick claimed every remotely well-groomed man was gay. It's totally not fair."

"We know, but what can you do but drool from afar?" Meri said. "Now quit stalling, what's going on that has you so flustered?"

No more avoiding the subject. "It's…it's my relationship with Jason," I confessed. "I feel like I'm on solid ground with the kids…well, as long as I don't try to cook."

"Oh, please, don't try an' cook. Nobody deserves that," Meri pleaded, and the others nodded their heads in agreement.

"How is it possible to reach the age of forty and not be able to boil water?" I asked rhetorically.

"Nobody knows, but you mastered that skill—or lack of thereof," Macy teased.

"But you can order out with the best of them," Tonya contributed the positive outlook to make me feel better.

I didn't know why I was so hung up on my inability to cook. Surely it had something to do with being the June Cleaver mother ideal, but that was never going to happen. The kids and Jason loved me anyway, so I must've been good at something.

"Stop getting off topic. What's your deal?" Meri once again prodded.

Finding the words was hard. I was fidgeting and hemming and hawing. "Out with it already," Bethany commanded.

"Jason and I have had separate rooms since I came ho—"

"WAIT!" Macy yelled, holding up her hands. "Does this conversation involve you, my brother, and sex?"

"Well, yeah," I confirmed.

"I'm gonna need another drink or twenty for this conversation," she said and started waving for the waitress. When the waitress arrived at our booth, Macy placed an order that would have put most people under the table. "Two shots of Fireball Whiskey and two vodka tonics, then keep the vodka tonics coming."

"Anybody else need anything?" the waitress asked.

"A Dr. Pepper, please," I requested.

"We don't have Dr. Pepper. Mr. Pibb okay?"

"Umm no, I'll take a sweet tea."

"I'll be right back with those drinks." She turned and made her way back to the bar.

"So, anyway—"

"Nope, not until I get my drinks. Talk about the weather or something," Macy instructed.

"I can at least talk about the lead up, can't I?" I asked Macy sarcastically.

"As long as it doesn't entail the two of you doing the nasty."

"How have we maintained such a close friendship if I can't talk about your brother?"

"We have boundaries, and sex between you and my brother is out of bounds, but I'm cutting you some slack tonight. Just let me get booze first so I can forget this conversation ever took place."

"I have to agree with her, Candy, I wouldn't want to talk to Johnna about Andy," Meri commented, and Macy slapped the table and nodded like *see I'm not crazy.*

"Jason has been sleeping in the guest room and we've been dating. Well, we've only had one real date, but we've had lunch and we talk a lot. I've avoided reading my diary, except, for the entries about how the two of us reconnected after high school. It's been great." I paused as the waitress came to deliver Macy's order. Macy swallowed the two shots back to back and then downed one of the vodka tonics without setting the glass down.

"Your liver is going to hate you," Tonya told Macy.

"Better than my mind haunting me with images of my brother in nefarious positions that I should never be subjected to," Macy rebutted with a shudder.

"I've stayed away from my diaries because I didn't want to confuse myself even more."

"How would reading your diaries confuse you?" Bethany asked.

"'Cause the more I hear about things that happened, the more real they become. Like there are some events that I've developed memories of just from being told about them."

"How do you know they aren't memories you're recovering from before?" This question came from Meri.

"They feel different than the things I know I remember. And they all come from things I've seen pictures of or been told about." I took a drink of my tea. "It's hard to explain, but I know the difference. But back on topic; I avoided Jason at first, but we had a few instances where things went a little further than I was comfortable with. From the time I woke up, I've known I was attracted to him, but I had more to consider than Jason and me. I focused on the kids and getting to know them and trying to figure out how to be their mother.

"Being around him made feelings come to life. I had a hard time admitting it to myself for a while, but I'm falling in love with him all over again." My announcement met a few squeals. "I realized it for certain last night when we were taking care of Dawson."

"So what's your problem then?" Tonya asked.

Voicing my intentions was more difficult than I thought it would be, so I went for diversion. "Am I a control freak?"

"Does a bear shit in the woods?" Macy said.

"Is the Pope Catholic?" Tonya asked.

"Cough—underfuckingstatement—cough," Meri coughed out.

"I'll take that as a yes." I frowned at their affirmative answers.

"You aren't so much of a control freak as much as you like a plan. You need a plan, and once you have a plan, you're okay," Meri explained more about my personality.

"You're attracted to and falling in love with the man you've been married to for fifteen years. What's the problem? I don't get it," Tonya pointed out.

264

"I don't know how to let him know I'm ready to move to the next step."

"Get naked, climb in his bed, and the rest will take care of itself. This isn't rocket science," Macy proclaimed as if Jason and me ending up in bed together was a done deal.

"Macy, you know your brother, he isn't going to make a move unless I blatantly say this is what I want."

"You're giving him too much credit. He's not a fucking saint; he's a dude who hasn't gotten laid in months. Has he pushed you away any of the times y'all have been together?" Macy pointblank asked.

"Well, no, but he did walk away."

"When did that happen?"

I gave them the details of our interactions during and after my date with Dawson.

"You're a moron," Meri stated, shaking her head. "What happened to your mojo? Did you learn nothing from me?"

"I dated three guys in college. I was never the one going out every night. And what the hell are you talking about learning from you? You married a guy you've known since the cradle."

"Well, I've kept him for three decades, haven't I?" Meri argued her point.

"Oh dear Lord, here's what you need to do; take your ass home, open a bottle of wine, invite him out to that hot tub of y'all's, and put the wham, bam, thank you ma'am, and be done with it." Macy's suggestion lacked subtlety, but it just might work.

"Yes, let's take advice from the woman who married her fuck buddy," Tonya drawled. Her words dripping in sarcasm.

Macy threw a hand up at Tonya. "I can't help he liked it enough to stick around."

Bethany interrupted the brewing argument, "As unsophisticated as the plan may be, she's on to something. If you don't think Jason will take a hint, just put it out there. It's not like he's going to turn you down."

They began throwing out different ways to seduce my husband. The later it got, the raunchier the suggestions became. Some were funny, but none of them felt right. In the end, I went home without a surefire option on how to take my relationship to the next level.

Out in the parking lot, Meri had stopped me and handed me a notebook of love stories she had gathered for me. She thought it would help me rediscover my own love.

chapter
twenty-eight

*S*imply because it wasn't a surefire plan didn't discourage me from implementing operation get naked in the hot tub.

Arriving home to a quiet house, I went straight to the wine fridge, pulled out a bottle, and set about finding the ice bucket and frozen mugs, since glass around a pool or hot tub is a no-no. Once that task was completed, I carried the tray bearing the chilling wine, mugs, and a small platter of fruit out to the deck surrounding the hot tub.

The lights in the pool were on, but the rest had been left off. Romantic ambience had been achieved. Or so I hoped.

In fear of rousing the natives, music had been left turned off.

Standing in my closet, dressed in a bikini and cover up, I psyched myself up for my pending attempt at seduction. "You can do this. It's not like he hasn't made it known he's attracted to you. That kiss the other night was more than enough foreplay to set the mood for weeks, or even fucking months, to come." With a nod of my head, I left the closet and made my way to the guest room door.

I'd hoped when I came home he'd have taken the hint to move back into our room. But I was going to have to be blatant.

Knocking on the guest room door, I continued my mental pep talk. I didn't have long before, "Come in," sounded through the door.

I pushed the door open and hovered in the doorway. Jason laid the book he'd been reading down on his lap. He stuck to traditional hardcovers and paperbacks.

"How was dinner with the girls? You're soberer than usual after one of these events. I half expected a call to come pick you up," he claimed with a laugh.

"Oh, well, I only had one drink. Macy had enough for all of us."

Gathering my courage to invite him to join me, I waited too long. "What's up, babe?" he inquired. "Going for a dip?"

"Um yeah," I swallowed, mustering my courage. "Would you like to join me?" Then clarified, "I'm going to relax in the hot tub—not swim in the pool."

He smiled and nodded his head. "Sounds great." He sat there without moving for a second as I waited. "Uhh, I don't wear anything in bed—"

"Oh, right," I sputtered and scrambled out the door, closing it behind me.

It wasn't until I was halfway down the hall that I mentally kicked myself in the ass. *You idiot, you had him naked in bed. Half the job was already done and you ran out of the room like a nincompoop.* No use beating myself up; it wasn't like I could turn around and go back in there, so I continued to the hot tub.

I'd settled in when Jason stepped through the patio doors. It was a good thing I was sitting down because I would have fallen on my ass. He was shirtless and his board shorts sat just low enough to show a hint of the V where his lower abdominal muscles met his hip flexors.

What is it about those lines that turns my brain to mush? Without a doubt, my mouth was hanging open and I was drooling. Reminding myself to play it cool, I snapped my mouth shut and busied myself pouring the wine.

"Would you like some wine?" I offered.

"Sure," he said as he slipped into the bubbling water and made his way to sit beside me.

"I brought some fruit out, as well."

"Good, I'm starving." He gave me a pointed look while reaching for a cluster of grapes.

My eyes followed a grape as it dropped from his fingers into his waiting mouth. I stared as he chewed, wishing it was my body feeling the caress of his tongue.

Nervousness rolled through my belly. Drinking a big gulp of chilled wine, I hoped it would quell the butterflies taking flight in my stomach once again. Maybe drunken butterflies wouldn't cause such a disturbance...

"How was your evening with the kids?" I asked, hoping he didn't notice the quivering of my voice, or maybe hoping he did and would recognize it for the invitation it was.

He popped another few grapes in his mouth and chewed before answering. "Not too bad. The five of us had a Wii bowling tournament."

"That sounds fun. Who won?"

"Dawson. His flamboyant style carries over into bowling. Amazingly," Jason said as he chuckled, "he got more strikes than all of us combined." My laugh joined his, mingling in the night air.

Then we were silent. He just kept chewing those damn grapes. And I just kept watching those damn grapes disappearing between his lips like it was the best show in town.

Boy oh boy were his lips something to watch.

I licked my lips in anticipation, tasting the slight hint of sweet wine.

Not giving myself time to think about what I was doing, I launched myself at him, crashing into him as my mouth somehow managed to collide with his. My hands rested on his muscular shoulders as I drank in the sweet taste of the grapes he just consumed. Grapes mixed with the flavor of Jason was delicious.

Pressing my chest against his, I kneeled with legs straddling his lap. One of his strong hands slid up between my shoulder blades while the other landed on my ass, rhythmically thrusting me against him. The ridge of his erection rubbed over my center, spawning a wondrous sensation. As the hand between my shoulder blades moved down and around my side to tease the side of my breast, I orgasmed and jerked my mouth from his and buried my mouth firmly against the juncture of Jason's shoulder and neck.

There was definitely a mark where my mouth had rested when I raised my head.

"So—umm—yeah—uh—thanks," I began to babble when I recovered somewhat from my high.

He leaned forward, capturing my lips in a gentle kiss, effectively cutting off my rambling words. "You're welcome. It was my pleasure," he said in a husky voice full of unfulfilled need.

As I returned to my senses, I zeroed in on the hard rod of his arousal lodged between us. Marshaling all of my gumption, I instigated the next round, hoping to propel our relationship forward.

My hand trailed down the contours of his chest to the ridges of his abdomen. When I reached the waistband of his board shorts, Jason grabbed my hand, stopping its progress. Denied my goal, I looked at him questioningly.

Jason shook his head, as if to clear his thoughts, swallowed and said, "Let's not go there."

"Why not?" He was aroused. I wasn't mistaking that, so why would he stop me?

It took a few moments for him to answer me. He looked me in the eye and answered my question. "Candy, I want you…badly…but we've never had just sex. We may have fucked each other seven ways to Sunday, but we've never done it without being in love with each other, and I don't want to start now." He looked me in the eye and said, "I love you and I have faith that one day—hopefully one day soon—you'll love me back. And when that happens, we'll use all the locks we put on all of the doors." He sighed. "But until then, I'd like to have you back in my arms when I sleep. That is, if you want to be there."

My first instinct was to blurt out that I loved him, but something in me told me this wasn't the time for that confession. Jason seemed to be more of the 'chick' in our relationship when it came to talking about feelings. I didn't think he would take my declaration of love on the tail end of trying to get him in bed as my true feelings.

"Okay," I replied instead of revealing my newfound feelings.

He blew out a huge breath. "All right."

We sat there less than a minute. My nerves flaring back to life. "I guess no time like the present. Let's get some sleep. Goodness knows the kids will be up bright and early."

For the first time in months, the two of us went to sleep in the same bed without a child sleeping between us.

chapter twenty-nine

"**H**ey, Sleepin' Beauty, wake up," along with warm breath floating across my ear, woke me from a very steamy dream.

"Good morning," I murmured in a sleep raspy voice as I stretched from the best night of sleep I remembered.

"Good mornin'," Jason's deep voice returned my greeting. "Get up and get dressed. We have reservations in two hours, and we need to leave in an hour to make it on time." Then he leaned over to give me a lingering kiss before he stood up and turned to leave the room.

Coming to my senses, I asked, "Where are we going?"

"Sunday Morning Gospel Brunch."

"We're going to church?" Even more puzzled as to why we needed reservations to go to brunch at church.

"Nope, just brunch," he replied as he sauntered out of the bedroom.

We parked in front of a windowless building with a red neon sign with pursed lips around a big straw and the name Lipstick. That was a double entendre if I'd ever seen one, and I knew I was in for something different.

Quirking an eyebrow, I inquired, "Come here often, do we?"

He shook his head and laughingly said, "Not really, but you and the girls come here every so often. You said they have the best cheesecake in town. And, well, you've always enjoyed the show, so I thought why not."

"Okay."

"There's only about ten minutes until the show starts, so we better get inside." Then he seemed to have second thoughts. "Unless you don't want to go."

"Oh, by all means, you went through all this trouble, we should

275

enjoy it." I was curious to see what lay behind the blacked-out windows.

Grinning, he climbed out of the truck and walked around to open my door. We stepped inside the foyer lit with flashing rainbow lights. I had to hand it to Jason, he never faltered.

We were checked in by a 'lady' in a huge church-goin' hat that had to have taken up two zip codes and then escorted to our table.

The emcee was a pregnant nun. When she stepped onto the stage, I knew there wasn't going to be anything politically correct about this experience. "Welcome, all you bitches! Are you prepared for a religious experience?" The crowd hooted and hollered. "I can't hear you, bitches, I said, are you prepared for a religious experience?" The bitches picked up the gauntlet and the place vibrated from all of the stomping, table beating, and yelling. "That's more like it. I'm Sister Merry-Fuck-A-Day-Away, and if you couldn't tell—" She caressed her 'baby bump'. "—I've been a little bit naughty, and I'll be your emcee for this morning's gospel brunch.

"We know a few of y'all are here celebrating your special occasion, and we have something special planned for y'all, so be worried." She looked out over the audience. You could see the shift the moment her eyes landed on Jason. It was like he was wearing a flashing sign in this crowd. "Oh, honey, there you are," she said, pointing at Jason as she rubbed the bump. "I've been searching high and low for you. We need to talk about that night eight months ago."

Jason played along. "I'm sure I wouldn't have forgotten that kind of night, but I've been fixed, so I'm afraid, as Maury would say, 'I am not the father'."

The Sister pshawed. "Sweetie, that don't matter, I got magic. But right now, I gotta get back to the show 'cause I got some fierce ladies waiting to take the stage, but you be sure and wait for me after the show and we'll exchange DNA again."

"I'll be sure to do that," Jason agreed, and she winked at him. I laughed so hard, but I loved that he was secure enough in himself to go along with the gag.

The entertainers were talented. They did so many different takes on gospel music with a little bit of raunchy thrown in.

Sister took the stage again accompanied by two young ladies wearing 'Bride to Be' sashes. "These lovely ladies have decided to give up—I mean, commit—oh what am I sayin'—I mean give up their lives for one cock to have and to hold and all that bull shit. So it's our responsibility to make sure you have the skills to keep that cock happy." The two women tittered with nervous laughter. "Sister Spends–Alota–Time–On–Her–Knees is gonna show y'all how to properly do a blow job. You bitches, get on ya knees."

Each of the women cautiously knelt on the stage. The new sister set a shot glass in front of each of them. One reached for the shot glass. "Oh no, no, no, honey. You never use your hands," Sister Merry chastised her. "If you're doin' it right, all you need is your mouth. Y'all listen to me now. I know what I'm talkin' about. How else do you think I caught that hunk of man meat right there?" She pointed and blew a kiss to Jason, and I wanted to bust out laughing for a different reason. Based on what I'd felt, there was no way she could use just her mouth. But I'd let her keep her fantasy. "Y'all are gonna give your blowjob using just your mouth, and make sure you swallow. Nobody likes a spitter. You bitches ready?" They nodded. "On the count of three—one, two, three, swallow, bitches," Sister Merry yelled, and the ladies followed the sister's instructions as best they could. "Not bad, but y'all need to practice, and you—" she said, pointing to one of the women, "you got a little something on your lip. Don't be wasteful. Waste not, want not, bitches."

The rest of the show was just as hilarious, and the vanilla bean cheesecake lived up to the hype.

That day was the first day in my life that I went on two dates with two different guys. Luckily, both knew about the other. Xavier had chosen to take me to a carnival. You would have never known he'd felt bad the night before. He had our agenda planned out. Evidently, this was not his first trip. I'd even been instructed to pin my change pouch in my pocket.

Xavier gave me a serious look once we were inside the gates. "First, we go to the big rides—"

"You don't want to eat first?" I was shocked that he wasn't thinking about food. This might have been a first.

He rolled his eyes. "Mom, you don't eat *before* you go on the rides or you'll get sick."

"Oh, that makes sense."

Xavier continued, "So, we go to the rides first. Then we go eat, hitting the major stands. After that, we go play games, then it's dessert time." He was already licking his lips at just the thought of what was to come.

I deferred to his expert carnival judgment. "Lead on, oh fearless leader."

With that he was off, dragging me behind him. I was all for it, until we got in line for the first ride. He wasn't taking it easy on me.

"Buddy, I'm not getting on that." I felt bad to be a poor sport on my date with him, but as I cast my eyes upon my worst nightmare—a roller coaster—I knew fear in the worst way.

Disheartened, the little guy's shoulders slumped. "It's all right, Mom. I was just hopin' you might have changed your mind 'bout them." He glanced up at me. "Can I still ride it?"

"Of course." I should've worn a sign that said loser mom.

The wait in line wasn't very long. When we arrived at the front of the line and Xavier held out his arm   to have his wristband scanned, the time was at hand to make a tough choice: I could either step aside and let the next person in line go, or I could suck it up and make my kid smile. Choosing the smile, I stuck my arm out for the attendant to scan my wristband.

Xavier had run ahead to select a car, so he hadn't seen me follow behind him. Once he situated himself in a car, he looked over and spotted me sliding in beside him. His smile was big enough to light the night sky, and there was no doubt that I'd made the right choice.

Trepidation filled my gut, and it didn't get any better once the ride began, and it wouldn't get better over the course of each ride on which we embarked. I hated and loved every minute of it. I can't say how many times my 'twenty-three' years flashed before my eyes, so that wasn't the best, but seeing the look of excitement and pride in Xavier's eyes would have made me want to walk through fire. When we stepped off the last ride, I wanted to kiss the ground.

"Wasn't that awesome, Mom? I can't believe you rode them all! Nobody's gonna believe it," he exclaimed, pride filling his voice.

"I'm so glad you're having a good day," I told him with a genuine smile. My legs felt wobbly as we walked the midway back toward the food pavilions and trailers.

I had no appetite, but Xavier's was in full force. His first stop was for a corn dog and fries, then it was a gyro, and then a Polish sausage with peppers and onions.

Xavier's appetite sated for a short time, we headed to the midway games. These I could do, not well but I could at least make a decent showing. We played toss the rings on the milk bottles, shot water pistols at targets, threw darts at balloons, tossed basketballs, and fished for plastic fish, at which we each ended up 'winning' a betta fish.

Our next stop on the carnival tour was for dessert. There were things I'd never considered, like deep-fried Twinkies, Oreos, and Snickers. They all looked disgusting, but just as with the rides, I joined in the smorgasbord. I felt like Templeton from the Charlotte's Web movie singing "Smorgasbord-Orgasbord-Orgasbord" as my stomach swelled with junk food. I was going to need to be rolled out of the gates.

Laughing, I said to Xavier, "So, are we ready to wrap this up and head home? I think we've eaten everything they have to offer."

Xavier shook his head and replied, "No, there's one last thing we have to do. It's tradition." He started to tug my hand back toward the rides. I must have groaned out loud, because he glanced back and reassured me, "Don't worry, you'll like this one."

"What about our fish?"

"We'll leave them at the gate. Nobody's gonna steal fish."

I trudged along as he tugged on my hands. Dread filled my every step until the familiar calliope of organ music from the carousel began. As I looked up at Xavier, he smiled and said simply, "It's tradition; the carousel is the last ride. No matter what." Seeing him displaying a typical nine-year-old's enthusiasm, when he appeared so quick to grow up, was refreshing.

As we picked out seats on our respective horses, I told Xavier, "This was always the tradition with Kitty and Paw Paw when we went to the fair when I was a kid. Did you know that?"

He nodded his head. "Yeah, you like to tell us about traditions and why they're important."

"They are important. I'm glad I have you and your brother and sisters to remind me of the ones we've created."

He nodded his head, and we continued our ride, listening to the music. This was a great date, scary rides and all.

chapter
thrity

The following couple of weeks were busy; everybody was wrapped up in preparing for the Summer Showcase. Since they both had training during the day, Sybany and Damaris were rehearsing after hours. Xavier kept his talent a secret, he wouldn't even confide in Jason.

Dawson and I were practicing with Charlotte from the dancing studio where we had our date. It was a work in progress. Due to his expectations, we had to work around the frustrations of things changing, but once we had the routine set, practice went smoothly. Getting there was worth the challenge when he knew he had a job well done. With me playing the 'straight' guy in the act, it gave him permission to ham it up.

Jason and I didn't have a lot of time to go on more dates, but he surprised me with a picnic in the park to listen to the symphony. I spent the evening asking Jason random questions to get to know him as Jason, not just as my husband or my children's father.

"Favorite color?"

"Green."

"Favorite food?"

"Lobster. Well, most any seafood."

"Favorite word?"

"Daddy." Awww!

"Favorite sound?"

"My family's laughter." That's when the thought 'Could I love him any more?' crossed my mind. But I got back on track with my questions.

"Favorite place to visit?"

"I don't know if there's one specific place, but probably anywhere that's quiet."

"Favorite book?"

"On the Road by Jack Kerouac."

"What's my favorite book?"

"You have two. To Kill a Mockingbird and Pride and Prejudice. But if I had to choose, I would say To Kill a Mockingbird is your favorite of the two."

"If you could relive one day, which one would you pick?"

"Damn, you aren't going easy on me," he said with a smile. "There are so many, but the day you said you would marry me."

"Why that day?"

"Because you said yes, and our life was together from that moment on, even if you thought my proposal was the worst one ever."

"Why did I say that?"

He looked a bit chagrinned as he answered, "Because, technically, I asked you offhandedly over the phone. Then I kinda sorta just said something like 'I got your ring' when I came to visit."

"Yeah, that's pretty unromantic," I agreed with a laugh.

"Well, I've been doin' my best to make it up to you. It was a lesson learned."

To lighten the mood, I asked a less serious question. "Favorite movie?"

"Full Metal Jacket."

"I should've known," I said with a roll of my eyes. "Favorite football team?"

"Forty-niners."

"Ice cream?"

"Cookies 'n Cream."

"Cake?"

"Oh that reminds me," he said as he turned to the picnic basket, pulling out a grease stained white bag.

I immediately knew what the bag contained. "You brought Pollman's brownies!" Grabbing for the bag, he pulled it back and quirked his eyebrow at me expectantly. In response to the silent challenge, I scooted across the blanket on my knees, leaned in, and gave him a kiss, which quickly became heated until a cough sounded from behind us. I drew away from Jason with my face flaming red.

He grinned and said, "I'd say that was worth the trip for the brownies."

I was mortified to get called out by a stranger for getting hot and heavy in public, so I became quiet the rest of the evening.

Since our days were so busy, our times to get away were slim, but we slept in the same bed and had great talks to end our busy days. We were all going in different directions, but we made a point to come together as a family. Even with all the stress, it was a great time.

When my cellphone rang during our rehearsal on Tuesday of the third and final week leading up to the showcase, I ignored it. The phone continued to ring with Macy's ringtone. On the third cycle of her ringtone, I broke away to answer it.

"Hello," I answered the phone.

"Candy," Macy's panic-ridden voice came across the line.

My heart began to race because I knew this wasn't good news. "What's wrong? What's happened?"

"Jason fell in the garage. He tripped over a bucket somebody left out 'cause the dumbass was looking at schematics instead of where he was going—"

"Macy!" I shouted to get her back on topic. "Is he okay?"

"He's on his way to the hospital. We aren't sure what all he hurt—"

I was already gathering up my stuff and waving Dawson over. The look on his face told me I needed to take my reaction down a few notches. Making a concerted effort to keep my voice calmer, I asked, "What hospital is he going to?"

"All Saints. They just pulled out of the parking lot. Mom's with him, and Dad and I are following behind."

"I need you to call my mom and dad for me and have them meet me there. Dawson's with me, and I don't want to alarm him. Okay?" I spoke softly.

"Okay."

"We'll work everything else out when I get there."

"All right. I'll call them right now."

"Thanks, Macy. I'm on my way." I disconnected the call and turned to Dawson. "Sorry, buddy, we have to call practice short for today."

"Why, we hab more practice?" he asked. He was perturbed by the interruption to his schedule. I knew I needed to put this delicately.

"Daddy had a little fall, and he has to see the doctor." I gave it the safest spin without lying.

His eyes got wide, and he asked "Is he gonna be okay?"

I gave him a reassuring smile and nodded. "Yeah, he's just got some boo-boos."

We made our way out to the SUV. He looked at me very seriously and said, "I hope dey hab da good BandAids."

"The good BandAids?"

Dawson nodded his head. "Yeah, the ones with Mickey Mouse."

"If they don't, we'll make sure we get some." I had no doubt what the first question out of his mouth was going to be when he saw a nurse or a doctor.

We walked into the waiting room, and Dawson took off at a run when caught sight of his grandma and grandpa. "Did Daddy get his BandAids yet?"

Jason's mom answered him. "I think they're taking a look at him

286

right now." Then she put excitement in her voice. "How about we go get some ice cream in the cafeteria? I heard they even have sprinkles."

"Sprinkles?" he repeated in awe.

"Mmhmm," she replied, and he looked over at me.

I smiled, and that was all the encouragement he needed. When they were out of hearing distance, J.W. filled me in on Jason's condition.

"They took him up to get X-rays and a CT scan. Pretty sure he broke his arm, and he's got a nasty cut on his head. Macy went to the restroom. She'll be back in a minute. You want me to wait here with you, or would it be better for me to go with Dawson?"

"I'd say it would be better for you to be with Dawson," then I added, "but thanks for asking."

"Any time, kid," he assured me and gave me a hug before following behind his wife and grandson.

I walked up to the desk to let them know I was there. The lady told me they would call me as soon as Jason was back from Radiology.

With nothing else to do, I called Bev to arrange for the girls to be picked up and to make sure Xavier had someone with him. I told her I would call her as soon as I knew something.

Macy sat down next to me. "Where'd my parents go?"

"They took Dawson for ice cream." She nodded. "I figured it would be better to keep him occupied and not sitting here focusing on his dad being hurt."

"Very true."

"What happened?" I asked, even though she'd already given me the basics.

"He'd gone into the garage to check on how the work on an engine compared with the plans. One of the new apprentices had set a bucket of old bolts and washers down while one of the mechanics showed him something he was working on. Jason was walking and looking over the paperwork, not paying attention to where he was walking. He tripped over the bucket and hit his head on the corner of a big tool chest. His head was bleeding, and we're pretty sure he broke his arm," she gave

287

me the details of his accident.

"But he was conscious, right?" I needed that confirmation.

"Yeah. Mom said he was bitching the whole way here because we called an ambulance instead of driving him here. Like I was going to let him bleed like a stuck pig all over my car." That last bit sounded like Macy. Sarcasm was a way for her to cover up her concern.

"Glad to know your priorities are in order." I nudged her shoulder with mine.

"Hey, I'm already sending him the bill for my blouse and shoes—"

"Oh Lord, do I even want to know which ones?" She was wearing flip-flops now.

"My purple, suede Louboutins," she said dramatically.

"Who in the hell wears seven hundred dollar shoes to work in a car garage?" I asked her incredulously.

She huffed and retorted, "I don't work in the garage, and just because I work in a masculine environment, doesn't mean I can't dress like a woman. And trust me, those shoes have snagged more than one client," she added as an afterthought.

I didn't have much room to talk in the shoe department, but it felt nice to joke around with her. It helped cover up my worry about Jason.

"Woodruff family," a lady in scrubs called out in the waiting room.

"That's us," I said, rising from my chair to walk over to her. Macy followed behind me.

"He's back from radiology. Y'all can come back and sit with him. Just follow me."

We followed her to room number eight. "They gave him something for pain, so he may be a little sleepy," she informed us.

Stepping into the room, I swallowed deeply. His right arm was splinted and resting on his chest, and he had a row of five staples lacing his scalp.

I walked over to the left side of the bed. Reaching down, I grasped his left hand. "Hey, babe, are you asleep?" I whispered.

His blue eyes fluttered a couple of times before they opened and focused on me. Confusion clouded his vision, and his brows knitted together. "Who are you?"

The floor fell out from under me. My eyes shot to Macy. This couldn't happen to us again.

chapter thrity-one

*T*hen he started to laugh, but it was short lived. "Damn that hurts," he said, grabbing his right arm with his left hand. "How can laughing hurt a broken arm?"

That's when I realized he'd been kidding, and I hauled off and slugged him in the left shoulder. "You ass! That wasn't funny!"

"OW! Damn, babe, take it easy. I'm injured," he cried while still choking back laughter. "Come on, it was a little funny." He clasped my hand, raising it to his mouth to kiss my knuckles. "Even Macy laughed," he pointed out.

"At least she has the grace to look sorry for laughing at my expense."

He kissed my hand again. "Ahh, babe, you looked so worried, like you were walking into a funeral parlor: I couldn't help myself."

Macy spoke up, "Dude, you're gonna be sucking up for that one for years to come. So what's wrong with your clumsy-not-watching-where-he's-walking ass?" Leave it to Macy to speak so eloquently.

Jason sobered up to answer her question. "Broke the radius. They said it looks like a clean break. I'll have to wear the splint for a few days before they can cast it. That gives the swelling some time to go down. And a gash on the head from catching the corner of an open drawer on the tool chest. No concussion. I'm just waiting for the doctor to sign off on everything, then I can get out of here."

I breathed another sigh of relief and said a prayer of thanks. Accidents happen, but given what happened with me, I couldn't help worrying something worse could happen.

"Oh, I need to see about getting you a Band-Aid," I said, remembering my conversation with Dawson from earlier, desperate to distract myself from my pessimistic thoughts.

"Why do I need a Band-Aid?"

"Dawson was concerned you wouldn't get a good Band-Aid. I told him we would see to it that you did."

"What makes a good Band-Aid?" he asked. "Or do I want to

know?" He laughed.

"Mickey Mouse or the like," I explained Dawson's rationale.

"I got some Scooby Doo," Macy offered, digging through a purse the size of a small suitcase. Finding what she was searching for, she looked up at us. "What? I have a kid, too, ya know." Our lack of faith in her annoyed her.

"I'm not surprised you have BandAids," Jason replied. "I'm just surprised you went with something as mundane as Scooby Doo."

Macy scoffed at her brother. "I'm not paying that much for something to be bled all over. Which, by the way, you owe me for a shirt and shoes. I expect an upgrade for my pain and suffering."

"What pain and suffering did you go through," Jason had the audacity to ask his sister, who might punch him in his broken arm if he kept it up.

With all her flare for drama, she replied, "You have no idea what I suffered while I watched you as you bled all over my *favorite* purple shoes."

"Blood's red, it'll work with purple. Just get one of those bingo things and put red dots all over them and you'll be a trend-setter."

I cringed at his suggestion. He had to know that would go over like a lead balloon in a hurricane.

"The day I take fashion advice from you, dear brother, is the day I hand in my ovaries and start wearing flannel and Doc Martens."

Thankfully, the doctor came in the room to interrupt the sibling argument. "Here." Macy handed me the Scooby Doo Band-Aid. "Make sure it gets the proper placement—preferably over his big mouth. I'm going to go get Mom and Dad." She left the room with a flourish at that pronouncement.

The doctor repeated what Jason had already told me. He gave Jason a prescription for a pain medication and a follow-up appointment with an orthopedic doctor on Friday to have the splint replaced with a cast.

Jason was in a quite a bit of discomfort that evening. Anxiety over Jason's injuries had Dawson's anxiety on the tipping point. Jason put in extra effort to show him that he was okay and that everybody gets boo-boos sometimes. He went so far as to download books and a couple of episodes of cartoons, which dealt with injuries. These re-enforcers went a long way in helping Dawson process the events. All Xavier cared about was when the cast was being put on so he could sign it.

Damaris and Sybany were mad at each other over some tiff that happened during rehearsals. Every perceived slight caused an argument. Things boiled over as they were getting ready for bed.

Yelling could be heard across the house in the kitchen, where I was cleaning up after dinner. Setting the plate I'd been washing back in the sink, I followed the noise and found the two of them in their shared bathroom.

They were facing each other like two fighters standing off before a cage match. All that was missing was the emcee guy to say, 'Let's get ready to RUUUUMMMMBLE!' to set the fist in motion.

"YOU DON'T HAVE TO BE SUCH A DRAMA QUEEN!" Rissa yelled.

"I WOULDN'T BE IF YOU WEREN'T SUCH A LAZY SLOB!" Sybany screamed back.

Approaching them, I asked, "What is going on with you two? I could hear the two of you all the way in the kitchen." They both began telling their sides of the story. "One at a time—calmly. Sybany, what's your issue?"

"Damaris—" Oh, she pulled out the real name. She was really mad. "—left a mess—"

"It was hardly a mess," Damaris interrupted her sister's version of events.

Sybany shot back, "It's my turn. Mom said I could go first. You'll get your turn." Rissa crossed her arms and huffed. "Anywaaay," Sybany continued, "this is my week to clean the bathroom. Damaris is always leaving toothpaste splatters on the sink. She doesn't put her stuff away."

"Damaris, what's your side of all of this?" I knew there was more to this story.

"I didn't leave a mess. I left a spot of toothpaste because she was standing behind me, tapping her foot and huffing, so I hurried up and got out of the bathroom. That's when she started yelling about me leaving stuff all over the sink," she finished her side of the story.

"Sybany, were you standing behind your sister, rushing her to finish?"

I saw the hesitancy in her demeanor. "I wasn't *rushing* her. I just wanted her to get finished, so I could clean up, but *she* was taking her time just to annoy me."

No doubt there was truth in both sides, but the culprit already knew what I was about to tell them. "Rissa, you should have asked your sister to wait. Sybany, you need to be more patient—"

"If patience is a virtue and ignorance is bliss, if you're stupid and don't mind standing in line, you should be pretty happy," Sybany recited, and my thought was, *Oh, she's my child all right.*

"Sybany, don't talk back." Oh, and now my mother is coming out of my mouth. This was going to require an even stiffer drink than I'd originally thought.

Taking a mental deep breath, I said, "Why are you really upset with your sister?" I hit pay dirt.

"She thinks just because she's in a ballet company that she knows everything about performing and gets to make all of the decisions and boss me around. She's always 'do this, do that, that's not right, you need to do it this way, blah, blah, blah' 'cause she's a know-it-all." While she'd been talking, her arms had been waving, accentuating her points.

If Xavier was Jason's mini-me, Sybany was my payback for everything I'd ever put my parents through as a kid. And she wasn't even a teenager yet.

"Damaris, is that true?"

"I wasn't bossing her around. I just wanted to help her do the moves better—"

"But you know your sister doesn't have the dance experience

you do. This was supposed to be something fun for the two of you. You're not performing on the stage in St. Petersburg. You need to relax and have fun and understand Sybany brings different talents than you do, and as the more experienced dance performer, you should foster her strengths, not just point out weaknesses. If you want respect, you have to give respect, and that goes for you too, young lady. Besides that, you know you wouldn't get in trouble for a spot of toothpaste," I ended by addressing Sybany, whom I knew was just as culpable.

"Now, you can either apologize, go to bed, get some rest, and start tomorrow fresh, or the two of you can go out in the yard and start pulling weeds. Which do you choose?" My head turned back and forth between the two of them. Damaris was on-board with the apology, but Sybany appeared to have an internal debate before settling on the apology.

My honeymoon period as a mother was officially over.

Returning them to their respective corners, I left to put Dawson to bed and check on Xavier.

"Everything okay?" Jason asked as I came back into the family room.

Collapsing on a chair, I whined, "I need a drink." He started to get up off the couch, grimacing as he moved. "Need some help?" I asked him.

"Sure. Would you mind helping me get ready for bed? I mean, I can't get my shirt off by myself, and I need help wrapping my arm so I can get a shower."

"Yeah," I said, rising to my feet. "Would you rather have a bath to soak?"

He shook his head, declining the offer. "I'll just take a quick shower. I'm beat, and my arm hurts like a bitch. It'll be better tomorrow."

"Okay, just let me get a trash bag and duct tape to cover your arm."

He waved that off with his good arm as he continued toward our bedroom. "I had Xavier get the stuff and put it in the bathroom already."

With nothing else to do, I trailed after him into our bathroom.

Jason sat on the bench and exhaled a deep breath. "Have you taken your pain pill?"

"No, I'll take it when I'm done getting a shower."

He wore a polo and a plain undershirt underneath. I contemplated whether to take them both off at once or one at the time. I decided on both. That way I only needed to manipulate his arm once.

The process was slow, but I managed to get his shirts off and his arm wrapped. When I picked up the scissors to cut the tape, I mentally kicked myself for not thinking to just cut the damn shirts off.

"Hold on a sec. I need to get the Vaseline," I told Jason.

"What do you need Vaseline for?" he asked, scrunching his face.

"To keep the duct tape from pulling off skin," I explained, not thinking anything of it until I looked back at him. "When you're friends with a drag queen and poor college chicks, you learn a few shortcuts."

It didn't take much longer to get him ready to shower. I turned on the water in the shower to get it warm. "I'll leave the door open in case you need me. Just yell, okay?" Not sure why I was allowing him such modesty. He'd certainly seen me at my worst.

He stood up and walked over to the shower. I turned to walk out of the bathroom. The swish of his pants falling to the floor caused me to glance over my shoulder, and I got an eye-full of Jason. The posterior view of his body was mouthwatering. I was so distracted, I hadn't paid attention to where I was walking until I walked into the doorjamb with a thud and a grunt.

Thankfully, Jason didn't hear me. I hurried into his closet and retrieved a pair of boxers and shorts. He slept naked but kept clothes close by. I dropped them on the bench and hightailed it out of the bathroom.

Keeping myself busy, I puttered around the room. The purse I'd carried to girls' night still rested against the chaise, the notebook of love stories from my sister sticking up over the edge. Needing distraction, I sat on the chaise and pulled it out.

I'd just read 'Love comes in many forms' when Jason strode into the room. I stood up and asked him if he was ready to go to bed.

"Yeah, I'm beat." He sighed. Gingerly he scooted into bed and lay down.

Standing at the end of the bed, I asked, "Can I get you anything?" I felt helpless to ease his pain.

His eyes were closed, and he cradled his arm, which was still wrapped in the trash bag. "Yeah. Can you cut this off and help me get the pillows right so I can rest my arm?"

Duh, Candice! "Oh, damn, I'm sorry. Let me grab the scissors." I ran into the bathroom to retrieve them from the counter and quickly made my way back to Jason to cut the bag and tape.

As I carefully placed his splinted arm on the stack of pillows, he began to softly snore. I studied his face. This was the man I'd fallen in love with not once but twice. We'd created a family I could have never imagined. He'd been my rock. I couldn't imagine what my life would be without him. Sighing, I got off the bed and returned to the chaise, seeking a way to distract my mind.

I couldn't tell him I love him now. He'd probably think I was doing it because he was hurt. Why hadn't I found the courage to tell him at some point over the past two weeks? Ugh, I'm officially a dumbass.

chapter
thrity-two

$\mathcal{I}$ flipped to the first page of the notebook and began reading.

Love comes in many forms. If you're lucky to have one version, you should consider yourself fortunate.

Candice,

I know you're struggling with all that has happened. I can't begin to know everything you're going through, but I do know that Jason and your children are your greatest joy. You're at your happiest when you're with them. I watched you grow from a young girl with her first crush into a mature woman falling in love with a real man instead of a fantasy. When you told me you'd reconnected with Jason all those years ago, I had my doubts and discouraged you from pursuing a relationship with him. I've never been happier that you ignored my sisterly advice and followed your heart. You found the one in six billion. Don't let him slip away because you're afraid. Love is always a risk, but anything worth having is worth working for.

I love you,

Meri

Turning to the next page, I recognized Pappy's handwriting.

At the age of seventeen, I convinced my mother and father to allow me to enlist. Our country was at war, and I felt it was my duty to do my part. After years of war, the ideals of my young mind had been replaced by horrors that haunt my dreams until this day. When I'd made it home to my parents' dairy farm, I couldn't find my place. I didn't belong there any longer. So I set out in search of peace. To do this, I thought I should give back to the world.

Just over two years later, I'd done some good, but not nearly enough. There were even some nights I managed to have a good dream. I didn't stay in one place too long, always chasing the elusive. I followed where the projects lead. Normally, I accompanied missionaries to wherever they were going.

I can't remember what village I was in, and it doesn't matter for the purposes of this story. The village was to the west of the closest town. I'd spent the night in town with one of the missionaries to get supplies. We intended to get an early morning start, so I was up before the sun rose, securing the last of our supplies. Even for the early morning, it was hot.

I may have forgotten the name of the village, but I remember everything that happened next with the clarity of a man being delivered from his personal hell.

As I'd rounded the corner of the town supply store, I removed my hat to wipe the sweat gathering on my forehead. I can remember every detail of that moment, but it's hard to put into words· My foot hit the boards of the porch, and I looked up into the early morning sun· As my vision began to clear, I saw a woman· She was a tiny thing dressed in a loose, man's work shirt and trousers, boots, and the biggest floppy hat· I had no idea what she looked like, I'd never heard her voice, never had a single conversation with her, hadn't even exchanged a hello, but I knew she was what I'd been searching for·

I stepped over to her, and she turned toward me· I said, "New around these parts?"

"No, actually, just returning· But you must be, or not very observant," she replied·

"If I'd observed you, I would have remembered·"

"As would I·"

I skimmed ahead to the last paragraph.

I'd found salvation in the rising the sun· From the time I spotted an unknown woman on the porch of the general store, she's never left my side· She's not only born our children, but my hope, my dreams, and my love with an innate grace and steadiness· Quite simply, she is my heart, she is my soul·

The next entry:

I came of age in the time of free love—

Oh dear Lord, the last thing I wanted to do was read about my relatives' sexual exploits.

It was a time when war wasn't popular. To take pride in serving in the military was frowned, and sometimes even spit, upon. My junior year of college, I had class with a young man enrolled in the R.O.T.C. Every week, he wore his uniform with pride. The derision he faced from our high-minded classmates became maddening. One day, I finally asked him why he didn't say something back to the assholes.

"I'm preparing for marriage," he responded.

"No, really, why don't you fight back?"

"Just because I'm proud to serve in the military, doesn't mean I'm seeking someone to fight. The pen is mightier than the sword."

We talked, debated, and argued and on occasion, fought like cats and dogs.

Yeah, that was definitely my parents.

Over the course of those weeks and months of debates, we discovered each other. Respect and friendship grew into love. It wasn't what I'd expected to find in college. I'd come to college prepared to learn the skills to fight for the causes of those unable to fight for themselves. Who knew I'd end up meeting a guy I'd have to fight with to get him to love me.

As I would come to find out, Carl and his close friends, who were all preparing to enter the military, had made a pact not to get into relationships. They didn't feel it was fair to impose their choices on someone else. There were to be no wives and absolutely no children.

To overrule his objections, I needed to use something more than logic; I used emotional blackmail. I simply explained to him that he'd made a bigger promise to me when he made me fall in love with him. It was the first time either of us had mentioned love to each other. Perhaps not the best way I could confess my feelings for him, but I wasn't about to let life pass me by while I did nothing to seize it.

He made a promise to me. It was the simplest, yet hardest, promise anyone could make. He promised to love me. He's loved when we were worlds apart and side by side. Keeping impossible promises is what separates the one you keep from the ones you throw back.

I, for one, was glad she hadn't thrown him back.

The following entry was from my Aunt Connie, or Sister Mark-Paul as she was now known.

My parents were poor, illiterate migrant workers. They followed the crops until one day they went to work for an elderly farmer and his wife. Mr. and Mrs. Clayton weren't wealthy by far, but they were fair and kind. Mamá and Papá stopped moving with the crops and stayed on with the Claytons.

When they learned my parents and their six children were living in the type of place that wasn't safe for young children, they offered us a place to live. It wasn't much, just an old two-bedroom trailer, but it was clean, dry, and safe.

We attended school regularly and helped around the farm when we could. We relaxed and began to imagine that we too could have the American dream. Summer passed and the autumn came, bringing the harvest.

The start of winter wasn't too bad, but the deeper we got into the season, the more we felt the drafts in the old trailer. We used kerosene heaters to warm the place. The Claytons couldn't afford to replace the windows, so we put Visqueen over the windows and filled in the gaps with caulk.

It also happened to be a very rainy winter. One rainy, winter day, four of my siblings and I left to attend school. Our youngest sibling, who was only three, stayed home with our parents. They weren't going to be working because of the weather.

Arriving home that afternoon, I sensed something was wrong when I opened the trailer door. It was too still and silent. I told my brothers and sister to wait outside. Calling out to my parents, I knocked on the closed bedroom door. When they didn't answer, I pushed open the door. Mamá and Papá lay on their bed. Neither moved as I approached. Panic filled me, and I ran from the room, yelling for someone to get the Claytons. Juan took off toward the main house. I screamed my youngest sister's name.

Bursting through the door to the bedroom I shared with my siblings at the opposite end of the trailer, I spotted Maria curled up on one of the beds. Her face wedged between the bed and a pillow. I stumbled my way to her. I don't know why, but I snatched her up and ran from the trailer. She was so cold.

As I ran out the door, Mr. Clayton ran up to us, asking what was wrong. I told him as best I could through my tears that my parents wouldn't wake up.

My Mamá and Papá had died from carbon monoxide poisoning. By covering the windows and sealing the cracks, we'd trapped the poisonous gas inside. Maria survived by the grace of God. When she went to sleep in our room, she'd found the safest place in the trailer because the heater in that room was shut off and a rolled-up blanket had been put in front of the door to keep the heat in the main room. Then she'd buried her face under the pillow, which helped act as a filter.

We became six orphans. The least likely to be

adopted, especially all together. The Claytons were in their eighties, but they didn't abandon us. There was a family that attended their church. Mr. and Mrs. Clayton asked them to foster us, and the couple agreed. Carl and Ellen Rogers had grown children, but they opened their doors and arms.

Being angry didn't make me easy to deal with. I rebelled and did everything I could to alienate Carl and Ellen. It made me mad to see my brothers and sisters clinging to them as parental figures. I was determined that they would never take the place of my Mamá and Papá.

Things boiled over one night with Carl and me shouting at each other. It took a turn when I yelled something like, "I bet if my name was Constance instead of Consuela, you'd like me better. Just like you're trying to make them," meaning my siblings, "like you."

Carl looked dumbfounded and yelled back, "I don't give a shit if your name is Constance or Consuela or Rosita Juanita Chiquita Banana."

Ellen slapped Carl in the arm. "Have you lost it? We're trying to convince her that we want her to stay and all you could come up with was the name of Mexican mouse's girlfriend and a fruit?"

Somewhere in that exchange, I began to see them as the genuine people they were. It wasn't always easy, but I came to love them as my parents. They've never wavered in their support. We found the love of adoptive parents and siblings, along with the surrogate grandparents, in the wake of losing our Mamá and Papá.

Mr. and Mrs. Clayton only had one child, who died as a young man. As they got older, they had to move into assisted living. They went into the home run by the Little Sisters of the Poor. Through this experience, I found my calling to return the blessing I had been given as a child by helping do God's work in taking care of the elderly. I wasn't meant for the love of a husband and children, but I've been graced with love too great to measure.

I'd known my youngest aunts and uncles had come into my family unexpectedly, but I'd never known the full story. My heart hurt for them.

The next entry was short.

Candy,

I don't have a lot of wise words about love, but I want to say don't miss your second chance. If I was offered one more day with Rick, even knowing I would go through the pain of losing him again,

I would do so in a heartbeat. None of us are guaranteed anything, so value what you have while you have it. Never miss a moment to tell those you love that you love them.

Devon

Devon's words made me think of the inscription on Rick's headstone: *I'm everywhere and I'm nowhere, but I'm always there.* I needed to be here.

I'm not sure how long I sat there in the quiet, but Jason distracted me from my musings with a groan.

"You need some help, babe?" I asked him.

"Trying to get comfortable. My arm's hurting."

"It's been long enough since your last dose, you can take something else for pain." I went into the bathroom to get his medication and some water. Going to his side of the bed, I handed him the pill and cup of water. "Do you want to try changing positions? You could lie on your side and prop your arm on the pillows."

"That might help a little. Why are you still awake?" he asked.

"Oh I was reading and lost track of time. I'm gonna curl up on the couch after I get you settled."

"Why are you sleeping on the couch? What's wrong with the bed?"

"Nothing's wrong with the bed. I just don't want to bother you."

"I'd rather have you in bed with me, even if my arm hurts." So, once he was in position, I carefully crawled into bed. I needed to be here.

chapter thrity-three

The day of the Summer Showcase finally arrived. I was admittedly nervous. Fortunately, the acts were arranged by age, so Dawson and I performed in the first group.

I was dressed in tails and a top hat. Kitty made a dress for Dawson. He wore a wig and sandals with tiny heels. When did they start making high-heels for little kids? Dawson fidgeted as we waited on the side of the stage for our cue.

Once we were introduced and our act began, it passed by in a blur. I loved watching him perform. This was one area where his need for things to be in a specific order helped him excel. He loved music and dancing, and he basked in the applause from the audience as we assumed our finale position with me down on one knee, arms spread, and him perched on my knee with his arms around my neck and lips pressed to my cheek.

He drew back as the curtain closed. "I wuv jou, Mommy," he proclaimed as he hugged me tightly.

"I love you, too, Dawson," I said for the first time since I'd regained consciousness.

Our time was cut short as the next act needed to come on stage. We ran off to get changed and then join Jason and our extended family to watch the remainder of the show.

The next act from our family was the girls, which was surprising to me. I'd thought Xavier would be next. As Damaris and Sybany began their rendition of The Maestro, I was mesmerized.

The puppet was seated in a chair; arms, legs, and head hanging limp. The maestro entered from upstage and approached the puppet in the chair. The maestro stood behind the chair and raised her arms. The puppet rose. As the act continued, the maestro became frustrated with the puppet's inability to perform the movements correctly. Neither spoke, but the body language spoke volumes.

The first part ended with the maestro giving up and going to sleep. Soon a tinkling sound could be heard and the puppet raised her head. She began gesticulating her frustration. Then she was suddenly free of the 'strings' and flitted across the stage with wonder before assuming her position as the new maestro. This was where my childhood experience in dance came in handy because I knew the movements.

The maestro and puppet *port des bras* together – right arm carries from first, through second, to fifth position, followed by the left arm. Arms in fifth position, the puppet rose slowly *sur les pointes*. The maestro moved downstage right, to the edge of the wing, and beckons to the puppet. The puppet steps gingerly *en pointe*, left, right, left, and then *arabesques* right. The maestro stepped forward and caught the puppet's waist as she *penchés* forward and melted into a plié. The puppet stepped across, *en coupé dessous*, and *bourrées en arrière*. The maestro piques *en arabesque, glissades, grand Jetés* across the front of the stage, and ran to stand behind the chair. She beckoned to the puppet, who *chassès* twice, then *chaînés* toward the chair. She finished the turns standing in first position in front of the chair, *bras bas*. Both *port des bras* through first, to fifth position. The maestro pressed her arms through fifth position down, and the puppet's arms fell limply to her sides as she slumped in the chair. The maestro repeated the *port des bras* while the puppet remained seated, first on the stage right, then on the stage left. The maestro *cambrés* back and opens arms. She *faillis, chaînés en diagonale* downstage and *stepeds* to *pique arabesque* at the edge of the downstage right wing, and then exited.

The very last act of the show was Xavier. He walked out onto the stage with his guitar. He sat on the stool and adjusted the mic.

Clearing his throat, he spoke to the crowd. "This song is for my mom." At the first chords, tears began to form in my eyes as I thought back to our conversation about how he knew we loved each other. By the time he sang the first line to Kenny Chesney's "You Had Me from Hello", tears streamed down my face. It was an all-out ugly cry. Jason wrapped his left arm around me and drew me close to him. He used the fingers of his casted right hand to stroke the arm I used to cling to him. Dawson patted my back and murmured, "Don't cry, Momma." When Xavier played the last chord, he sat the guitar down and walked down the stairs to where we were sitting. I stood and reached for him, hugging him to me.

"I love you, Xavier," I said close to his ear. Then I saw Sybany and Rissa standing about a foot away. Waving them over, I absorbed them into our hug. "And I love you," I declared to Sybany. "And I love you," I repeated to Rissa. "I'm so blessed to be your mother. I don't know how I got so lucky." Then I felt another small set of arms wrap around me from behind. I turned to bring him in front of me. "I love you all."

"I love you more," they said in unison.

The tears pooled again, but I smiled and laughed. "I love you through infinity," I recited the next line in the familiar routine.

"I love you through infinity and beyond," they once again said in unison. Dawson added a wave of his hand to his declaration, which made me laugh.

These words made me feel better than any balm ever could. The 'I love you' routine had been started by my pappy. The first person said, I love you. The second person said, I love you more. Then the first said, I love you through infinity. It stayed that way for decades until the movie "Toy Story" came out. Buzz Lightyear's tagline was, 'To infinity, and beyond!' After seeing the movie, I added 'through infinity and beyond' to it, adapting the line to fit our through infinity I love yous.

None of us wanted to hang out and socialize after the emotional revelation between the children and me. We were all on a high, and laughter filled the rest of our night. When the kids went to bed, the 'I love yous' rang out, giving me the confidence to be honest about all of my feelings.

I didn't care what happened; there was no way I was letting another night pass without telling Jason what I'd been trying to find the right moment to say. I knew, in my heart, that no matter when I told him, it would be the right moment.

Once in our room, I called his name and he turned to look at me. My eyes locked with his, and I said, "I love you." You could've heard a pin drop, so I kept talking. "I mean, I've fallen in love with you."

He slowly crossed the small distance between us. His fingers curled in my shirt on my left side, and his left hand raised to cradle my head, the fingers wove through my hair. "Say it again," he pleaded quietly. His eyes peered into mine.

"I love you, Jason Woodruff."

He swallowed, and his hand shook. "I love you more."

"I love you through infinity," I recited as my voice trembled.

"I love you through infinity and beyond," he said just before his lips crashed into mine.

As had happened previously, my reaction to his touch was instantaneous. When he withdrew, my body followed in search of his out of instinct. My eyes opened and I saw a face full of so many emotions. The one that surprised me was peace. It was as if he could relax and trust that I had returned to him.

"I want to sleep with you in my arms tonight. The rest will come later," he said. "Please, come to bed with me."

I nodded, and he took my hand and walked to my side of the bed. He stood back and allowed me to get in bed and scoot to the center. With his arm in a cast, we didn't have to worry about keeping it propped up. He lay down on his side, facing me. I did the same with my head resting next to his on the same pillow. Raising my hand, I stroked my thumb across his jaw.

"I don't know how to make sense of all of this, but I'm done questioning it. I've made peace with the fact that I may never remember our previous life together. I want to focus on what we can have now and what we can create in the future. I fantasized about a boy with dimples for years, but you aren't what I imagined; you're so much more. I don't know what made me fall in love with you the first time, but I know I love the man you are now. You're my best friend, my partner, and the best father I could have ever hoped to have children with…and even without my lost memory, I feel you know me better than I know myself, and I want to know you that well, too."

"I'm a pretty simple guy. I've just done something good enough to deserve more than one chance with the love of my life. Life with you has blessed me with more than I ever could have dreamed of achieving. As a young man, I wanted to leave a mark on the world. But now, if the only place I leave an impression is in the hearts and minds of my wife and kids, I'll be a contented man. Loving you and you loving me, gave me the best of myself. If we don't make it past tomorrow or we make it forever and a day, you'll always be the love of my life."

I let his words wash over me and thanked God for the man I shared my life with.

chapter thrity-four

$\mathcal{A}$ knock at the door woke me the next morning. Relishing cuddling with my warm pillow, I ignored it and snuggled closer to Jason. The second knock snapped me out of my dream state when the kids dawned on my sleep-addled brain. Sitting up in bed, I called for whoever was at the door to come in and glanced at the clock. Nine thirty-seven shown back at me. I couldn't believe we slept so late or that the kids let us sleep that late.

Jason pushed up in the bed to rest against the headboard. "Can't believe we slept so late," he said in a sleep raspy voice.

"Me either."

The kids entered the room single file. Rissa and Xavier slowly and carefully carried trays across the room.

At the smell of food, my stomach rumbled.

"Good morning, guys. Look at all this," I said as Xavier set my tray over my lap. "Did y'all make all of this?"

"Yes, ma'am," Xavier answered. He was proud of their accomplishment.

"Looks delicious, kids. I'm starving," Jason commented, grinning at the kids. "This is the best way to wake up."

Dawson walked up to Jason's side of the bed. "I brahwd jou da new paper, Daddy."

"It's a *news*paper, Duck," Sybany corrected him.

Dawson cocked his head to the side and squinted at her. "Das what I said, da new paper."

Patting the bed, I said, "Climb up and tell us about your morning." That was all the urging it took to create a dog pile on the bed. "Careful, remember Daddy has a broken arm."

"Sorry, Daddy."

"Whoops, sorry, Dad."

"It's all right, just don't spill my food," Jason joked, earning a

323

laugh.

We chatted with the kids as we ate. There was a ton of food. Fortunately, they had not inherited my lack of kitchen talent. As I sat back against the headboard, I noticed Xavier eyeing the leftovers on my tray. "Oh, I'm stuffed. There's no way I can eat another bite," I said. "I hate for it to all go to waste, though. Ugh." Making eye contact with Xavier, I encouraged him to help himself. "Y'all want any of this?"

Xavier pounced like a lion on its prey. Dawson wasn't far behind, entreating his brother not to hog it all. "Dohn eat all da bacon. I wan' some."

Why I was shocked they were hungry, I wasn't sure. "Didn't y'all eat breakfast?"

"Yeah," Xavier said around a mouth full of biscuit, "but that was like two hours ago."

Rissa offered an explanation, "He eats on the hobbit schedule."

"The hobbit schedule," I inquired for clarity.

"The schedule the hobbits from *The Lord of the Rings* ate on," she clarified.

My head bobbed up and down. "Ah, I read those when I was much older than you. I had a hard enough time reading them."

She shrugged and said, "You don't have to read the books. They made them into movies."

"Yeah, Mom, the movies are really good," Xavier added his two cents. "You should watch them."

"I'll have to do that, but what do y'all want to do today?" Suggestions started flying.

Bowling was the idea we settled on as our activity for the day. Jason's broken arm concerned me, but he assured me it would be fine.

It didn't take me long to realize that as competitive as the kids were, they enjoyed good-natured rivalries. Silliness took precedent over score. The kids did their best to top each other, but Jason scared the shit out of me when he almost busted his ass trying to impress the kids while throwing a bowling ball with his left hand.

I laughingly said to him, "You're gonna break your other arm if you aren't careful."

"Getting sponge baths might be worth the pain." He waggled his eyebrows up and down suggestively.

I licked my lips at the thought. I opened my mouth to tease him right back when, "Momma, i's jour turn," rang out across the bowling alley, even though I was less than ten feet away.

Turning to the kids, I said, "Bud, I'm right here. There's no need to yell."

"But, Momma, I was cawin' jou' name, but jou was ignorin' me," Dawson argued. I felt even more embarrassed, like everyone could read my mind, which had currently taken up residence in the gutter.

"Buddy, I wasn't ignoring you. I was talking to Daddy, and I didn't hear you. You need to be patient and not interrupt."

"But you wasn't talkin'. An' how am I suppowsed ta tell jou I wanna talk ta jou if I don' tell jou?" Dear God, I'd given birth to this generation's version of F. Lee Bailey. "Jou wasn't wookin' at me, so I coudn't waise my hand."

I didn't know whether to be annoyed that a five-year-old had bested me in an argument or proud of his skills of turning the tables on me.

"Buddy, you just walk over and tap someone on the shoulder then wait for them to acknowledge you before you speak."

"Okay." He walked over to me, tapped me, and looked at me expectantly.

It was nearly impossible to smother my laughter, but I managed to and said, "Yes, Dawson?"

"I's your turn," he responded, giving me a pointed look.

"Thank you, buddy." I stood up and took my turn, expertly not hitting a single pin.

"Momma, I don't think we've ever seen somebody have a zero at the end of the game," Sybany observed. Her face scrunched like she didn't actually believe someone could play a game and not hit a single pin.

I made a 'what can I say face' and said, "I'm just good like that."

Rissa put her arm around me. "Don't worry. You can make up for it next game."

"Thanks for the vote of confidence, Rissa." I smiled at her, going back to sit next to Jason, who snickered as I sat down.

"Shut up," I said, kicking his foot. That just made him laugh harder.

Successfully getting his laughter under control, he said, "Good to know some things don't change."

"Yes, it is," I concurred, agreeing with my whole heart.

chapter thrity-five

$\mathcal{W}$e bowled a few more hours then went to dinner. The time was filled with laughter and happiness.

When we pulled up to our house, I noticed my dad's truck out front.

"I didn't know they were dropping by," I said, pursing my lips as I considered why they were here.

"Kitty texted me," Jason said offhandedly, easing my concern.

Dawson chose then to make a contribution to the conversation. "Yeah, Kitty and Paw Paw are gonna spend thwee sweeps wid us," he let the cat out of the bag. Rissa, Sybany, and Xavier started giving Dawson a hard time about spilling the beans.

My head snapped around to Jason. "Are we going somewhere?"

"Surprise," Jason deadpanned.

Dawson began to cry at the realization he told me something he wasn't supposed to tell. "I'm sowwy, Daddy. I forgot. I sowwy, Daddy."

"Dawson—buddy, it's okay." I reached back and rubbed his leg. "Really, it's all right. You didn't hurt anything."

Once we pulled into the garage and the doors opened, it was like a switch had been thrown and he forgot about his slip up as he took off to find his grandparents.

Jason opened my door, and I asked him. "Where are we going?"

"Now that is a surprise," he denied my request for the destination.

"But how will I know what to pack," I argued.

"No need to worry about that. I've got it handled," he brushed off my concern.

"What if you forgot something?"

Jason shook his head and laughed. "We aren't going to the wilds of the frozen tundra or the jungles of Borneo. I'm sure there will be a Wal-Mart or a Target or some sort of store you can pick up whatever you need nearby. Although, you won't be needing much."

HALLEJUAH!!!!! The boy was getting with the program.

"All right," I conceded and let it go. "Lead on."

He stood there disbelieving. "That's it? You aren't going to pump me for details?"

"Nope."

"I guess some things do change."

Thrilled that I'd managed to surprise him, I smiled. "So when do we need to get going?"

Jason glanced at his watch. "As soon as we say bye to the kids."

We flew into a small airport—not really even an airport, more like an airstrip. Thank goodness I'd had some wine on the plane and had no idea where we were flying to. It had been bad enough when we'd walked up to the plane. I'd balked at getting on the small jet.

Digging my heels in, I'd said, "I'm not getting in something the size of a tin can. You're out of your ever-lovin' damn mind." I've never been a good flyer, so that jet pushed my nervousness into code red territory.

Thankfully, the flight was behind us. We walked across to a small parking lot. A lady stepped out of a car. "Mr. Woodruff," she said, as if asking for confirmation, as she walked toward us.

"Yes," he confirmed, extending his hand to her.

She stretched her hand out to him. "Hi, I'm Jeanette. It's nice to meet you."

"Nice to meet you, Jeanette. This is my wife Candice," he introduced me.

Jeanette smiled even bigger and extended her hand to me. "It's nice to meet you. We've been anxious to put faces with the names." I shook her hand, but I was in the dark since I'd never spoken to her. "Here are the keys to the car and the house. Everything you requested has been set up. If you need anything, you have mine and Cheryl's numbers. I won't keep y'all. I know you must be anxious." She sort of teehee'd like a prepubescent girl. "Such a sweet story," she said with a sigh, pressing a hand to her chest.

"We will," Jason said. "Thanks again. Have a good evening." Then he directed me to a waiting sedan.

No sooner did he get in the car before I asked the burning question. "Not that I don't find all of this whirlwind romance stuff great, but it's Sunday and we spent most of the day with each other in the bowling alley. How did you set all of this up?"

"I set it all up a while back. I contacted a rental company and told them everything I wanted, but that I just didn't know when I would need it. I paid them a fee for each month to be on standby. Then, when the time was right, I called them and set everything in motion. I just had to wait until you gave me the sign. It was only a matter of time," he explained the plan he'd set into motion long ago.

"Am I that easy to predict, or are you that sure of yourself?" Unsure which scenario I would prefer.

He playfully scoffed. "Candy, you're anything but predictable, and no, not so sure of myself, but sure that what we had was stilled embedded in your heart somewhere, even if it was gone from your mind. I'll never lose faith in that…ever."

What was I supposed to say to that?

"I don't have your way with words, but I love you," I told him. "However, if you don't hurry up and get us the hell out of here and where we need to go, we're going to turn helpful Jeanette's PG13 romance into an X-rated skin flick."

"Hold that thought," he cranked the car and hightailed it out of the airport.

It wasn't long before we pulled up to a two-story aqua-colored beach house. The place was massive. We drove into the garage. I didn't bother to wait for Jason to come around and open my door. I was out of the car as soon as Jason turned the engine off.

He wasn't far behind me. I got to the third stair step when an arm came around my waist, pulling me back against Jason's firm chest as he spun me around. "Where do you think you're going in such a hurry?" he said, his cheek pressed to the side of my head, his breath caressing my ear. A shiver traveled its way through my body as he loosened his hold, allowing me to slide down until my feet touched the floor.

I turned to face him as I laughed and said, "Just getting a head start." Raising my face to look at him, I lost my breath at the look on his.

Jason guided me the few steps back until my butt hit the side of the car. Slipping his left arm lower to rest just below my ass cheeks, he lifted me to sit on the hood of the car, my legs parted. He stepped between my thighs, coming to rest against me. The intensity in his eyes took my breath away.

"No need to rush, we've got the rest of our lives." His voice husky with desire. His breathing as rough as mine.

Unwilling to wait any longer, I pulled his lips to mine, sealing our fate in a kiss. The kiss became heated. Soon my legs wrapped around Jason's waist, and my back made contact with the hood of the car. Throughout the passionate kiss, the fingers of Jason's injured right hand softly stroked the side of my face. The gentleness of that touch was in stark contrast to the fierceness of the rest of our embrace.

"Damn," I exclaimed, jerking away from Jason and slapping at the sting of my exposed thigh. "I'm getting eaten alive by mosquitoes." Jason raised us up. "And we didn't close the garage door. Hope the neighbors enjoyed the show." I laughed at his flustered face. "But let's move this inside before we get arrested for indecent exposure," I suggested.

"That's a great plan." He swept me into his arms and walked up the stairs.

"Jason," I squealed, "you have a broken arm, put me down before you hurt yourself."

"I could carry you with one hand tied behind my back. Close the garage, babe, and open the door."

The first part was easy, but when I reached for the doorknob, it didn't turn. "It's locked."

He braced me against the wall and started patting his pockets. "Shit!" He looked back down the staircase. "I dropped the keys." Putting me down, he charged down the stairs, retrieved the keys from the garage floor, and charged back up the stairs.

Unlocking the door, we stepped into the mudroom. I could see the glow of flickering light of candles, so I continued into the open first floor. There had to be hundreds, if not thousands, of LED pillar candles. A path of flowers started at the door, going as far as I could see around a corner.

"Oh my God," I murmured breathlessly in awe of the scene I saw laid out before me. Spinning to look at Jason, I said, "You never cease to amaze me."

"I hope I never do." He stared at me. His gaze earnest and loving.

"Do you love me?" I asked, even though I knew the answer.

"Forever and a day."

"Then that's all I need because you're all I want."

Jason crossed the distance, lifted me in his arms once again, and began walking.

"Jason," I groaned, "I can't take this much longer."

"Less than a minute. I'm not going to make love with you for the first time on a couch or a floor or a counter top. I'm gonna have you in a bed, where I can take my time and catch up on all that we've been missing."

Not wanting to waste time, I began to trail kisses along his neck and jaw. "Damn it, Candice, you're gonna kill me."

Mmmm was the only sound I made in response.

He laid me down on a bed in the closest bedroom he could find. Jason placed a kiss on the center of my chest then moved up my neck. "Jason," I moaned. And that was the last coherent word to cross my lips.

I awoke to Jason leaving brief kisses against my lips. "Mmm, this might be the best wakeup call ever," I declared in my dreamy state.

"Come watch the sunrise with me," Jason entreated.

I opened my eyes and smiled. "Sure," I responded as I stretched, delighting in the unfamiliar soreness.

We threw our clothes on from the night before. We hadn't taken the time to bring up our luggage. Once dressed, we made our way outside to the beach to watch the sun rise over the Atlantic Ocean.

As the orange ball of light topped the horizon, Jason began to talk. "Candice." I adjusted myself so I could see him. "I didn't know what I did to deserve a second chance with you seventeen years ago, and I don't know what I did to deserve a third chance with you, but I know, without a shadow of a doubt, that I love you more now than I did when I asked you to marry me the first time." He sort of laughed to himself. "You've always teased me that my first proposal was the worst proposal ever, so I hope I do a better job this time." He pulled away from me and rose up to kneel on one knee beside me, keeping my hands in his. "I brought us back to the place we began, because April first, two thousand-one was the beginning of the best seventeen years of my life. I had no idea what sunrise that morning would begin. The more years that pass, the more I love you. You amaze me in ways I can't describe." He let go of my right hand and reached behind him. When he brought his hand back around, he held a small box in his hand. Tears left trails down my cheeks. "I want you to remember the day I make my vow to you for the second time.

"I don't know what the future holds for us, but I know I will love you more, through infinity and beyond…forever and a day." Jason flipped the lid open to show the most unique ring I'd ever seen. The multicolored stones were arranged in the shape of a flower. "The center is a diamond because we began in April. Each of the seven petals is the birthstone of one our family. The aquamarine and tanzanite stones in the bands around the flower represent our March wedding and our meeting in December. I chose a flower because they mean love, hope, friendship, faith, and so much more. You are my more." Then he slid the ring on the bare ring finger of my left hand.

Through the crying, I said, "Every day, I think I can't possibly love you more, but every day I do. Loving you is like my heart beating;

I can't live without it. I don't want to." I paused to catch my breath, knowing these words would make my most important commitment. "I love you more, through infinity and beyond…forever and a day."

I didn't know why it was so easy to fall in love with Jason, but I'd like to think it was because my soul recognized its mate, even when my mind couldn't. Believing that gave me the comfort to make peace with the past I couldn't remember, because I knew it was still a part of me.

Against the odds, we'd made it through the improbable. Our love would last through infinity…and beyond.

The End

epilogue

Jason

April first, two thousand one, I was given a second chance to discover the love of my life. Once I realized what I had, I never let her go.

Seventeen years later on April eighteenth, somehow against all the odds, I was granted a third chance with the love of my life. But this time, if it was what she needed to be happy, I would let her go.

There was no guarantee our love would last through infinity…

& beyond....

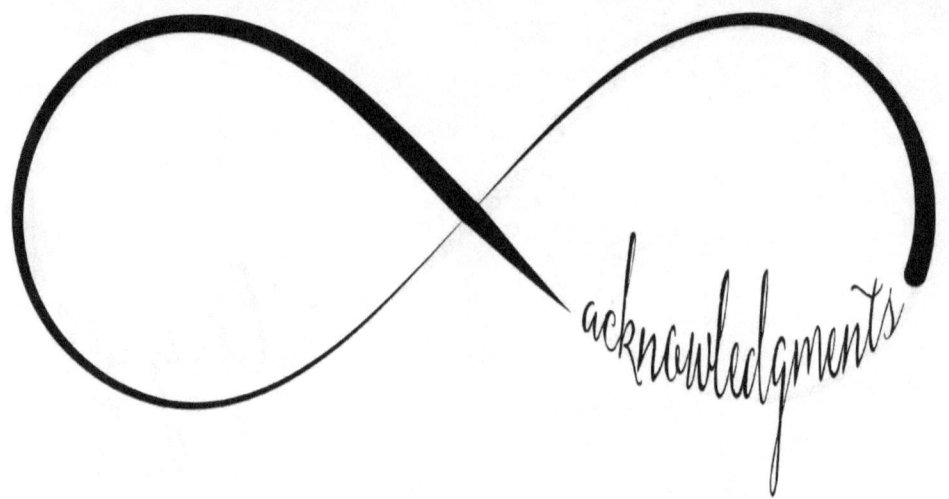

My greatest thanks goes to my family. You are the loves of my life, and I'm grateful for every day I get to spend with you.

Thank you to Martha Howard Morgan for giving a lot of dance advice to someone with two left feet.

Thank you to the betas, Valerie, Corinne, Jaimie, Heather, Kerri, Tiffany, and Luci. I appreciate the fact that y'all put up with my crazy schedule and never-ending questions.

Thank you to the ARC readers, Pam, Nina, Becky, Janet, and Nicole, for having the patience to suffer through the unpolished manuscript.

To my 'sister wives', Kate and Courtney, you're my 'sister wives' for a reason. Can you believe where we all were five years ago to now?

To the other vendors I've worked with on this journey, thank you so much for working with me.

Aimie Grey and Lisa Poston Murphy, thank you both so much for your advice and suggestions to help make *through infinity* its best.

Murphy, thanks for creating a beautiful cover to capture the feel of my story.

Elaine, you are perhaps one of the most gracious people I've ever met. Thank you for putting so much hard work into my book simply because you're a nice person. One day, I'll repay you.

Last, but no means least, thank you to the readers who took a chance on an unknown author's debut novel. I hope you enjoyed reading *through infinity* as much as I enjoyed sharing it with you.

Dear Reader,

A few of the places and people mentioned in the book are real, so if you're ever in town stop by and take a peek. We're a friendly sort of bunch, unless you pronounce the name of our fine city incorrectly —it's Mo-beel, like banana peel— or you mistakenly tell us that New Orleans is the home of Mardi Gras. We'll gladly correct you on both accounts.

Crescent Theater is a neat little art house theater.

www.crescenttheater.com

Lisa Warren is a multi-talented artist, and she does it all beautifully.

www.lisacwarren.com

ArtWalk is an impressive array of local talent.

www.facebook.com/pages/LODA-Artwalk

The LoDa Bier Garten serves up delicious German food…and beer.

www.facebook.com/pages/LoDa-Bier-Garten

Libby's Web page

www.libbyaustin.com

Facebook Author Page

www.facebook.com/Libby.Austin.Author

Facebook Friend Page

www.facebook.com/Libby.Austin.Author.Personal

Twitter

@Author_Libby

Instagram

@Libby_Austin_Author

Libby Austin Google+

Goodreads

https://www.goodreads.com/libby_austin

books by Libby

forever and a day series

coming soon

standalone

www.ingramcontent.com/pod-product-compliance
Lightning Source LLC
Chambersburg PA
CBHW030409180626
46812CB00005B/1980